Blood Typed

Jane Doucet

Vagrant
PRESS

Vagrant Press is an imprint of
Nimbus Publishing Limited
3660 Strawberry Hill St, Halifax, NS, B3K 5A9
(902) 455-4286 nimbus.ca

Printed and bound in Canada

Vagrant Press is based in Kjipuktuk, Mi'km'aki, the traditional territory of the Mi'kmaq People.

Editor: Whitney Moran
Design: Bee Stanton
NB1797

This story is a work of fiction. Names, characters, incidents, and places, including organizations and institutions, are used fictitiously.

Library and Archives Canada Cataloguing in Publication
Title: Blood typed : a Val Jenkins mystery / Jane Doucet.
Names: Doucet, Jane, 1968- author.
Identifiers: Canadiana (print) 20260100501 | Canadiana (ebook) 20260101753 | ISBN 9781774715154 (softcover) | ISBN 9781774715161 (EPUB)
Subjects: LCGFT: Detective and mystery fiction. | LCGFT: Novels.
Classification: LCC PS8607.O9143 B56 2026 | DDC C813/.6—dc23

Canada Council for the Arts | Conseil des arts du Canada

Nimbus Publishing acknowledges the financial support for its publishing activities from the Government of Canada and the Canada Council for the Arts.

ADVANCE PRAISE
for Blood Typed

"A classic whodunit, clever and propulsive, blending the puzzle-box pleasures of Agatha Christie and Richard Osman with warmth, humour, and the genuine heart of a Lesley Crewe novel. It's Nova Scotian to its core, but it travels beautifully. A triumph, and the start of a mystery series to savour."

EDIT MAGAZINE

"When a murder interrupts Halifax's NOVA Prize literary gala, journalist Val Jenkins can't resist chasing the story of a lifetime, even if it means snapping into sleuth mode. Packed with Jane Doucet's signature sharp wit, *Blood Typed* is a fast-paced, genuinely funny cozy mystery full of colourful characters, cheeky publishing insights, and surprises that keep the pages turning right to the end."

TOM RYAN

bestselling author of *The Treasure Hunters Club*

"Spot-on banter and continuous intrigue pair nicely with expertly placed clues and red herrings to create a delightfully satisfying mystery. However, it is the unique characters and their endearing quirks that provide insight into the human condition as Doucet tackles themes of grief, found family, and generational trauma, all with warmth and graceful wit."

B. R. MYERS

Edgar Award–winning author of *A Dreadful Splendour*

"A delightfully sly concoction of murder and sleuthing set at a literary awards gala, with plenty of twists and banter courtesy of a lively cast of quirky characters and a quick-witted journalist-turned-detective who just won't quit. Plenty of wit, local flavour, and familiar settings anchor this romp in Nova Scotia and propel the fast-paced plot to a very satisfying conclusion."

JO TREGGIARI

Crime Writers of Canada Award–winning author of *Heartbreak Homes*

"With its maritime charm, local settings, and even a touch of Nova Scotia history, people who love amateur sleuths, such as Jessica Fletcher and Agatha Raisin, will appreciate Val Jenkins."

THE MIRAMICHI READER

"A humorous, engaging, bright-eyed mystery that rips through Nova Scotia like a scalded bandit. Highly recommended."

C. S. PORTER

Crime Writers of Canada Award–winning author of *Beneath Her Skin* and *Salt on Her Tongue*

PRAISE FOR Lost & Found in Lunenburg

"With her latest novel, Jane Doucet brings us a whip-smart, sweet (and salty) tale of love, loss, and starting over. Brimming with heart, humour, and hope, *Lost & Found in Lunenburg* is a pure delight."

BOBBI FRENCH

author of *The Good Women of Safe Harbour*

Fishnets & Fantasies

"[*Fishnets & Fantasies*] proves prolific journalist Jane Doucet can write a very funny novel."

TORONTO STAR

"I haven't had this much fun reading a book in a long time. Irreverent, wise, and more than a bit cheeky...an absolute delight."

AMY JONES

author of *We're All In This Together*

"The spirit of Stephen Leacock meets a colourful pantheon of contemporary Nova Scotia characters simmering in a sexually charged Lunenburg pheromone chowder!"

RON JAMES

author of *All Over the Map*

For Duke, my faithful writing companion

Prologue

FOR YEARS AFTERWARD, THE YOUNG MAN WHO MADE the discovery would have nightmares about what he had seen.

On the floor next to the desk, a body lay crumpled on its side.

Skull smashed.

Legs twisted.

Face covered in blood.

Features frozen in...horror?

No. Not horror.

Surprise.

Next to the body lay a beautiful antique typewriter, its keys mangled and bloody.

Sally: The Author
Wolfville

SALLY MACPHEE COULD FEEL THE CANCER IN HER BONES long before the doctor confirmed it. At church, the pain prevented her from lowering herself to the padded kneeler in her pew. It prevented her from genuflecting in front of the altar and during the stations of the cross. Most of all, the pain prevented her from looking inward, and from asking the priest for absolution for a secret she couldn't bring herself to share in the confessional.

This pain is my penance, Sally berated herself silently.

St. Francis of Assisi was a ten-dollar taxi ride from Sally's seniors' apartment in the tiny university town of Wolfville, if she included a modest tip. As a senior on a fixed income, she paid for everything with cash. Each month, she rolled her coins, then took them to the bank to exchange them for bills. Penny-pinching had gone out with pennies, she supposed. When it came down to brass tacks, she was still practically penniless.

While Francis of Assisi had aspired to lead a Christian life of poverty, Sally had not. When she was young, she'd had grander plans for herself than working as an elementary school secretary for fifty godawful years. Most of the staff were nice enough, but the day-to-day tedium was torture. And all those children. Good Lord.

In high school, when Sally told her parents she wanted to be a writer, they laughed. They were hardworking apple farmers who listened to Wilf Carter and Hank Snow on the radio. They believed writing was a hobby. Not a career.

Her options? Teacher. Nurse. Secretary. The latter cost the least to train for and took the least amount of time. So.

Now, at seventy-six, Sally found herself twice widowed, with only modest monthly government pensions to pay the rent on a small, overpriced, one-bedroom apartment on the outskirts of town. Over the past decade, the cost of absolutely everything had risen exponentially. To try to keep up, she had sold her car the year before.

Seated on the slipcovered loveseat in her living room, Sally gazed wistfully at her collection of flea-market finds. Porcelain Hummel and bone china Royal Doulton figurines smiled at her from an antique mahogany glass-fronted corner cabinet that had belonged to her grandparents. In pride of place on the cabinet's middle shelf was a chipped Old Country Roses teacup with matching saucer that had belonged to her mother. A plain glass bowl of purple dollar-store potpourri gave the room a pungent punch.

Placed delicately on the coffee table were lace doilies she had crocheted as a young bride. Because it had been expected of her. And Sally MacPhee was dutiful, if nothing else. Always aiming to please. First, her parents. Then, her husbands.

It had taken all of Sally's savings to prepay for her cemetery plot. Because that's what good Catholics did. She supposed she could try to sell the figurines. And the cabinet, if it came to that. But she couldn't bear to part with them yet.

Above the dining table, where she had eaten every meal alone since her second husband had gone to meet his maker, hung a print of the Last Supper. Next to it, the plain gold cross that had been both of her wedding cakes' topper.

That crucifix was cursed, it had turned out.

In hindsight, both of Sally's husbands had been extremely poor choices. Number one, an alcoholic. Number two, an adulterer. What little money they ever had slipped through their fingers and into the ether.

During her fertile years, Sally had secretly taken the appropriate measures to make sure she would bear no children. People silently pitied poor "sterile" Sally. But she'd had the last laugh. Shortly before she turned fifty, she found herself living alone for the second time in her life. And loving it.

Two slim yellow-gold wedding bands were stowed away in a box at the back of her sock drawer. There had been no money for diamond engagement rings. On her fiftieth birthday, she made a promise to herself: no more relationships. She felt her husbands had gotten the endings they deserved. They were both interred in her parish cemetery. After their burials, Sally had never gone back.

In her twenties and thirties, instead of raising a family, Sally spent her spare time writing a novel. In secret. So no one would laugh at her. Mostly during her summers off from her job at the school. *That wasn't a career either, Mom and Dad*. When she was fifty-three, her debut was published to modest reviews. Much to Sally's great disappointment, however, the royalty payments didn't pad her bank account. Instead, they paid for a few groceries. But that first book had lit a fire in her. Three more novels followed, each one better than the last. All had been nominated for provincial awards, two even reaching the shortlist. None had won.

I am the Susan Lucci of book awards, Sally kept telling herself.

But with this novel, her fifth, it wasn't a prize payout Sally was after. She knew she wouldn't live long enough to enjoy it. Although she knew what she'd do with the money. Oh yes, she did. Recently, she'd added a codicil to her will. Just in case. Fame and fortune? Those weren't in the cards, either. Her readership was loyal, but small. Mostly based in the region.

What Sally truly longed for filled her with shame. Every night, she lowered herself to kneel beside her bed. Arthritic fingers intertwined. Head bowed toward her heart. The searing pain from her swollen knees was punishing, but that wasn't the only thing stopping her from sleeping peacefully.

Every night at her bedside, Sally spoke these words aloud:

> *Dear Lord,*
>
> *I bring before you the specific sin that weighs heavy on my conscience. I ask for your forgiveness and the strength to turn away from the action I am contemplating. Thank you for the promise that if I confess my sins, you are faithful and just to forgive me. Grant me the power to live in the freedom of your forgiveness for my remaining days.*
>
> *Amen.*

Making the sign of the cross, the old woman hauled her cancerous body up from the floor and crawled into bed.

When Sally read the email that mid-May morning, she was relieved to be sitting down, and not just because her knees were throbbing.

Thanks to a literature-loving grocery-store philanthropist, the NOVA Prize for Historical Fiction was worth one hundred thousand dollars, with twenty thousand for each of the two runners-up.

And her newest novel was on the shortlist.

For a writer, let alone one in the rural Maritimes, that kind of cash was much more than chump change. Rumour was, writers sometimes moved to Nova Scotia just to be considered. The NOVA Prize might be the pinnacle of an author's writing career. Receiving the award meant added pressure to produce something equally original, compelling, and literary with their next novel. It was a punishing act to follow. Many froze. And failed.

Sally's nominated novel, *Alex Cage*, was inspired by Cape Breton's coal-mining legacy. In the twentieth century, "Alex Cage" was the nickname given to the man who operated the mine's elevator shaft. Sally had spun the story around this character, who was based loosely on her paternal great-grandfather, a rough, uneducated coal miner with a tender heart.

Of all of her books, Sally was most proud of *Alex Cage*. The research had been exhaustive. It had taken five years to produce a final draft to submit to Greenwich Press, her small independent publisher in nearby Hantsport. And, of course, publication took another two years. And now the nomination had arrived nearly a year after that. At this rate, she'd poured almost a decade into this project. Her last.

Five minutes after reading the nomination notification, Sally called her editor.

Bev: The Editor

Hantsport

FOR TWENTY YEARS, BEV HAD COLLABORATED WITH Sally to massage her manuscripts into the bound books they would become. As an editor, Bev loved everything about the process—from working on the manuscript with the author to writing promotional copy to proofreading and consulting with the designer on cover concepts. Finally, two years after reading a manuscript's first sentence, she'd open the box of books in the publisher's warehouse, lift out the first copy, and hold it tenderly in her hands. It was better than Christmas, and it never got old.

Bev had been thirty-three when she first edited one of Sally's manuscripts. Now, there was a sacred trust, and a bond, between author and editor. And a certain shorthand.

When the phone rang in her bungalow, she hurried to search for it. "I just heard," said Bev breathlessly, after finding the phone buried on her desk under a pile of papers. "Congratulations! This is big!"

"I won't win," said Sally, her voice flat. "Hang on, I have to adjust the volume on my hearing aids." She could do that through her cellphone now. Technology was marvellous, when it worked. "There now, that's better."

"You don't *know* you won't win," countered Bev, running her fingers through her blond bob. Behind her tortoiseshell cat's-eye frames, her blue eyes were bright. "Who are the other nominees?"

Shifting in her chair in an attempt to get more comfortable, Sally scanned the email. "Sonya King, Alexander Fitzgerald, and Victor Comeau."

Over the years, Sally had appeared on various panels with Sonya and Alex. Vic was a newcomer. The local authors' community was microscopic. Many were members of the provincial writers' association. Everyone knew everyone, and most of them got along well enough. Friendly, if not friends. They celebrated each other's successes and mourned each other's disappointments. But if you looked more closely, you'd sense a spoonful of simmering jealousy that often came to a boil during awards season. Surely that wasn't unexpected? Writers were only human, after all. And as an editor, Bev knew how fragile their egos truly were.

Bev grunted. "Not a very diverse list this year. And doesn't Sonya write romance? Odd choice. Who's on the jury?"

"I've only read the summary, but Sonya's new novel is centred around the Halifax Explosion," Again, Sally consulted the email. "The jury members are Sunil Patel, Delmore Davis, and Steven Silver."

"Some cultural diversity there, but all men," Bev pointed out. "What was the committee thinking? Those decisions don't make them look progressive. Sunny and Del are young talents, but Steve is a fossil…and a pissant."

"Steve's my age," Sally pointed out.

"Yes, but you aren't a narcissist," said Bev, recalling a long-ago unpleasant encounter with the man. "Which makes you seem younger. And as for Sonya's novel, hasn't everything there is to say about the Halifax Explosion been said? Harbour, ships, collision, explosion, destruction, death. It's like everything ever written about the *Titanic*. The ending is never a surprise."

"Well, yes, you would think so," Sally agreed. "Anyway, thanks for the vote of confidence, but we both know I won't win. And…it's my last chance, too."

Bev picked up on the barely concealed bitterness. Sally had shared her cancer diagnosis, and prognosis, with her. And only her. Over the years, Bev had also shared the author's frustration at her failure to win awards, as both her editor and her friend.

More than any of the past awards, Bev desperately wanted this win for Sally. First, the prize was massive. And maybe, just maybe, Sally would bequeath a portion of the winnings to her long-time, loyal editor. There was no question that the extra cash would help ease her out of a tight corner.

Does that make me a bad person? Bev kept asking herself, ignoring the answer.

Also, if Sally won, Bev would finally get recognized for editing an award-winning novel. Some well-earned pats on the back from her peers. Maybe even a feature in the local newspaper. She envisioned herself and Sally on the cover of the *Valley Chronicle*, lining mailboxes across the county.

A good editor's work was invisible. Readers had no clue that Bev spent her days polishing prose. Suggesting pithy prologues and epic epilogues. Fixing grammatical errors, timelines, and tenses. Looking at a manuscript through mental macro and micro lenses. And while Bev considered herself to be a good editor, she was fed up with donning that tiresome old cloak. She wanted more.

Bev hadn't shared her secret desire with a single soul. All she knew for sure was that she would stop at nothing until she got it.

Sonya: The Author
Lunenburg

SONYA KING SMILED WHEN SHE READ THE EMAIL. NOT because she was surprised. After all, she knew her novel was good. Very good, in fact. Far better than the other nominees', which she had read as soon as they'd landed in stores. Long before the NOVA shortlist was announced, avid readers had a sense of which books would appear on it. Authors, even more so. There was always talk.

In Sonya's opinion, she was a shoo-in for the big prize. Not that she needed the money, of course. A retired anesthesiologist and national award-winning romance author didn't lust after one hundred thousand dollars. Or even the accolades and attention, although she always appreciated those. No, Sonya was pleased for another reason altogether. Even though she didn't need the money, she had plans for it. And they were almost entirely self-serving: funding a new wing in the town's hospital, with her name appearing on it in big, bold letters. *My legacy*, she thought.

Sonya's novel, *Frances Coleman Carries On*, was narrated by the wife of Vince Coleman, a train dispatcher who famously died in the Halifax Explosion on the sixth of December in 1917—but not before he sent a message to an incoming passenger train with a warning to stop outside the range of the disaster. His final, heart-wrenching telegraph message read:

> Hold up the train. Ammunition ship afire in harbor making for Pier 6 and will explode. Guess this will be my last message. Good-bye Boys.

Every time Sonya read that passage, her eyes grew moist and goosebumps dimpled her arms. Vince had died a hero. And although his widow, Frances, and the youngest of their four children suffered serious injuries, all of them survived and recovered. Frances lived for another fifty-three years, dying in 1970.

The Colemans were buried at Mount Olivet Cemetery in Halifax, along with others who perished in the Explosion, plus nineteen bodies recovered from the *Titanic*. During her research, Sonya had spent time sitting near the Colemans' resting place. Contemplating Vince's courage. Wondering how his widowed wife had managed to raise their children alone. How she had rebuilt their damaged home, and their lives, without their beloved husband and father. From there, Sonya had spun Frances Coleman's story.

At home in Lunenburg, on Nova Scotia's scenic South Shore, Sonya watched the sun sparkle like diamonds on the water of Front Harbour. She was sitting in a padded patio chair outside the stately Kempt Street home she shared with her husband, Booth. Located on one the highest points in town, their house had a clear view of both Front and Back Harbours.

"Just beautiful," she said aloud, turning up the collar of her lightweight down coat and taking a deep breath of the fresh spring air. She texted Booth to meet her on the patio.

Sonya had decided to use her real name on the cover of this novel. When writing contemporary romance, she went by S. R. Kingsbury. For her historical fiction romance, her pseudonym was Silke Solange. She was on a book-a-year contract with her Toronto publisher, Romantic Escapes. Sales continued to be brisk. Despite this, and numerous awards to her credit, Sonya still kept two shifts a week working as a sales associate at Fishnets & Fantasies, the upscale sex shop on Pelham Street. More than a decade ago, her friend Wendy Hebb had opened it. Two years ago, Wendy's widowed friend Rose Ainsworth had bought it and taken over management, not long after Rose's husband died suddenly in a cycling accident in Halifax. For the most part, Sonya and Rose worked together well.

"What's up, buttercup?" said Booth, lowering his lanky frame into the chair next to his wife.

"You've been spending too much time with the kids at the community garden," said Sonya, laughing. She was referring to the raised bed that Booth tended on the Lunenburg Academy's grounds, at the top of Gallows Hill. Once a big-shot corporate lawyer in Toronto, Booth was now a town councillor who had discovered a later-in-life love of planting, cultivating, and harvesting flowers and vegetables.

"I guess I have, I keep picking up their lingo," he said, grinning. "It's wonderful to see young people so engaged with the natural environment."

Booth looked wistful. Sonya's biggest regret was focusing exclusively on her career and not on starting a family with her husband, who had longed for one. It relieved her guilt slightly to know he'd found a passion that allowed him to connect with children.

"I don't think you called me out here to ask after my rutabaga, although I could wax poetic about it all day," said Booth. Crossing his arms and legs, he said, "Shoot."

When Sonya finished reading the nomination note, Booth pulled his wife out of her chair and wrapped his arms around her.

"Congratulations, honey! We'll be rich!" said Booth, locking his lips with hers.

Booth never failed to make her laugh. "We're already rich," said Sonya, breathless, when she could speak again.

"Then we'll be richer!" said Booth, rubbing his hands together. "I'll be able to grow a bigger crop of rutabagas and donate even more of my harvest to the food pantry."

"You're already beyond generous with your donations," said Sonya, returning to her chair. "Although I'm not sure rutabagas are top of their list of needs."

"My rutabagas are *epic*," said Booth, pouting. "But so are you. Seriously, Sonya. The NOVA Prize? This one's a doozy! Does this nomination feel different?"

Absentmindedly twisting a strand of her shoulder-length, professionally coloured auburn hair, Sonya carefully considered her answer.

"Yes and no," she said finally. "Yes, because it's the province's biggest prize, which comes with a certain measure of prestige. And it's always nice to be recognized, especially since this is my first foray into traditional historical fiction."

"And no, because...?" Booth prompted.

Sonya shrugged. "And no, because I don't need the prestige or the money."

"My beautiful wife is so humble," said Booth, holding a hand over his heart.

Smiling, Sonya remained silent. Truth be told, she wasn't terribly humble. She hadn't shared her plan for the prize money with her husband. And she wouldn't, unless she won.

"Who are the other nominees?" asked Booth.

Sonya told him.

"And the judges?"

Sonya told him.

Booth tilted his head. "Who's Victor?"

"A professor at Sainte-Anne University on the French Shore," said Sonya. "This is his debut novel."

"Really?" Booth raised his eyebrows. "His first novel, and he's up for the NOVA Prize? Isn't that odd?"

Sonya pursed her lips. "Now that you put it like that…yes, I suppose it is."

Booth frowned. "And is Steve Silver the misogynist?"

"Yes," said Sonya. "He won't vote for Sally or me. But Del and Sunny will be fair."

"Book awards sound as political as…well, small-town politics. Or figure-skating competitions," said Booth, shaking his head. "May I take you out to dinner to celebrate?"

Sonya smiled. "That would be lovely. The Beach Pea?"

Booth looked at his watch. "How's seven?"

"Perfect. That'll give me time to freshen up," said Sonya, mentally planning the outfit she'd put together from her spacious walk-in closet. "And I want to call the girls to tell them. Maybe they can meet us for a drink later?"

"That'd be great. See if Paul and Allan can come, too," said Booth, who got along well with Wendy's husband and Rose's partner. "And you know I'm proud of you no matter what. You're always a winner to me." Standing up and stretching, Booth went to kiss Sonya again. "I'm going to check on my *epic* rutabagas before I head to town hall for a meeting. I'll book us a table before I leave."

"Thanks, honey," said Sonya.

Almost at the door, Booth turned around suddenly. "Hey, one more question. When will the winner be announced?"

Sonya glanced at her phone. "The third weekend of June, at the gala ceremony and dinner in Halifax. The four of us will sit on panels, do readings and media interviews, and be on hand to sell and sign our books." She sighed. "The usual dog and pony show."

Booth pulled his phone from his pocket. "I'll put it in my calendar now. I'm looking forward to being your plus-one at the dinner, if you'll have me."

Sonya's heart swelled. Not so long ago, she and Booth had been on the brink of divorce. Bygones, now. Thankfully. "I can't think of anyone else I'd rather have by my side," she said, smiling warmly.

As Sonya watched her husband head back into the house, she picked up her cellphone to search her contact list for the chair of the hospital foundation.

Victor: The Author

Université Sainte-Anne, Pointe-de-l'Église

TEN MINUTES BEFORE HIS ZOOM INTERVIEW WITH A TV reporter, Victor Comeau was in the bathroom down the hall from his office. Gazing in the mirror, he combed what remained of his once-thick head of hair. The thinning strands would be completely grey if not for liberal bimonthly applications of Just For Men in Dark Brown.

Vic thought his eyeglasses—big, bold, black plastic frames with fake lenses—made him look scholarly. Turning his head to the left, he glanced at his profile. *And just like...* He scanned his memory for the name of that handsome Chilean actor. *I've got it.* He smiled and stroked his moustache. *Pedro Pascal.*

At sixty-four, vanity was a race against time. Vic didn't want his roots showing. Nor did he want to look old enough to retire. There were some in his faculty who would enjoy nothing more than to push him out now, but he had tenure on his side. Before he called it quits, he had plans for himself.

Big plans.

Head of the Acadian Studies program in the Faculty of Arts, *le professeur* was a journalist's dream source. Articulate. Charming. Witty. Fluent in both official languages. Available on short notice. Instead of asking reporters to reach out to the university's communications director to book an interview, he encouraged them to text him directly. Which annoyed the director to no end.

Vic was not a team player.

Today, the reporter wanted to review the highlights of the upcoming Congrès mondial acadien. The Acadian World Congress was a festival of Acadian and Cajun culture and history, held in August every five years. Vic hadn't missed any of them. The best one had been in Louisiana, more than twenty years ago. The university had paid his travel expenses. The week was filled with music, food, dancing, workshops, reunions, revelry, and comradery, all shared by Acadians and Cajuns from around the world. The events were a strategic spot for him to see and be seen. By politicians, in particular.

Vic had plans for himself, all right.

Big plans.

This year, the Congress would be held in southwestern Nova Scotia, which meant that Vic could sleep in his own bed every night.

Which also meant that he couldn't sleep with a woman who wasn't his wife. They had a rule: no lovers in their own bed.

Quel dommage, thought Vic, shrugging at his image in the mirror. Although the more he turned his thoughts toward yet another tryst, the more he realized that, yes, it would be tricky, but not impossible. Raising his eyebrows and peering at his furrowed forehead, he wondered if it was time for another shot of Botox. He'd have his secretary make an appointment.

Patting pressed powder with an organic-cotton puff over his shiny skin, Vic glanced in the mirror one last time, nodded in approval, and returned to his office. There, he quickly scanned his inbox before launching his Zoom meeting. He liked to join five minutes after the start time. Fashionably late, but not so late as to be disrespectful.

An email from the NOVA Prize committee caught his eye. Opening it, he grinned like a cat that caught the canary after torturing it first. The reporter would get a scoop: his debut novel, *The Reinvention of René Thibauld*, about the Acadian immigration from France to Louisiana, was on the shortlist. As far as he was concerned, there was no contest. His would take the top prize. *Fin de l'histoire*.

As soon as the interview was in the can, he'd call his old nemesis, Steve Silver, to thank him. Silver had owed him, big time. And Vic would never let him forget it.

Then Vic had another important call to make. Pronto. To someone he needed to ensure remained silent.

Alexander: The Author

Dalhousie University, Halifax

SITTING IN HIS CRAMPED OFFICE, ALEXANDER Fitzgerald swapped his regular glasses for computer glasses. Then he powered up his PC to prepare for his afternoon courses in contemporary fiction and creative writing.

"I feel old," the professor said aloud. Sighing, he adjusted the height of his ergonomic chair to help pinpoint the sweet spot of his new lenses on his monitor.

Two years shy of fifty, Alex had been happy to shell out big bucks for his sixth pair of funky frames in west end Halifax. The upscale shop was a short walk from his two-storey Victorian. He liked to keep his look fresh for his online-dating profile. Now that he was middle-aged, he needed all the help he could get to snag a boyfriend. So far, no luck. At his age, premium pickings were slim.

Alex's office, located on the third floor of Dalhousie's McCain building, was filled with books. Crammed tightly on the shelves behind his desk. Stacked in piles on the floor. On his visitor's chair, in a Jenga-like tower on the verge of toppling. When Alex was twenty-five, his debut novel had won the provincial "first book" award. Since then, he had pumped one out every other year. After joining the faculty, he was able to devote the summer months to working on his manuscripts. It was a sweet schedule that came with a defined benefit pension plan.

Over that quarter century, federal and provincial arts organizations threw grant money at Alex. His academic colleagues and author acquaintances whose funding applications were regularly declined were resentful, he knew. If the roles were reversed, he would be, too. But everyone knew that writing was a cutthroat, competitive business. Certainly not for the faint of heart. And definitely not for quitters. To get anywhere as an author, you had to persist.

An incoming email notification chimed. Clicking on it, Alex scanned it quickly, then clapped his hands in glee. "This is terrific news!" he announced to the potted palm in the corner.

The prize money would be welcome. And timely, since the absent-minded professor found himself in arrears of tens of thousands of dollars in unpaid income tax.

"Everything okay in here?" Usha, a bubbly graduate student Alex was supervising, poked her head in his doorway. Her desk was in a closet-like cubbyhole across the hall.

"Never better!" said Alex, beaming as he switched his glasses. "I've been nominated for the NOVA Prize."

"That's amazing!" said Usha, pumping her fists in the air and doing a happy dance. "Congratulations!" She had, of course, read his novel and given it a glowing five-star Goodreads review. Even though she'd skipped the middle section, which dragged. She'd never tell him that, of course. She was more of a Jane Austen fan.

In media interviews, Alex described *Cape Breton Calls Him* as a cross between Anne-Marie MacDonald's *Fall on Your Knees* and Linden MacIntyre's *The Bishop's Man*: a family, a priest, a scandal. A tale as old as time. A history too often repeated. But this time, with a spectacular twist.

Alex had been born and raised in Sydney, the son of a provincial court judge and a homemaker. A later-in-life only child, his parents—his mother was forty-two when he was born, his father, fifty—called him "a happy surprise." His upbringing had been privileged. For more than a decade, John and Margaret Fitzgerald had been resting in Resurrection Cemetery in Sydney Forks. They'd be proud of him, he knew.

Alex sighed, thinking of the upcoming media interviews.

Yes, he would tell every reporter who ever asked (and they all did), he was related distantly to the late, great Cape Breton fiddler Winston "Scotty" Fitzgerald.

No, he wasn't the least bit musical; he only played the radio (that always got laughs).

Yes, he was related distantly to the owner of Fitzgerald's Restaurant, overlooking the beautiful Bras d'Or Lake.

No, he had no culinary skills, unless ordering gourmet take-out counted.

Reporters were always looking for links to the past.

To connect dots.

And to dig up skeletons.

Alex had long made his peace with having only two talents: writing and teaching. After Usha returned to her cubbyhole, he swapped glasses again to read the NOVA Prize email more closely. Of course, he knew Sally and Sonya—over the years, they had appeared on panels at conferences and workshops together—while Vic was a new author. Though Alex knew the man peripherally through provincial academic circles.

Alex had read all of their books. It was a good idea to check out the competition, right? He would grade them as follows:

Alex Cage was well crafted but not outstanding: B-

Frances Coleman Carries On was well researched but pedestrian. *I mean, more Halifax Explosion? Enough already*: B

The Reinvention of René Thibauld rubbed him the wrong way, although he couldn't pinpoint why: C+

He'd watched some of Vic's interviews. He came across as pompous. Self-important. Slick and sleazy. From what Alex had read of Vic's academic journal articles, the French professor wasn't a good writer. Whoever edited his book must have taken an incredibly heavy hand. He liked Vic's glasses, though. Which he'd try to remember to tell him when the nominees gathered for the gala weekend in a few weeks.

No reason to be nasty, Alex thought. *Until there is*.

Del and Sunny: The Judges

North End café, Halifax

"I'M RELIEVED THAT'S DONE AND DUSTED," SAID Delmore Davis, draining the dregs of his coffee. "Binge reading is exhausting."

Sunil Patel sipped iced tea through a compostable straw. "I hear ya. I don't want to look at another novel for the rest of the year. Not even the one I'm working on."

"Same," said Del, laughing. The pair were relaxing at a bustling café in Halifax's North End, celebrating the public announcement of the NOVA Prize's shortlist.

Del did a quick shoulder check, then leaned in. "Should we have invited Steve?"

"Nope," said Sunny, taking his glasses off to polish them with a cloth. Del's sense of fair play was always at the forefront. It's what made him an ideal book-award judge. But Sunny had no patience for their third juror. "We've spent more than enough time dealing with that guy. He's on my last nerve." For a practicing Buddhist with a twice-daily meditation practice, that was saying something. Sunny's mantra throughout the last few months had been *Try not to kill Steve*.

Since January, Del, Sunny, and Steve had spent countless hours discussing the NOVA Prize submissions. All forty of them. It was a lot of work. Now, with the shortlist out, they only had the winning book to reveal. That announcement would take place in four weeks. Until then, the winner was top secret.

Before Sunny spoke again, he glanced furtively over both shoulders, then lowered his voice, as if he were a spy in Cold War Berlin. Del rolled his eyes, half expecting his friend to tap out Morse code under the table.

"Some of the novels were pure dreck," whispered Sunny. "And from respected—quote, unquote—authors. I quit after the first chapter on more than a dozen of them."

"Same," said Del, biting into a cookie-dough ball. "The first round of elimination is always the easiest part."

"I found several of Greenwich's submissions particularly weak," said Sunny, still speaking in a hush. "Do you think Bev Clarke is losing her edge?"

Del shrugged. "Dunno. Maybe they farmed out some manuscripts to freelance editors?"

"Maybe," said Sunny, scanning the room again.

Just then, Sunny's cellphone buzzed. Picking it up off the table, he glanced at the number. "Shit, it's Steve."

"Let it go to voice mail," said Del.

"Yup," said Sunny, tossing his phone in his courier bag. "I mean, if he wasn't such a prick, people wouldn't avoid him. He doesn't know I'm in the city, by the way."

"Your secret is safe with me," said Del, popping the last piece of cookie into his mouth. "Unless you posted something on socials?"

"Damn," said Sunny, grimacing. "Social media is a necessary evil, but…"

"…but evil just the same," finished Del. "I get it. Free publicity and promotion. I feel the same way, and I grew up with it." Del was a fresh-faced twenty-eight.

Sunny was in Halifax for a long-awaited MRI on his left knee; the impromptu celebration at the café had just been a bonus. Over the years, Del had become like a younger brother, and a mentee of sorts. That said, Sunny had certainly learned a thing or two about literary writing from the younger author's novels. He was proud to be friends with such a rising star. When they found themselves on each other's home turfs, they always got together for a coffee.

Three years earlier, Sunny had been shortlisted for the NOVA Prize. Now thirty-nine, he was hoping his next novel would win it so he could take a leave of absence from his gig as a part-time literature professor at the University of Cape Breton. This time, he was focusing on plot elements that were almost always present in prestigious book-award winners. Sunny called them "the three S's": self-harm, sexual assault, suicide. There had to be suffering, and plenty of it.

Sunny's current work in progress was loosely inspired by his parents' love story. His father, Jatinder, who was from Jaipur, had met his mother, Donalda, in her hometown of Port Hawkesbury while vacationing there with his parents. The Patel family had stayed at the Maritime Inn, and Donalda was their waitress in the dining room. It was love at first sight—and at the first bite of Jatinder's breakfast bacon—although it took Jatinder's parents some convincing. But unlike Sunny's parents' happy lives, he had written a Romeo and Juliet–style ending for his lovestruck young protagonists.

There was suffering, and plenty of it.

Del was a writing wunderkind. The previous year, he had taken the top NOVA Prize for his third novel. Now, he was adapting that book into a play for the local theatre. Born and raised in Uniacke Square in Halifax's North End, his stories were rooted in his African Nova Scotian heritage. The area of the city around the square was gentrifying. He'd stayed, to be close to his parents. And he set his stories there, to preserve the oral histories he'd grown up hearing.

In the author community, because of his youth, Del was often called "one to watch." CBC Books had spotlighted him. George Elliott Clarke had defended the young man's award-winning novel on Canada Reads. He had been profiled in all of the top daily newspapers. The NOVA Prize shone a national spotlight on its authors. And yet the more public accolades Del received, and the more he was pushed into the limelight, the worse his anxiety and sense of imposter syndrome became. The antidepressant his GP had prescribed helped, but only a little. Therapy did, too. That's why he preferred judging awards. It was behind-the-scenes work.

Del and Sunny wore their talent with humility and grace. Steve Silver, not so much. Thirty years ago, when his third novel won a provincial award, he became even more insufferable. After that, his writing matured, and his confidence grew alongside his ego. Sure, he had talent. But his arrogance overpowered it.

Then there was the misogyny. Over the years, Steve had revealed his true nature multiple times, both in public and in private. There had been whispers about his poor wife. It was a sad story that had largely been buried. Along with her.

But there was one person who had never forgotten that sad story. And who never would.

Val: The Journalist
The Halifax Post's *office*

VAL JENKINS PAUSED IN HER BOSS'S DOORWAY. "YOU ARE aware that smoking was banned in office buildings twenty years ago, right?"

"Yes, Mother" said Kevin Lewis, the cigarette between his lips moving up and down as he spoke. "Actually, it was in 2006. Fact-checking really has gone the way of the dodo bird. And this puppy ain't lit."

"First, I can't believe you said *ain't* and *puppy* in the same sentence," said Val. Dropping her knapsack and bicycle helmet, she plopped down in Kevin's visitor's chair. "Or at all. And second, you can probably get oral cancer just from chewing on that."

"What, all of a sudden you're a health expert?" Kevin's chair squeaked under his bulk as he swivelled sideways to face her. "Stick to what you know best, Mary. Entertainment and books."

"Lip cancer, then," Val persisted. "Do you want to lose a lip?"

"I wish *you* were less lippy," Kevin muttered.

Val watched the older man turn back to his computer to bang out an email with only the index finger on each hand. He was the fastest two-finger typist she'd ever seen. And the only one left.

Val took a sip from her water bottle. In good weather, she enjoyed the short bike ride from her apartment to the *Halifax Post*'s office on Hollis Street.

Recently, Kevin had nicknamed her Mary Tyler Moore. "Because you've got spunk," he said. "And I hate spunk."

"Ha," Val had replied. "Thanks for the compliment. I think." She knew that being given a nickname by Kevin—even if it was, apparently, fifteen years in the making—was a big deal. He didn't like most people enough to even learn their real names.

Kevin raised his eyebrows. "I'm impressed you know that reference, since you weren't even born when that show aired."

"Everyone knows that reference, Lou," Val said patiently. "It's on YouTube."

Just like Mr. Grant, if Kevin Lewis had been a dessert, he would have been crème brûlée: hard shell, soft centre.

Kevin grunted, "Oh, yeah? Go get whatshisname. The new intern. Todd."

"Tyler," Val said, rolling her eyes as she stood up.

When Tyler appeared, Kevin greeted him with his usual charm. "You don't look old enough to shave," he said. "Pop quiz. What's the reference for this quote: 'You've got spunk. I hate spunk'?"

Tyler frowned. "What's spunk?"

Kevin pointed a pudgy finger at the young employee. "You're fired. Pack your things, or I'll call security."

Tyler laughed. "No, you won't. I'll call my father first. You know, head of the *Post*'s legal counsel? Which is how I wound up with this lousy summer gig instead of working at a law firm."

"Yeah, well, your old man isn't doing such a great job with the bankruptcy-protection negotiations, now is he?" Kevin replied, always quick with a comeback. "If he doesn't step it up, we'll all be out on our asses, and you'll be flipping burgers at McDonald's."

Without breaking eye contact, Tyler raised the middle finger of his right hand and slowly scratched the bridge of his nose. Then turned on his heel and sauntered out.

"Law school's for wimps!" Kevin called after him. "He's got spunk," he added with what sounded to Val like admiration as soon as Tyler was out of earshot. "He'd make a damn fine legal reporter."

"You hate spunk," Val reminded him.

"That's right, I do," Kevin agreed.

The highlight of Val's workday remained the verbal sparring with her boss. Their banter helped her creative juices flow. It also boosted morale. Which, considering the pitiful state of print journalism, was in the shitter. (Tyler, who did end up going to law school, got out just in time.)

In spite of print publishing's decline, Val still loved working at the *Post*. After graduating from journalism school, she started her career as an intern and never left. Now forty-four, she lived in a small, ground-floor, one-bedroom apartment in a Victorian house near Halifax's old grain elevator with Sherlock Holmes, her three-year-old Maine coon cat. She had one broken romantic engagement behind her and was likely facing unemployment, if Tyler's dad and the rest of the legal team couldn't save the *Post* from financial ruin. Not a lot to look forward to, really.

As if no time had passed, Val's boss looked up from his two-finger-typed email. "Hey, why are you still here? Don't you have work to do? Like write a piece of fluff that'll put our readers to sleep. No wonder the paper is bankrupt."

"It isn't fluff, it's the NOVA Prize, the biggest book award in the province," Val pointed out, feeling as though she should defend it. Picking up her backpack and helmet, she added, "You know the top title gets one hundred thousand Gs."

"NOVA doesn't even stand for anything," said Kevin. "No, scratch that. I'll tell ya what it stands for: Neurotic. Obnoxious. Verbose. Authors."

Then he laughed so hard he started coughing. In spite of his crankiness, Kevin had been Val's mentor and advocate from her very first day. Still was. Now, at sixty-four, the senior managing editor was hoping the paper could hang on for one more year so he could retire with a full pension. He'd refused an early retirement package. *Fuck that,* he'd said to himself. And out loud. To anyone within earshot. Repeatedly.

"You okay, boss?" asked Val. "Want some water?"

Val worried about Kevin. Like her, he lived alone. Unlike her, he was a recovering alcoholic and a type 2 diabetic who ate poorly, didn't exercise, and smoked a pack a day (just not in the office). If he didn't wise up soon, he'd lose more than that infected toe on his right foot.

"I'm fine, Mother," said Kevin, when he'd caught his breath. "Fit as a fiddle. Never better. Don't worry about me."

"My concern for you is entirely self-serving," said Val. "I need to keep you alive until you retire so you can get me moved to the crime beat."

It wasn't the first time Val had brought up her not-so-secret dream of being a crime journalist. And it wouldn't be the last.

When Val was ten, she begged her parents for a spy activity kit for Christmas. The kit came with a booklet to collect fingerprints using ink strips, a magnifying glass to search for clues, an invisible-ink pen, a periscope, and other cool investigation tools.

Val fingerprinted her parents.

She fingerprinted her classmates.

She fingerprinted her cat.

She fingerprinted herself.

In the spy notebook, Val would make up stories about her "cases," including the crimes, along with detailed descriptions of her detectives and suspects. That led to her discovery of Nancy Drew mysteries. After she finished the series, she didn't want to be *like* Nancy. She wanted to *be* Nancy.

While other girls her age were focused on experimenting with makeup and noticing boys, Val was hooked on solving crimes. In junior high and high school, while her classmates were tuning in to *Dawson's Creek*, she was glued to reruns of *Murder, She Wrote* and working on the student newspaper. Later, she eagerly awaited new installments of Sherlock Holmes movies and series (Robert Downey Jr. and Jonny Lee Miller were her favourites).

Val's fascination with solving crimes, plus her love of reading and writing, led her to enrol in journalism school, with her sights set on becoming a crime reporter. Covering crime wasn't where a reporter started their career, however. First, you had to prove your worth covering city council and writing news-desk copy. On a small city paper, you had to bide your time if you wanted to switch beats. Wait for the right opportunity. After two decades, Val's patience was worn thin.

"But you're so good in entertainment," said Kevin, grumbling. "Who would take over? Besides, Joel's hanging on for the full pension."

Long-time crime reporter Joel Holt was sixty-three. Like Kevin, during the last round of layoffs he had flipped the bird at being packaged out.

"You could give entertainment to the intern," Val suggested. "It's a great place to make a name for yourself."

"I'm not confident that kid can read," said Kevin, turning back to his computer. "But I'll put in a good word for you when the job comes up. Should only be a coupla years."

"Thanks," said Val, grimacing. "I'm so glad we had this talk.

Shall I file it under 'career growth plan'? I've recorded it." Poker-faced, she held up her cellphone.

Kevin looked surprised. "Seriously?"

Val laughed. "Nah, just kidding."

As she put her belongings away at her desk and turned on her iMac, Val silently begged the universe to find a way to keep the *Post* afloat long enough so she could prove to Kevin—and, more importantly, to herself—that she was worthy of covering crime. And ready. She was fed up with being pigeonholed in entertainment.

What she needed was a break. Some kind of way in. And it had to be something big. That morning, as she began preparing to profile the NOVA Prize nominees, she had no clue that at the gala ceremony in a few short weeks, the crime beat would find her.

Val's apartment, Halifax

SHERLOCK HOLMES LOVED WORK-AT-HOME Wednesdays. Val's cat was affectionate, but only with her. She knew that if Sherlock could speak, he'd say: "Sure, I'll sit on *your* lap and purr, but let's be clear—I don't want anyone else touching me."

Hovering around a hefty twenty pounds, Sherlock took up all of Val's lap, with some overflow. He tolerated her regular brushing of his long, luscious grey fur coat. His tufted lynx-like ears made him look like he belonged in the wild. Yet Sherlock was strictly an indoor cat. For good reason.

It wasn't until Val had brought Sherlock home from the breeder that she noticed her kitten's emerald-coloured eyes were crossed. The vet insisted that crossed eyes was a common condition in cats. That imperfection made Val love Sherlock even more. Sadly, however, it meant he wasn't a mouser. Which was unfortunate, because Val was currently waging a war with a large family of rodents in her apartment.

Val was working on her laptop at her small dining-room table, putting the finishing touches on the profiles of the NOVA Prize nominees, when she spotted Mouse Number Twelve skittering along a baseboard and running into a low kitchen cupboard.

"Goddammit," Val muttered. Sitting on the chair pad next to her, Sherlock lazily licked at a paw.

In the past three weeks, eleven mice had stumbled stupidly into three kinds of traps: snap, sticky, and electronic. Plus, Val had set out several boxes of poison pellets, all placed safely away from Sherlock's prying paws.

Val felt like a murderer, but there was no way around it. The disease-ridden vermin that kept gnawing holes in her bags of oatmeal, rice, and pasta—now in the best lock-top storage containers money could buy—had to go.

So far, Number Twelve was eluding her efforts to capture it. Her landlord was indifferent. There was so much construction happening in the city that rodents were migrating from building sites in droves, seeking shelter in old heritage houses with cracked foundations, no longer just in winter to keep warm but *all year long*.

And so, the war waged on.

Reluctantly, Val turned her gaze away from Number Twelve's flight path and toward her laptop.

"Today, Sherlock, my goal is to finish the Q&As for each NOVA Prize nominee," she said, cracking her knuckles before placing her hands on her keyboard.

Despite Kevin teasing Val about her "puff pieces," he was fully aware that the paper's subscribers loved her *Book Briefs* column. As soon as their praise landed in her inbox, Val forwarded it to Kevin with the cheeky subject line: "Time for a raise?"

Normally for author spotlights Val wrote straight narrative profiles with quotes, but this year she'd decided to mix it up with Q&As. For a writer, they were easy to draft, and as a reader, she loved them (she always read the "Proust Questionnaire" first in *Vanity Fair*).

To get in the zone, Val reviewed the notes she had taken during her phone interview with Sally MacPhee. Because Sally was old, and therefore old-school, she preferred a phone call to a video interview. Unlike many reporters, Val had always chosen note-taking over recording her interviews. Who could be bothered transcribing tape or deciphering the typos in voice-to-text printouts? Not her.

Two hours later, Val stood up to stretch, walking the few steps to the galley kitchen to plug in the kettle. After dropping a bag of green tea in a mug, she got herself a chocolate chip granola bar from the cupboard. Sighing, she grabbed a tissue to scoop up Number Twelve's latest "evidence" from the shelf, then tossed it in the garbage can.

Returning to her laptop, Val reviewed what she'd written. The Q&As had to be short, because they would run with an author headshot and an image of the book cover. *My kingdom for a higher word count*, Val often thought.

Author: Sally MacPhee
Hometown: Wolfville
Nominated novel: *Alex Cage*
Publisher: Greenwich Press

Book Briefs: Where did you get the idea for *Alex Cage*?

Sally MacPhee: From the stories I heard growing up about my paternal great-grandfather, who left school in grade eight to work in a Cape Breton coal mine. 'Alex Cage' was the nickname given to the man who operated the mine's elevator shaft in the twentieth century. I set my novel around that character—a rough, uneducated teenager with a tender heart. Cape Breton coal miners had hard lives, and I wanted to honour them.

BB: Over the years, you've been nominated for several awards, but you've yet to win. What would winning the NOVA Prize mean to you?

SM: Everything. Absolutely everything.

BB: What's next for you?

SM: Right now, I'm busy promoting *Alex Cage*. After that...I'll have to wait and see, I suppose.

Author: Victor Comeau
Hometown: Meteghan
Nominated novel: *The Reinvention of René Thibauld*
Publisher: Acadian Editions Publishing

Book Briefs: Where did you get the idea for *The Reinvention of René Thibauld*?

Victor Comeau: *C'est l'histoire de mon peuple, les Acadiens*—the story of my people, the Acadians—and it called to me. I have always wanted to write about the Acadian immigration from France to Louisiana in the late eighteenth and early nineteenth centuries. It is an important tale of trauma, tradition, and transformation that must never be forgotten.

BB: You're a first-time author. How does it feel to be nominated alongside more seasoned novelists?

VC: *Je suis honoré, bien sûr*. I am honoured, of course. May the best book win. But if I may be so bold—I hope it is mine!

BB: What's next for you?
VC: *Le ciel est la limite.* The sky is the limit. And I am planning to reach for it.

Author: Sonya King
Hometown: Lunenburg
Nominated novel: *Frances Coleman Carries On*
Publisher: Yesteryear Press (Romantic Escapes imprint)

Book Briefs: Where did you get the idea for *Frances Coleman Carries On*?
Sonya King: I've always been fascinated by the Halifax Explosion. Much has been written about Vincent Coleman's bravery, but I couldn't find anything in-depth about his wife, Frances, and what her life looked like after Vincent died. I wanted to convey her courage in raising their four children as a widow during such a tumultuous time in history.

BB: You're an award-winning romance novelist. Why switch to historical fiction?
SK: My protagonists have always been strong women, and my last novel was historical-fiction romance. So, it felt like a natural evolution for me to transition from one genre to the other. To be honest, I was ready for a change, and I think my readers were, too...or at least I hope so!

BB: What's next for you?
SK: I'm midway through a new manuscript, but the premise is under wraps for now. My lips are sealed!

Author: Alexander Fitzgerald
Hometown: Halifax
Nominated novel: *Cape Breton Calls Him*
Publisher: Ceilidh Publishing

Book Briefs: Where did you get the idea for *Cape Breton Calls Him*?
Alexander Fitzgerald: I love a period drama set in Cape Breton, so I decided to write one. The setting is an homage to the beloved part of the province where I was born and raised, although the story and characters are entirely fictional. There's a twist that should knock readers' socks off!

BB: Have you read the other nominated authors' novels?
AF: I have, and I can honestly say that they're all terrific. I don't envy the judges!

BB: What's next for you?
AF: A long-overdue vacation [chuckles]

Val rubbed her eyes, then closed her laptop. At the office tomorrow, she'd review the Q&As once more before filing the drafts to Kevin. One Q&A would run every Saturday in the four weeks leading up to the awards weekend.

Sherlock purred loudly on Val's lap. Gently rubbing his head with two fingers, she held one of her usual one-sided conversations with him.

"Sally is sweet and grandmotherly, and I really hope she wins," she said, shifting to better support her furry friend's bulk. "But I admire Sonya's evolution as an author, and Alex has put in the work."

Wrinkling her forehead, Val paused, lost in thought. "Then there's Vic, who came of out nowhere. If he wins, he'll be a dark horse for sure. And I bet a lot of people will be royally pissed off. If I were a betting woman, I wouldn't know which horse to put my money on."

Bev's house, Hantsport

BEV CLARKE WAS DOING HER BEST TO DODGE MESSAGES from her bookie. The one who had recently loaned her an enormous sum of money. Because Bev couldn't pay it back.

If there was one thing Bev had learned since she began betting on horses online, it was that you didn't mess around with Big Bernie Brown. At eighty-two, Bernie wasn't interested in someone else's sob story. That's because no one could beat Bernie's: childhood poverty, absent father, abusive mother, foster homes. Quit school at sixteen to work as a paddock assistant at the Truro racetrack, quickly promoted to paddock judge. That's where she'd been introduced to betting.

Rising from a tragic beginning, Bernie had become the top bookmaker in the province. A young Bernie had first operated from ramshackle digs in Stewiacke. Now, mission control was the most expensive suite at an exclusive nursing home in Halifax's South End.

Bev knew from first-hand experience not to dick Big Bernie Brown around. That's because Big Bernie was a relative. Her aunt: Bernice Alice Brown. Babs to her friends. And at her age, the old woman could count the friends she truly trusted on fewer than four fingers.

"Dammit," said Bev. Another text from Bernie demanding she pay up: **Not now. Not tomorrow. Yesterday.**

Bernie hadn't made a direct threat, but Bev had heard rumours about the nefarious ways her aunt elicited payment from debtors.

"How did I sink myself this deep into quicksand?"

It was a rhetorical question. As long as Bev could remember, she had loved horses. There were posters on her bedroom walls in elementary school. *Black Beauty* and *My Friend Flicka* were her favourite books. Watching horses race on TV, then live in Truro.

When Bev was twelve years old, her aunt took her to the racetrack and taught her to bet. Gave her a ten-dollar bill. Treated her to an ice cream when her horse crossed the finish line first. Bernie had looked at Bev with such pride that the impressionable young girl's heart swelled. That was all it took. Bev was hooked. Throughout her youth, she regularly went to the track with her Aunt Bernie. It seemed unusual to outsiders, but that's how Bernie bonded with her niece. And Bev's mother was happy to have her introverted daughter out of the house, doing something besides reading books.

Then, when Bev was in high school, the outings stopped when her seat next to Bernie was taken over by a young paddock assistant named Patrick. The slight stung. But all of that was a long time ago.

Now, because Bev needed more money than her editor's salary provided to pay for her "hobby," she took on side hustles for cash. Legitimate ones, of course. Freelance editing projects. Occasional pet sitting and dog walking. A few times, she'd even cleaned houses. But the money wasn't great, and there were only so many hours in a day. Plus, now that Bev was menopausal, she tired easily. So, against her better judgment, she'd asked Bernie for a loan.

Lowering herself slowly onto the living room loveseat, Bev was careful not to spill her mug of coffee. Situated on Hantsport's main drag, the back of her bungalow overlooked the muddy Minas Basin. Her gaze lingered on Cape Blomidon, looming large in the background. With her money woes, was it time for a hike that included a swan dive from Lookoff Loop onto the rocky beach below?

Shivering, Bev wrapped her hands tightly around her mug. Suicide wasn't the solution, she supposed. Mostly because she was a coward. Would anyone even miss her if she disappeared into the ether? She had no parents (dead). No partner (couldn't keep one). No kids, nieces, or nephews. No pets. Few friends. Sally was dying. And now, sleepless nights worrying about paying Bernie back.

It'd be a shame to have to sell her home. Bev had already refinanced it once to pay previous debts. With the housing crisis and dearth of affordable apartments, if she did sell, she'd have nowhere to go.

I need Sally to win the NOVA Prize, thought Bev. *Then I'll ask her for a loan. And then, if I'm lucky, she'll die before I have to pay it back*.

These thoughts made Bev feel ashamed. But not paying Bernie back in a timely fashion would have unpleasant consequences. Bernie had always been big; her bulk in and of itself was intimidating. After a young Bev saw *Return of the Jedi*, she realized her aunt looked like crime lord Jabba the Hutt, but with drugstore reading glasses, pink lipstick, and a perm.

Therefore, guilt was a luxury Bev simply couldn't afford.
Sally simply had to win the NOVA Prize.
But what if she didn't?
Bev didn't have a Plan B.

Big Bernie Brown: The Bookie

Penthouse suite, South End, Halifax

BIG BERNIE BROWN DIDN'T TAKE CRAP FROM ANYONE. Tipping the scale at three hundred and twelve pounds on a five-foot-eight frame, the acerbic octogenarian was in full command of her faculties, and her fiefdom.

Bernie took no crap from the nursing home staff. Or from her friends. Or her family. *Especially* not from her family. And especially not from her least-favourite brother's daughter, Bev. What a privileged childhood that girl had. Both parents home and working (until Bev's brother was incarcerated, that is). Never went hungry or wore threadbare clothes. *Buck up, buttercup.*

Oh, sure, Bev was okay, Bernie supposed. Right on time with cards for her old auntie's birthday and Christmas. Probably hoping to inherit a little *je ne sais quoi*. Visits? Nope. The occasional text when she needed money was pretty much what their relationship amounted to now.

When it came down to brass tacks, the bookmaking business was just that—a business. And the tacks that Bernie had loaned Bev recently were the brassiest of the bunch.

"C'mon, kid, pick up," said Bernie, punching her niece's number into her cellphone. "You know ya can't outrun me."

From her perch on the sofa, Bernie looked at the walker parked in front of her.

"Well, maybe *run* isn't the right word," she said, chuckling.

Bernie didn't bother leaving a message. Bev would see who'd called. And know why.

There were other bettors who owed Bernie big money. In fact, Bev and one other gambler—a well-known author who had gotten mixed up in something shady—knew each other in a professional sense, but Bernie had a policy to keep her "clients" confidential.

Bernie sighed, shifting her bulk awkwardly on the sofa. What was wrong with these literary types? Didn't they earn enough royalties to cover their "hobbies"? They should get off their high horses and write erotica. *Fifty Shades of Grey* had done all right. Hadn't it?

The Pay Bernie Back Clock was ticking at ear-splitting decibels. See, if Big Bernie's clients didn't reimburse her, then she had to foot the money herself until they did. And while her reserves were deep, they weren't infinite.

To be fair, Bernie had never put a hit on a client who hadn't ponied up in a timely fashion. No, she wasn't *that* kind of bookie. Because over the years, she'd discovered that there were other ways to make people pay.

You know the saying *You can't get blood from a stone*? Turns out you can, if you pound its hand hard enough with a hammer. Or back over its foot with a tractor. Or stick a sharp knife in its neck.

Sometimes, all you had to do was light a little fire.

Leaning heavily on her walker, Bernie shuffled her way down the hall to the bathroom. As she lowered herself onto the toilet, her cellphone rang. Glancing at it, she saw it wasn't Bev. It was the author.

Grunting as her bunged-up bowels released slowly—she'd forgotten to take her Lax-A-Day—Bernie heaved a sigh of relief before answering the call.

"Big Bernie," was her trademark greeting.

"I know you asked for full payment, but I have half now," said the caller.

Or at least that's what Bernie thought she heard.

"Speak up, for Chrissake, it sounds like you're in a tunnel." Technology gave Bernie a rash.

She heard a click, then a clearer voice. "Sorry, I was on speakerphone. Where should I make the drop?"

"Same place as usual," said Bernie, rolling her eyes. *Amateurs*. "When will you have the rest?"

A nervous cough, followed by, "Same time next month okay?"

Standing unsteadily, Bernie flushed the toilet. The way she felt right now, she was ready to flush her financing business, too. For good.

The hell with it.

The highs and lows Bernie used to thrive on now cancelled each other out. What used to be exciting was now...not. Might be time to retire. But like all potential retirees, she worried about what she'd do to occupy her time. Macramé in the arts-and-crafts room? Cribbage in the games room? Chair yoga in the exercise room?

Not on your fuckin' life, Bernie thought. *Just feeling sorry for myself. It'll pass.*

"Yeah, one month from today for the rest," said Bernie, trying to sound tough (even that took effort). "I'm marking it on my calendar." She mimed writing it down, but she never had to. Safer, too. No paper trail that way.

Ending the call, Bernie shuffled over to the bookcase. Taking a photo off a shelf, she wiped the dusty frame on her belly.

"There, that's better," she said, staring sadly at the greasy-looking man on a motorcycle. Grinning wickedly at the photographer. Now, he had been gone longer than they'd been together. "You were an asshole. But I loved you."

Friday afternoon
Lord Nelson Hotel, Halifax

SALLY UNPACKED HER SUITCASE SLOWLY, SAVOURING the moment. Her battered blue Samsonite was open on the queen bed in her room at the Lord Nelson Hotel. From the window, she gazed wistfully upon the Public Gardens in its late-June splendour. The rhododendrons were in full bloom, the sun beaming down on them. High school graduates in prom finery were having photos taken in front of the beautiful bell-shaped purple and pink petals.

They're so young and healthy, thought Sally. *Their future is anything they want it to be. Not like when I was their age.*

Sighing with envy, she lifted her bible out from under a folded cardigan and placed it reverently on the bed, caressing the worn cover with a wrinkled hand. She never left home without it, even though hotels still tended to keep one in the nightstand drawer. Then she took her toiletries to the bathroom. No longer able to walk without a cane, she moved with trepidation. Tripping and breaking one of her brittle bones wasn't an option. Not this weekend. It was important for her to tread carefully, and to hang on.

As she placed each pill bottle next to the sink, Sally mentally reviewed the weekend's itinerary. Supper and small talk tonight in the hotel's restaurant with Sonya, Vic, and Alex. Saturday afternoon, an hour-long Q&A with Bev in the main-floor Admiral Room. Saturday evening, a panel discussion with all of the nominees in the Britannia Room, in conversation with that nice newspaper columnist, Val Jenkins.

For an hour on Sunday morning and in the afternoon, the authors would be set up at tables in the main-floor Regency Ballroom, selling and signing their books. There would be lineups of loyal readers, no doubt. Sunday evening was the main event: the gala in the grand Imperial Ballroom, a three-course supper followed by the awards ceremony.

Sally prayed she had enough stamina to get through the next two days. She had to summon the strength. She knew it was her final festival. She'd rest in her room when she could. And double her pain medication. Triple it, if she had to. It didn't make her sleepy. Because one thing was certain: she had to keep her wits about her. Now, though, it was time for a little lie-down.

Passing the desk on her way to the bed, Sally noticed a typewriter sitting on top. Drawing closer, she saw that it wasn't just any typewriter. It was an antique. And there was a sheet of paper in it. With words on it.

Gently pulling the paper from the roller, Sally moved with her cane to the chair. Pushing her glasses up higher on her nose, she read the following:

> Congratulations, Sally MacPhee, on being a finalist for this year's NOVA Prize! We are pleased to gift you this fully functional 1920s Underwood typewriter to provide inspiration on your next book. Best wishes in all of your future writing endeavours.
>
> Sincerely,
> Emilie Craig
> Chair, The Westby Foundation for the Arts

Tears filled Sally's eyes. What a generous, thoughtful gift. Expensive, too, she imagined.

Sadly, there wouldn't be another book. *Alex Cage* was her swan song. For weeks, Sally had been preparing to write her own final chapter. Soon, she would be meeting a very personal deadline.

Before Sonya King even opened her suitcase in her hotel room, her long legs carried her swiftly to the desk.

"What's this, now?" she mused aloud. Leaning forward, she pulled a piece of paper from a vintage typewriter. Then she sat in a corner armchair to read it.

"What a lovely gesture!" she said, placing the note in her lap. She took a photo of the typewriter and the message, then texted them to Booth. He was arriving on Sunday for the gala.

Booth's reply arrived a few minutes later:

Nice! That was thoughtful of them.

Sonya sent a smiley face and a heart back.

As much as she was looking forward to the gala, her mind couldn't help but turn toward the future. She already had the plot of her next book mapped out.

As Victor lathered his armpits with shampoo in his hotel room shower, he sang loudly and off-key. Five minutes earlier, the young, shapely front-desk clerk had slipped out of his king-sized bed, ready to return to her shift.

The song he was butchering? "The Winner Takes It All."

He wasn't normally an ABBA fan, but when the shoe fit…

Vic's outfit for that evening's author dinner was draped over an armchair. Black dress pants and shoes. Dark grey shirt, with enough buttons open to reveal a hint of chest hair. Lighter grey blazer. À la Pedro Pascal.

Pursing his lips like a runway model, Vic whispered to his reflection in the full-length mirror: "*Je suis un tueur de femmes.*" *Oui.* A lady killer. When Vic won this award, the babes would be lining up around the block, begging him to sign their books. Maybe their breasts, too. Those, he would initial in private.

He felt a stirring. *Non. Pas maintenant. Plus tard.* To distract himself from lascivious thoughts, Vic pulled the piece of paper from the old typewriter on the desk. Reading it, he laughed. He crumpled the sheet and tossed it at the garbage can. He missed. And shrugged.

Merci, mais non merci. He didn't want a rusty old typewriter. What use would he have for it? Certainly not to write his next book. For there *would* be a next book. Of that, he was certain. When he won this award—and there was no doubt in his mind that he would—publishers would be banging down his door. There would be a bidding war. Journalists would be tripping over themselves to interview him.

Vic had no idea what his next novel would be about. But he knew who would write it.

Alex had packed his most colourful clothes for the awards weekend, plus a matching pair of bold eyeglasses frames for each outfit. Lifting his suitcase onto the bed, he thought, *If I don't win, at least I'll look sharp in the photos.*

If the judges were political in their voting, he thought Sally was a shoo-in. One: She was old, and this might be her last book. Two: She had been nominated many times for other awards but had never won. Three: Her novel was good. Good enough for the Governor General's Award? No. Good enough for the NOVA Prize? Probably.

If Sally did win, Alex thought of the irony of her title: *Alex Cage*. The first name mocked him. It was her story, but it could have been his, given his Cape Breton roots.

Alex was proud of his novel, of course. It wasn't that. But he wasn't sure it was good enough to place first.

Cape Breton Calls Him was captivating, but not entirely original: B+.

Sighing, he noticed the vintage typewriter on the desk and knew right away that it was an Underwood. A classic. It was thought that Ernest Hemingway had written *A Moveable Feast* on a 1926 Underwood Standard Portable. Gently pulling the piece of paper from its carriage, he sat in the armchair to read it.

"So sweet," Alex said, softly. "I guess the grocery business continues to be brisk. Even if ordinary folks can barely afford to buy bananas. But we won't dwell on *that* this weekend. In fact, the Westbys were so generous that each judge also received an antique typewriter, with a note thanking them for their talent, time, and contribution to the award."

Checking his watch, Alex saw that it was time to meet the others in the restaurant. He'd go to the fitness room later to work out. The Westby Foundation was picking up the tab on accommodations and meals, but he tucked his wallet in the inside pocket of his suit coat out of habit.

As he picked up the key card to his room, Alex spoke a final reminder out loud: "Remember to compliment Vic's glasses."

Friday afternoon
The Halifax Post's *office*

STANDING IN HER BOSS'S DOORWAY, VAL JENKINS watched Kevin Lewis two-finger-type furiously. Banging the send button with something akin to aggression, he turned toward her. "What?"

"I have a tummy ache," said Val, pressing a palm to her abdomen and grimacing.

"No, you don't," said Kevin.

"Yes, I do," Val insisted. "And I'm gonna report you to HR for not taking my ailment seriously."

Kevin snorted. "Good luck with Human Remains. Buncha palookas."

Val paused. "It's…female troubles. Yeah. I'm pretty sure my uterus is trying to kill me. I should go home and spend the weekend in bed with Advil and a hot water bottle."

Kevin sighed. "Buck up, Mary. And quit fibbing. You're so transparent I can see right through you to Trent scrolling on his goddamn phone instead of doing whatever it was I asked him to this morning."

Val plopped herself in the chair in front of Kevin's desk. "You shouldn't swear at the office, the intern's name is Tyler, and why can't you send *him* to cover this weekend's events instead of me?"

"I'm going to have to get rid of that chair," Kevin grumbled under his breath. Louder, he asked, "Why the sudden change of heart? I thought you were looking forward to getting all gussied up and schmoozing."

Val shrugged. "Yeah, I was, but I'm just not feeling it anymore," she admitted. "I know it's the tenth anniversary, and that's a big deal. But to me, it's just one more year of the same old thing. I've been there, done that, nine times already. I'm…*tired*. If I can't write about crime, I'd rather stay home and curl up with Sherlock and a good book."

"I'd rather curl up with a rum punch on a beach in Punta Cana, but if wishes were fishes…yada yada." Kevin frowned. "What a stupid saying. So, you'll go and do a bang-up job, like you always do. And hey, since it's a milestone anniversary, maybe it'll be a real showstopper."

Val rolled her eyes. "You're a tough boss, Lou. May I take Monday off in lieu of overtime?"

Already banging away on his keyboard again, Kevin grunted.

"I'm taking that as a yes." Val jumped up and made a quick exit before Kevin could protest.

Neither editor nor reporter knew exactly what kind of showstopper the awards weekend would turn out to be. And that Val certainly wouldn't be able to take Monday off.

That evening, after feeding Sherlock and herself, Val did curl up on her sofa with a cup of chamomile tea, her cat, and a local murder mystery. Because she was a book columnist, publishers sent her advance reading copies in the hopes she'd review them. Her TBR pile on the floor next to the sofa nearly reached the ceiling.

Personally, Val would rather be reading Sir Arthur Conan Doyle for the umpteenth time. But since her employer was a far cry from *The Strand Magazine*, duty called.

"All right, Sherlock, let's recap." Val picked up her book to accommodate the furry feline doing doughnuts in her lap. "A spry retired high-school teacher goes missing in the backwoods of Nova Scotia, and one of her former students with a criminal record is the prime suspect. Which means, of course, that he didn't do it. So… who did?"

Just then, Mouse Number Twelve raced across the living room floor and into a baseboard crack. "Fuck!" Val said as Sherlock licked a paw.

The tiny rodents were revolting. Trying to keep up with killing them reminded Val of fruit flies: you might win a battle or two, but never the war. Val made a mental note to stuff steel wool in the hole later. And call her landlord. Again.

Val wondered how many other single forty-four-year-olds were at home on an early summer Friday night. With their cats. Their books. And their mice.

"I'm kinda lonely, buddy," said Val, reaching down to scratch Sherlock's head. "But I'm glad I have you."

Sherlock showed his mutual affection by stretching and yawning.

"Not that you'd understand, but dating sucks," said Val. "Maybe I'll meet someone at the book awards. He'd have to be gainfully employed, handsome, and not allergic to cats."

Val had no idea she would indeed meet a handsome man with a good job and a recently departed tabby cat that weekend. And that the event leading to their meeting would be the catalyst to revamping her career.

Friday late afternoon
Lord Nelson Hotel

"I LOVE YOUR GLASSES, VIC," SAID ALEX.

"It's Victor, *mon ami*," said Vic, barely glancing at Alex across the table.

Pretentious prick, thought Alex.

What a dick, thought Sonya.

That wasn't very nice, thought Sally.

An awkward silence followed.

Alex sipped white wine.

Sonya nursed a cocktail.

Sally stared at her water glass.

Vic downed a shot of whisky.

Alex wouldn't allow himself to be baited by the arrogant Acadian who reeked of expensive cologne. "Now that the pleasantries are out of the way, I propose a toast."

"That's a wonderful idea," said Sonya, gripping her glass with pale pink fingernails polished to perfection.

Vic motioned for a second shot. When it arrived, the four nominees raised their glasses.

"We've all worked long and hard on our novels, and there's no doubt we're all equally proud of them," Alex began. "And while there can only be one grand-prize winner, I think *everyone* at this table has already won."

Vic drained his second drink and snorted. "Well, you've got one thing right, *mon ami*. There can only be one winner." *Et ce sera moi*, he thought.

I'm not your friend, thought Alex.

This man is dreadful, thought Sonya.

I'm not feeling well, thought Sally.

Except Sally had said it out loud.

As soon as Sonya had seen Sally, she could tell the older woman was ill. Cancer, she suspected. Whatever kind it was, it had likely metastasized. Once a doctor, always a doctor.

Sonya laid a cool palm on Sally's warm hand. "What do you need?"

"To go lie down," said Sally, with a wan smile. "The trip up on the shuttle took more out of me than I anticipated."

"I'll take you to your room and get you settled," said Sonya, standing. "We can order room service if you feel up to it."

Sonya looked at Alex and Vic. "Go ahead and enjoy your meals. We'll see you in the morning."

Great, now it's just the two of us, with no buffers, thought Alex.

Great, thought Vic. *If the old woman kicks the bucket this weekend, it'll mean less publicity for me when I win.*

"Well, *mon ami*, if you don't mind, I've got a little business to take care of, so *excusez-moi*," said Vic, standing. "*Bon soir et bonne chance.*"

Fuck off, jackass, thought Alex. Smiling, he raised his glass and nodded.

Now Alex could enjoy his meal in peace. At a table on the other side of the room, he spotted the judges having drinks. Steve Silver appeared to be arguing with the other two. Alex watched a red-faced Steve push his chair back and stand up unsteadily.

There's another jackass, thought Alex.

"You'll be shorry," slurred Steve, jabbing a finger at Del and Sunny. Loudly enough that heads turned toward their table. Holding on to the backs of chairs, Steve stumbled his way out of the restaurant under the baleful eyes of the front-of-house staff.

Shorry for what? wondered Alex. *What a clown.*

Just then, a server brought his entrée to the table: squash puttanesca.

"I'm afraid my companions could only stay for drinks, so I'll be dining alone," Alex apologized. Lifting his wineglass with a flourish, he added, "I'll have another one of these, when you have a chance, please."

Alex would make sure he saved room for coffee and dessert, too. Clearly, he wouldn't be dining out on good company. Might as well milk the weekend for all it was worth.

Friday evening
Lord Nelson Hotel

SONYA HELPED SALLY SETTLE INTO BED AND WAS ONLY slightly surprised when the older woman began to weep.

"What's wrong?" said Sonya, pulling a chair close to the bed.

Wiping her eyes with a tissue, Sally shook her head back and forth. *No.*

"It might help to talk about it," said Sonya softly.

Sally's chest lifted as she inhaled, then exhaled slowly. Composing herself.

Sonya decided to be blunt. "You're dying, aren't you?"

The tears flowed again as Sally shook her head up and down. *Yes.*

Sally said something so softly, Sonya had to bend forward and ask her to repeat it.

"I have a plan," Sally whispered.

"It's helpful to have a plan," said Sonya, placing a hand on Sally's arm. "It gives you some control, and time to prepare."

"But my plan is a sin in the eyes of the Catholic church," said Sally. Her words thick with shame.

Sonya raised her eyebrows. This was no time to mince words.

"Are you planning to take your own life?" asked Sonya.

"No!" replied Sally, horrified.

Good, thought Sonya. *So much can go wrong. I've seen it in the emergency room.*

Trying to think like a Catholic, Sonya tried again. "Have you arranged for a medically assisted death?"

Sally felt safe with Sonya. Like she could trust her. Maybe it was because the elegant woman had spent her career caring for people. Maybe the pain and shame were just too much, and the thought of sharing it with someone else finally too irresistible. Whatever the reason, she chose to tell Sonya the truth. About everything.

Sally nodded up and down. *Yes.*

Sonya gave a gentle pat on Sally's arm. "Have you chosen a date?"

Tears. Up and down. *Yes.*

Sonya considered herself agnostic, with a hard lean toward atheism, but she knew Sally needed comforting.

"I think your God will forgive you, Sally. But first, you have to forgive yourself."

Tears. Back and forth. *No.* Sally swallowed. "I'm scared. That's why I'm doing it. I don't want to die alone at home. In pain. With a guilty conscience."

Sitting back in her chair, Sonya placed her hands in her lap. "Will a relative or friend be with you?"

"You're the first person I've told," Sally admitted, arthritic fingers clutching the bedsheet.

Sonya processed that information. Deciding what to do with it.

"What about Bev?" Sonya thought the author and her editor were close.

"Oh, no, I couldn't ask her," said Sally. "I wouldn't want to upset her."

Sonya's face softened. "I've never attended a MAID death, but I know doctors who perform them. They've told me the person's passing is peaceful. And that while it's difficult to bear witness, it's a comfort to whoever is present because there's no suffering. Booth and I plan to have one ourselves, if the circumstances call for it."

"You do?" asked Sally, eyebrows raised.

"Yes," said Sonya. "We're seventy-two, Sally. Only a few years younger than you."

"Yes, but you're both healthy," said Sally, shifting a bit. "And... you have each other."

Sonya helped Sally lean forward so she could rearrange her pillows. "We're healthy today, but there are no guarantees for tomorrow, or the days after that," she said. "I was a doctor and Booth was a lawyer. We don't have children. So, we have all the appropriate legal documents drawn up."

Sonya paused. Then she made a decision. Putting her hand on Sally's arm again, she asked, "Would you like me to be there?"

Tears spilled from Sally's eyes. She nodded up and down. *Yes.*

"All right, that's settled," said Sonya, passing Sally a tissue from the box on the bedside table. "When this weekend is behind us, we can talk about it."

"Thank you," said Sally. "But first, there's something else I need to tell you. Something that happened a long time ago that has filled me with guilt, and shame, ever since. Something I can't bring myself to confess to my priest. Then you can decide if you still want to be there."

While Sally was confessing, neither woman noticed that someone lurking in the hallway had silently slipped the toe of their shoe in the door to prevent it from closing. And that person was hanging on to every word.

Saturday morning
Val's apartment

SHERLOCK HOLMES WAS PAWING THE BOTTOM cupboard next to the kitchen sink.

"Why can't you eat mice instead of treats, you cross-eyed cutie?" asked Val, squatting to open the drawer where Sherlock's food was kept. "I should have returned you for a refund when I had the chance."

Placing four Temptations on the worn pine floorboards, Val looked at her watch. Almost noon. She'd have a quick bite, then take a cab to the Lord Nelson for the afternoon of Q&As with the nominees. To ensure maximum media coverage, the Westby Foundation was springing for transportation and meals.

It would be a long day of small talk, but Val didn't mind chatting with the other authors and reporters she knew. Overall, it was a pretty close-knit community. Most of the events were free for the public to attend. For the gala, people had to buy tickets to sit at tables with starched white cloths and wineglasses to find out first-hand who would be crowned the winner of the province's top prize.

To witness which author had a sincere smile on their face.

And which three did not.

But that was tomorrow. Tonight, at seven o'clock, Val would conduct a casual "in-conversation" with the nominees. Ever the old-school journalist, her questions were in her purse on paper, plus on her phone as a backup. The Westby Foundation was paying her a generous stipend for her time, the least she could do was be prepared.

Normally, Val didn't dress up for author events. However, since it was the NOVA Prize, and the gala's dress code was formal, she had made an effort. Plus, she was moderating a panel. In the full-length bedroom mirror, she inspected herself.

Long, flowy blue dress with paisley print (steamed on the bathroom door while she showered).

Strappy sandals (toenails painted red post-shower, several already smudged).

Mascara (expiry date unknown; would she get pink eye?).

Caramel-coloured lip gloss (which would wipe off the first time she sipped water).

Hair (chin-length black curls damp and untameable).

Accessories: notepad and pen.

It was a step up from her usual casual uniform of T-shirt, jeans, and sneakers.

The Westby Foundation had arranged for a photographer, but Val would snap shots on her phone for her personal social media accounts and record part of the session for background material for her story.

Tucking a dishtowel into the neckline of her dress, Val sat at the kitchen table to devour a ham-and-cheddar sandwich on Italian sourdough from the German bakery in her neighbourhood. She enjoyed a hearty, savoury breakfast. It was a good thing she had the metabolism of a greyhound.

After brushing her teeth and reapplying her lip gloss, Val grabbed her purse and bent down to scratch Sherlock behind his ears. "All right, buddy, I'll see you at bedtime," she said, over his purring. "Hopefully, I'll have a good story to share with you and with my readers. And, hey…try to kill a mouse, will ya?"

As Val locked her apartment door, she had no idea that she would soon be involved in a very different kind of story. One unlike any that she had ever written before. One that she had been dreaming about writing for years.

Saturday morning
Bev's house

AT 7:00 A.M., BEV CLARKE WAS IN HER BASEMENT WORKout room, running on a treadmill in front of the washer and dryer. Every ten minutes, she slowly increased the speed and incline until the settings were on par to a brisk sprint up and down Citadel Hill. After an hour of cardio, she'd move to the weight-lifting bench.

In university, Bev had won track-and-field medals for shot put and discus. Now, at fifty-three, those glory days were firmly in the rear-view mirror. And while she no longer had the physique of an elite athlete, she liked to stay in shape. She didn't want to be old with brittle bones.

Like Sally.

The poor woman, thought Bev, as her heart and lungs pumped oxygen-rich blood to her muscles and cells. Sweat beaded on her forehead and dampened her T-shirt. While her feet flew faster, she wondered how long Sally had left to live. One thing was certain: their collaboration on *Alex Cage* had marked the end of their professional relationship.

Attending the NOVA Prize gala ceremony as Sally's plus-one would be bittersweet.

Pondering Sally's demise led Bev to think about her own future in the industry. Was her own editorial death on the horizon? Only the owner/publisher, Eve MacIntosh, was older than Bev, in her early sixties. It was no secret that Eve was coaching her daughter, Heather, who had recently earned a master's in publishing, to take over the business.

After they first worked together, Sally had only wanted Bev as her editor. They were a dream team! In between Sally's manuscripts, Bev had worked with other authors. In the early days of her career, there had been a skeleton staff at Greenwich. During any downtime, she had happily pitched in with production and promotion. As the company grew, so did the number of employees, and Bev's "other related duties" fell away.

Oh, sure, after Sally was gone, Eve and Heather would make an effort to rustle up more authors for her to edit. But for how long? If they were searching for somewhere to slash the editorial budget, Bev's position was at the top of the salary scale. She was also acutely aware that she was at risk of aging out of a struggling regional book-publishing system that was recruiting junior editors with low salaries to match their minimal experience, but who had excellent digital and video skills.

Only recently, an intern had been hired on a temporary contract to handle social media, exclusively, and to expand those accounts. Bev simply couldn't keep up with the technology. Nor did she want to. During the pandemic, she had despaired when video meetings and online editorial calendars were instated. And she couldn't design a promotional poster if her life depended on it, no matter how many times a younger coworker told her that Canva was "user friendly."

Bev had to face the facts: she was an old-school editor—a one-trick pony. If she lost her position at Greenwich Press, what would she do?

There was always the dreadful task of ghostwriting. Bev had only done it once, and it wasn't a process she wanted to repeat. Dealing with an author with a massive ego who wanted results but refused to carve out an adequate schedule was not an effective use of her time and talent. Even if it paid well. *Really* well.

I should never have signed the NDA, thought Bev. Not that she would have told anyone anyway. It wasn't something she was proud of. But she needed the money.

Glancing down at the display on her treadmill, Bev reminded herself to stay calm so her blood pressure wouldn't spike. Instead of fretting about the future, she tried to focus on the present. And on her secret project. Something she had been working on in her spare time for a decade. On evenings, weekends, and vacations. On "sick days." Something that she fantasized would help wipe out her debts.

The project? Her own novel. When she was finished, it would be a six-hundred-page masterpiece. One she prayed would someday win the NOVA Prize.

Bev would show everyone then.

Of course, she was writing under a pseudonym. In the publishing world, editors were often thought of as "wannabe" writers. The assumption was that if you weren't good enough to get published, you edited or taught the craft. Often, you did both to help make ends meet. Over the years, Bev had led several editing workshops. She didn't love teaching. Mainly because while most aspiring writers had heaps of enthusiasm and ambition, they had no talent. And as every good editor knows, you can't teach talent. But she was always happy to deposit the honorarium cheques.

It was no surprise, then, that Bev didn't want to submit her manuscript to potential publishers with her own name attached to it. She knew only a handful of top-notch editors who also happened to be crackerjack writers. Bev believed she was one of them. Which didn't explain why her manuscript had been rejected by three regional publishing houses so far. Efforts to land a literary agent had been fruitless, and the multinational publishers didn't accept submissions from authors without one.

There was always self-publishing, Bev supposed. The option of last resort. Even if she wanted to go that route (she didn't), she couldn't afford to pay a freelance editorial team. The expense of having copies printed? Out of the question. Paper and printing costs had skyrocketed in recent years. Hybrid publishing wasn't much cheaper, but it would reduce some of her workload.

No.

To feel like a real author, Bev needed to land a traditional publisher. A proper contract, with an advance. But already she felt defeated by the discouraging submissions process.

And yet.

Bev knew that Stephen King's novel *Carrie* was rejected by thirty publishing houses. *Harry Potter* was rejected by twelve. *Chicken Soup for the Soul* was rejected by one hundred and forty-four (having once received it as a Christmas gift, Bev could understand why). All successful authors advised persisting. In fact, one of them maintained that the best reaction to a rejection slip was sitting in front of your keyboard with an evil grin, muttering, "Okay, you bastards. Try rejecting this!"—and then writing something brilliant.

Starting her cool-down, Bev picked up the bottom of her T-shirt to wipe the sweat from her face.

She planned to persist, all right.

Turning off the treadmill and catching her breath, Bev said bitterly, "One day I'll show those bastards who the best writer in Nova Scotia is."

Checking her cellphone for messages, Bev saw that Bernie had called several times, but had left only one voice mail: "Hey kid, the sharks are circling. Well, one hungry, pissed-off shark. Me. You have one week to cough up the cash, or I'll be sending Boris to have a little chat with you."

Bev sat on the weight-lifting bench. Held her head in her hands. And sobbed.

Saturday evening
Lord Nelson Hotel

IN THE LORD NELSON'S STATELY BRITANNIA ROOM, THE audience's applause was deafening. Smiling broadly at the four authors surrounding her, Val placed her notes on her lap and clapped, too.

That went well, thought Val, rolling her shoulders to release the tightness.

The authors had been engaging and entertaining. Val glanced at them, still sitting in their chairs in a semi-circle on the stage. Talking among themselves.

Sonya was glowing like a South Shore sunrise.

Vic was turning his head from side to side as cellphones snapped shots of him.

Alex was laughing as he waved to someone across the room.

Sally looked spent.

A brief reception followed. Coffee and tea flowed into cups, and hungry hands dipped into trays of sweets and melon skewers. Val filled a plate, then hung back to hug a wall and eat.

Del Davis spotted her. Raising a hand, he made his way across the throng toward her. "Great panel," he said. "You're a natural moderator."

Val smiled. "Thanks, but the nominees are the stars," she said. "As you know first-hand. I just ask the questions."

Del returned her smile but said nothing.

So humble, thought Val. *And so talented*.

From their vantage point on the sidelines, Val and Del watched as groupies lined up to gush over their favourite authors. Some had brought gifts: cards, homemade cookies, flowers. They had been asked not to bring their books—those would be signed the next day, when the authors appeared in the Regency Ballroom. They were just available now for a quick hello before retiring for the evening.

"I know better than to ask you who the winner is," said Val, patting her mouth with a linen napkin. "But of the four books, can you tell me if you have a personal favourite?"

Del pursed his lips. "Off the record?"

"Of course," said Val. "Just curious, really. My favourite was *Alex Cage*. I think Sally outdid herself."

Del relaxed. "In that case—and only because I trust you—I really enjoyed Vic's book."

"You sound surprised," said Val, setting her empty plate on a table.

Del scanned the room. No one who mattered appeared to be within earshot. You could never be too cautious, though.

"Is this whole conversation off the record?" he whispered.

Val pretended to look confused. "What conversation?"

Del shrugged. "Well, then, yeah, I *was* surprised. The guy's a rookie. No previous novels. Not even a short story or a poem to his name. Just ho-hum academic papers. It's…weird."

"Hmm," Val replied. Noncommittal. When she'd read *The Reinvention of René Thibauld*, she'd felt the same way. Unsettled. It was an impressive book, there was no disputing that. She wondered if the editor had taken a heavy hand.

Also, although he was fluent, English was Vic's second language. It was odd that he hadn't written his first novel, about a Frenchman, in his first language.

Then again, sometimes writing talent lay dormant. Like a volcano. Waiting for the right hot-magma moment to erupt. Maybe that was Vic's backstory. He had been biding his time. In secret.

Except, from what little Val had learned about Vic, that didn't seem like his style.

Del finished his coffee, then set his empty mug next to Val's plate.

At that moment, a staff member wearing a black blouse and black dress pants slipped past silently to put the dirty dishes on a trolley and take them away. Lingering here and there, longer than necessary. Listening. Val glanced away from Del to thank the woman and noticed her luminous green eyes.

"Are you coming to the gala?" Del asked Val, hopefully. He more than trusted the newspaper reporter. He had a crush on her, but was too shy to ask her out.

"Yup," she replied. "I'm skipping the book signings, though."

"Yeah, me too," said Del, stifling a yawn. "I need some serious sleep. My duty is done until the ceremony."

"Are all of the judges staying at the hotel tonight?" Val asked, curious. She could see Sunny deep in conversation with a dapper white-haired gentleman wearing a tweed suit coat with a multicoloured pocket square.

At the drinks table, Steve was standing alone, filling a water glass with a shaky hand. Looking like death warmed over.

"Yes, we're all staying overnight," said Del. "The Westbys are beyond generous. I plan to empty the minibar and order one of everything off the room-service menu."

Val threw her head back and laughed. "Well, have fun…I think?"

Del smiled, his pulse quickening at the thought of seeing her again. "See ya tomorrow."

Oblivious to Del's well-hidden feelings about her, Val waved him off and surveyed the space. Vic and Alex were busy working the room. Sonya was handing Sally her cane. One measured step at a time, the two women made their exit. Offering polite greetings to admirers along the way.

Sally looks quite sick, thought Val. *I hope it isn't anything serious. That's kind of Sonya to help. I wonder where Bev is?*

Unbeknownst to Val or anyone else, Bev had slipped into the room late, hid in the back row, then left when the applause began.

Bev was on a secret mission. One that would climax later that night with its very own hot-magma moment.

Sunday afternoon
Val's apartment

"WHAT SHOULD I WEAR, SHERLOCK?" ASKED VAL, STANDing in front of her closet. "I have what you'd call a capsule wardrobe. Which means I hate shopping."

Lying on the bed, Sherlock lifted a back leg and licked it. Indifferent to his favourite person's plight.

Val sighed, pushing hangers aside to better view her choices. Although it was hot and humid outside, the hotel was air conditioned.

"This," said Val, pulling a burgundy cotton sleeveless dress with a lacy bolero jacket. Peeking down at her feet, she decided she didn't need to touch up her pedicure. No one attending the gala would be paying any attention to her toes. Or to her, for that matter. Which suited her fine.

A chime announced an incoming text. Kevin. Which was odd. He never messaged off-hours.

Hey, Mary. Have fun tonight. Don't forget to take tomorrow off.

Val watched three dots swimming as her boss typed some more. The dots stopped. Then started again.

I'm out of the office for the next week or two. Don't worry, I'm not getting axed, but two of my toes are. Be in hospital for a bit. Marianne will cover.

Marianne Phillips was the deputy managing editor. Early sixties. Smart. Built like a brick shithouse. Wrote the best headlines in the business.

Val frowned. While she liked Marianne, she was worried about Kevin. Amputation was serious. Her appeals to him to stop smoking and start eating fruit and vegetables were tantamount to Sisyphus pushing a boulder uphill.

Frustrating.

Futile.

Roger that, Lou. Take care. I'll check in next week.

Glancing at the clock on the kitchen wall, Val showered, dressed, and applied minimal makeup. After she fed Sherlock, it was time to call a cab.

Although she'd rather stay home tonight, curled up with a Stephanie Plum novel and her cat, Val found herself curious which book would win the NOVA Prize. There had been a lot of buzz at the events all weekend, and when she thought about it, they really were so lucky to have such a prestigious award in their small province. Even if she'd rather watch the ceremony's livestream on her laptop from bed.

Picking up her purse, Val gave Sherlock one last ear scritch. Then she was off. For a night that would change everything.

Sunday evening
Lord Nelson Hotel

IT WAS SHOWTIME.

Just before 6:00 P.M. in the Imperial Ballroom, more than one hundred hungry guests in various interpretations of finery were finding their seats. The tables were laid with white linen cloths and napkins, shiny silverware, wineglasses and bottles of Tidal Bay on ice, coffee cups, and fresh floral centrepieces.

Val located her place card at a table in the middle of the room with two other reporters. Together, they represented newspaper (her), radio (Bob Landry), and television (Janice Murphy). Like Val, Bob and Janice had been covering the NOVA Prize right from the start. They were friendly professional acquaintances who genuinely enjoyed each other's company. Which couldn't be said for all of the reporters in the city.

"God, I'm starving," said Bob, grabbing a warm roll from a basket and slathering it with a decorative pat of whipped butter. "I came straight from the studio. Are we laying a friendly bet on the winner?"

"I'll put ten bucks on Sally," said Janice, sipping a glass of water. "She's due."

"I'll match your ten but put it on Vic," said Val. "He's the dark horse."

"Guess that leaves me with Alex or Sonya," said Bob, grabbing a second roll as soon as he finished the first.

"You won the pool last year, right?" asked Janice, glancing at the table in front of the stage where the authors would sit. Still empty. Behind them, at the judges' table, were Del, Sunny, and Steve, plus Emilie Craig, the chair of the Westby Foundation.

"Yup," said Bob, crumbs flying from his mouth. "I think I'll go with…Alex. I mean, that twist! Didn't see it coming."

"I know, it floored me, too," said Janice, nodding.

"Bets on the table," said Val, pulling a ten from her wallet. The others did the same. Janice put the sugar bowl on top of the bills as a paperweight.

Turning around in her chair, Val scanned the room. She spotted many familiar faces. Seated at one table were some of her favourite independent booksellers. Val gave them a wave. They all worked incredibly hard to support and promote local authors, and she often reached out to them for commentary. Since the nominations were announced, the shortlisted novels had been flying off their shelves.

"Oh, look, there are the authors," said Janice, nodding toward the door.

The reporters' heads swivelled to see Sonya helping Sally walk to their table, with Alex bringing up the rear.

"No Vic?" said Val.

"Not surprised," said Bob, cracking open the bottle of wine. "He's been late for every interview I've done with him." He poured each of them a glass.

"Same," said Janice, lips puckering like she'd bitten a lemon. After glancing over her shoulders, she whispered, "He's a pompous ass."

Val laughed. "Shh! Not now. Hey, there's Sonya's husband."

Booth King, looking sharp in a tailored light-blue suit, sat next to his wife and kissed her cheek.

"Who's Sally's plus-one?" asked Bob, reaching for a third roll after refilling his already empty wineglass.

Janice slapped his hand. "Leave some for the rest of us!" she scolded.

"I'm pretty sure the Westbys can afford another basket," said Bob, tossing the roll in the air with his right hand, then catching it with his left.

"Why do men feel the need to juggle things?" mused Janice.

Bob shrugged. "It's in our DNA. Although technically, it wasn't juggling. It was tossing."

Janice rolled her eyes and took a sip of wine. Val smiled, aware that the two reporters had a long-ago romantic history. They had since settled into a comfortable friendship.

The same could not be said for Val and her ex-fiancé. Who had returned home to Calgary after their breakup. Thankfully.

Interrupting the pair's playful bickering, Val nodded toward the empty seat in question. "Sally told me Bev was going to be her date," she said, scanning the room. "But I haven't seen her today."

Swallowing his mouthful of buttered bun, Bob shrugged. "Maybe she's sick."

"Maybe she's sleeping with Vic," said Janice, swivelling to scan the room. "My spidey sense is tingling."

Val grimaced. "For her sake, I hope she isn't," she said. "I don't know why his wife stays with him."

"Now, now, we shouldn't judge," said Bob. Remembering how hard *his* wife had worked to earn his forgiveness and regain his trust after her affair.

When a server passed by, Bob held up the empty bun basket and pointed to the wine bottle, signalling that they needed more.

Val couldn't judge. Perks were rare in journalism these days.

Now that three of the four authors were seated, the audience was getting restless. It was fifteen minutes past the start time. At the judges' table, Emilie Craig looked concerned. Conversation there appeared strained.

"Look, there's Bev now," said Bob, pointing. The reporters saw the editor slip into the empty seat next to Sally. Breathless. Face flushed. They continued watching as Bev leaned over to whisper in Sally's ear.

The older woman's eyebrows rose to her recently permed hairline. Then she patted Bev's hand.

"Who's that doe-eyed teenager dressed like she's at the Oscars sitting next to Alex?" asked Janice, squinting. "Stupid cataracts. I need binoculars."

"No clue," said Val, moving sideways for a clearer view. "Maybe his niece? I heard he and his boyfriend broke up."

In fact, Alex had brought Usha, his graduate student, as his date. It was the least he could do to make up for the pittance she was being paid from the grant money he'd received to hire her.

Over at the judges' table, Del and Sunny seemed to be having an intimate conversation.

Sunday evening
Lord Nelson Hotel

DEL AND SUNNY WERE CHATTING ABOUT THEIR WORKS in progress.

"What's your word count?" asked Del, who obsessed over his.

"I'm about halfway to the finish line on the first draft," replied Sunny, his relief evident as he sipped strong coffee.

"That's great. But how many words are we talking? Thirty thousand? Forty?" asked Del, pressing the point.

Sunny shrugged. "Somewhere in between, I think," he said. "You know I don't keep track like you do. I just go with the flow."

Del sighed. "Yeah, I know. I check the word count after I finish each chapter. It helps me see how far I've come."

"It would make me realize how far I have left to go," said Sunny, chuckling. "I do a tally when I finish writing each day, but I can never remember the number."

Steve wasn't taking part in their conversation. He was too busy chugging the complimentary wine. Emilie Craig was trying hard not to notice. Reaching into the purse on her lap, she covertly palmed a tiny white pill and placed it under her tongue. While the anxiety medication was dissolving, she checked her cellphone.

"I wonder what's keeping Vic?" Steve shouted out of the blue, just this side of slurring. "Probably his wandering dick."

"Please lower your voice," said Sunny between gritted teeth.

If Steve heard him, he didn't let on.

"Vic's late for everything," said Del, moving the wine bottle away from Steve.

"Yeah, but you think he'd want to be here to make a grand entrance," said Sunny, frowning. "It *is* odd."

Pushing his chair back, Sunny walked over to crouch next to Emilie. After a brief whispered conversation, he returned to his seat.

"Emilie says their publicist knocked on Vic's door but there was no answer," he said. "She's been trying to reach him on his phone. I offered to go talk to someone at the front desk."

"I'll come with you," said Del, standing up. Anything to be rid of Steve for a few minutes.

"Our good man is probably schtupping the help," said Steve, reaching for the wine.

When Del and Sunny arrived at the reception desk, they explained the situation. The on-duty manager, Jamal, accompanied them to Vic's room on the third floor. He looked like a student. It's because he was one, they learned as they rode the elevator together, doing a co-op placement at the hotel for the summer.

When they reached Vic's room, Jamal knocked loudly three times before calling out: "Mr. Comeau, are you there? It's time for the awards ceremony to begin."

Crickets.

Jamal knocked again. Repeated himself.

Looking at Del and Sunny, he said, "We'll give it another minute, in case he's…indisposed."

Still no response on the third try.

"Mr. Comeau, we're coming in now to see if everything is all right," said Jamal. Using his master key card, he opened the door.

Three pairs of eyes were drawn downward. They didn't have to walk any farther to find the missing author.

"Jesus Christ," said the Buddhist.

Del's vocal chords were paralyzed.

For years afterward, Jamal would have nightmares about the scene in front of him. But in that moment, he felt an odd sense of calm. He pulled out his cellphone, called 911, and gave details to the dispatcher.

On the floor next to the desk, Vic lay crumpled on his side.

Skull smashed.

Legs twisted.

Face covered in blood.

Features frozen in…horror?

No. Not horror.

Surprise.

Next to Vic lay a beautiful antique typewriter, its keys mangled and bloody.

Sunday evening
Lord Nelson Hotel

WITH SHAKING HANDS, JAMAL ENDED THE 911 CALL.

"The police are on their way," he said, his voice trembling. "We aren't to touch anything. I'll call the front desk to let them know what we...discovered...and stay here to secure the...scene."

"What should we do?" asked Sunny, keeping an eye on Del, who looked like he might faint. Or throw up. Or both.

"Don't go back to the ballroom, because people will have questions that you shouldn't answer right now or they'll panic," instructed Jamal. "Go sit in the mezzanine until I come get you. I'm sure the police will need to speak with everyone while they're here."

"Oh god," Del whimpered. Sunny placed a reassuring hand on his friend's arm.

"What about everyone in the ballroom?" asked Sunny.

"The hotel will handle that," said Jamal, looking relieved. "We have a team that responds to...*delicate* situations."

As Del and Sunny made their way to the mezzanine, they were lost in their own thoughts. When they reached a sofa, Del collapsed onto it as though the backs of his knees had been whacked with a baseball bat.

"I wonder what other kinds of 'delicate situations' have happened here?" Sunny mused aloud, thinking back to what Jamal had said.

"Now is *not* the time to ask," said Del. "And anyway, I don't want to know. I think I'm gonna pass out." Spreading his legs apart, Del lowered his head inch by inch until it was between his knees.

Sunny patted his friend's back. "Hang in there, pal."

Del grunted. When he stopped seeing stars, he sat up slowly. "What do you think will happen to the gala? I mean, will they still announce the winner?"

Sunny frowned. "I didn't even think of that. I don't know. I doubt it. Maybe they'll hold off until the police interview everyone. I can't imagine the event will go ahead after people find out about Vic."

Del scratched his head through his thick, curly hair. "Do you think Vic's death could have been an accident?"

Sunny frowned. "What, he was typing a thank-you note to the Westbys when he fell backward, banged his head on the typewriter, and killed himself? Like Bob Saget? Although come to think of it, there was no blood in Bob's case."

"No, not like Bob Saget," said Del weakly. "And that's not funny."

"It's kinda funny," said Sunny, shrugging. "Given the victim. Vic, I mean. Not Bob. That was tragic."

"I realize that Vic was murdered," said Del, shuddering at the word. "I meant, do you think it was an accident? Like, whoever did it didn't plan it?"

"A crime of passion, you mean?" said Sunny.

"Yeah," said Del. "But who would want to kill Vic?"

The friends looked at each other. Poker-faced.

Sunny tilted his head and grimaced.

"Hey, he was an egotistical pig, but that doesn't mean someone hated him enough to kill him," said Del. "Does it?"

Sunny sighed. "No. If that was the case, half the writers in the province would have hits out on them. Unless…"

Del waved a hand for his friend to speed it up. "Unless?"

"Unless Vic had a nefarious secret," said Sunny, shrugging. "And someone was threatening to expose it."

"Okay, but why here?" Del said, then added, after a beat, "We should talk to Val."

Sunny squinted at him. "We were literally just told not to speak to anyone until the police get here, and you want to go straight to the press?"

"Not like, officially," Del explained. "Off the record. I trust Val. She's probably interviewed everyone here at some point," he added. "If anyone knows an author's secrets, it's Val. Plus, she's a reporter. If she doesn't have the answers, she can dig for them."

"Worth a shot, I suppose," said Sunny, considering. "Let's look for an opportunity."

Just then, a commotion in the lobby caused the two judges to look over the balcony railing. Four uniformed police officers had arrived ahead of the homicide detectives.

"Thank god," said Del, exhaling audibly. "I feel safer now." And yet his right foot hadn't stopped tapping since they sat down.

"Why wouldn't *you* feel safe?" asked Sunny, perplexed. "No one has an axe to grind with you. Or wants to bury one in your back."

Del turned to face him. "Good grief, would you knock it off with the gallows humour? I don't feel *safe* because an author was just *murdered* at an event full of *authors*," he said. "What if there *is* a target on someone else's back?"

Sunny slumped back onto the sofa. "I hadn't actually thought about it like that. But if Vic was killed for, say, the prize money, the murderer won't be coming after us."

"But no one knows who the winner is," Del pointed out. "Except for us, Steve, and Emilie Craig."

"Right. Shit." Sunny sighed. "Do you think Steve blabbed?"

"Wouldn't surprise me," said Del. "But if he did, it still wouldn't explain why Vic was killed."

A knowing look passed between them.

"Don't say the winner's name out loud," whispered Del. "The room could be bugged."

"Man, you're paranoid," said Sunny, closing his eyes dramatically.

"You know I have anxiety," said Del, his foot still tapping. "Maybe someone wanted to ensure that, if Vic *was* the winner, he wouldn't live to enjoy the money."

"There's really no point in speculating," said Sunny practically, removing his glasses and rubbing his eyes. "I'm hungry and tired. None of this makes any sense. We need to talk to Val."

Bourque and Slade: The Homicide Detectives

Sunday evening

Lord Nelson Hotel

DETECTIVE CONSTABLE WADE BOURQUE OF HALIFAX Regional Police had set up an incident command room in the Lord Nelson's stately Georgian Lounge. Over the mantel hung a portrait of the hotel's namesake, Admiral Horatio Nelson. Bourque wasn't aware that the mantel had never changed since the hotel's grand opening in 1928. However, he did know that Nelson was a commander responsible for several naval victories during the French Revolutionary and Napoleonic wars.

Hands clasped behind his back, Bourque stood in front of the painting. "Bet you could tell some good stories, Admiral," he said.

"They say talking to a portrait of a dead man is a sign of senility." At a nearby table, an attractive woman in a grey pantsuit was typing on a laptop. "Sarge," she added as an afterthought to show respect.

In her mid-thirties, Detective Constable Sarah Slade's blond hair was coiled at the nape of her neck in a neat bun. In a makeup-free face, her blue eyes were bright and missed nothing. At the police college on PEI, she had been top of her class. Smart. Ambitious. A team player.

"Ha, I'm not senile yet," said Bourque, striding toward the table. "Just thinking out loud."

At forty-two, Wade Bourque was the lead of the criminal investigation division's homicide unit. Born and raised in Pubnico on the Acadian Shore, he was the fourth of six sons of a commercial fisherman and a homemaker. Unlike his father and his brothers, a life on the sea had not called to him. Bourque decided he wanted to be a police officer in elementary school, since the day a francophone cop had visited his grade-five class to talk about bullying. With a gentle

German shepherd by his side, the kind but authoritative officer had won him over.

Sarah Slade didn't know Wade Bourque's backstory. Only that he was a good leader and mentor. A recent recruit to the homicide unit, she knew she would learn a lot from observing him. Physically, he was handsome. Tall and fit, with short, curly brown hair and brown eyes. Tonight he was dressed in a navy blazer with a light-blue short-sleeved shirt and dress pants. Too hot for a tie. Brown leather brogues. Unless he was speaking to a fellow francophone, Bourque's accent was barely detectable.

Thankfully, Slade's assessment of her boss's good looks was purely objective. Her wife, Daphne, was a deputy sheriff at the courthouse. They had met there during a murder trial. Sarah had testified, and Daphne had escorted the prisoner to and from the courtroom to the cell block. Their eyes had met across the courtroom. A cop's idea of true romance. Both women had chosen careers where they sought justice for victims through proper process and procedure. But the path to justice wasn't always clear-cut.

Sometimes the good guys lost.

Sometimes the bad guys walked.

Sometimes the victims were bad guys.

Sometimes, in spite of the good guys' best efforts, justice was never served.

Which will it be this time? Slade asked herself. As she always did at the start of a case.

Lowering his lanky frame into a floral-patterned armchair on the other side of the table, Bourque said, "Let's review what we've got."

"Right," said Slade, glancing at her notebook. She read out what they knew about the victim, Victor Armand Comeau, then moved on to the medical examiner's preliminary comments.

"He's saying it looks like homicide, but we'll need to wait for the autopsy report in a few hours to know for sure. He thinks time of death was likely two hours before Mr. Comeau's body was found, so around 4:00 P.M. No sign of forced entry. Presumed murder weapon: the typewriter lying on the floor next to him."

"Right. That's something to start with, but we'll need more in order to begin profiling potential suspects. Did you reach his wife?"

"Yeah," said Slade, referring to her notebook. "Simone Maillet. Also a Sainte-Anne professor. Said she's been in Chéticamp doing research all weekend. With her *boyfriend*."

Although nothing surprised Bourque anymore, he raised his eyebrows.

Slade shrugged. "According to Ms. Maillet, she and her husband had an open marriage. Mr. Comeau also had lovers. She didn't sound too upset when I told her he was dead."

"Could be shock," said Bourque, scratching the back of his neck. "Or could be that their marriage wasn't as open as she wants us to believe."

"Revenge?" asked Slade, tapping her pen on her notebook.

"Maybe," said Wade. "Is she on her way home?"

"Yes, she'll be back..." Slade flipped open her notebook and glanced at it. "...tomorrow at around lunchtime. I'll set up a time to interview her when she returns. And check her alibi."

"Very good," said Bourque, lifting his lanky frame from the low, soft armchair "Now, we have to deal with a roomful of writers who have spent the last two hours sitting in the ballroom, wondering what the hell is happening. Probably making up all kinds of stories in their heads."

Slade stood next to him. "Don't they say truth is stranger than fiction? What's the plan?"

"I've already asked Ms. Craig not to announce the winner until our investigation is complete," said Bourque, perching on the edge of the desk. "First, a celebration isn't appropriate considering the circumstances. But it'll also give us an opportunity to interview everyone who attended, and draft a list of potential suspects, before a big, fat cheque hits the fan."

Now Slade's eyebrows rose. "You know there are at least one hundred people in that room? Plus staff and other guests."

"Yeah, we'll need to call in the investigative team to help conduct interviews and take statements," said Bourque, rubbing the scratchy chin he had shaved that morning. "It's gonna be a long night. We'll need a floor plan. A list of guests and their room numbers. Restaurant reservations. Video surveillance, from within the hotel and the exterior. And make sure no one leaves the building until we've gotten names and phone numbers for everyone. Given the number of people here, our team will have to conduct several of the interviews at the station. You and I will stay on scene, run things from here."

"On it," said Slade, pulling out her cellphone. As she dialled, her favourite Columbo quote sprang to mind: *There's no such thing as a perfect murder.*

Sunday evening
Lord Nelson Hotel

BEV HAD NEVER BEEN SO SCARED IN HER LIFE. AND THAT was saying something, given that Big Bernie Brown was her aunt. The rumours that Bernice Alice Brown had made Vinnie "The Vulture" Capello cry like a baby were true. Afterward, the notorious mafioso from Chicago always walked with a limp. Vinnie never lived it down. When their honeymoon was over, he never played poker with Bernie again.

"It was the sixties," said Bernie, as if that was a reasonable explanation, whenever she told the story (in certain company only, of course). "Everyone was hooked on heroin. Except for me. I noticed very quickly that drugs made people stupid. And when you're stupid, you make mistakes. Serious mistakes. *Deadly* mistakes. So, I decided to stay smart and sober. Back then, as a young woman in this business, you had to find innovative ways to get a leg up on your rivals. Or break a few legs."

Then Bernie would sigh, look wistful, and say, "Those were the glory days."

Thinking about her aunt, Bev took her seat next to Sally in the Imperial Ballroom. Her entire body was trembling. Her mouth was dry, but her hands were shaking so badly she worried if she took a sip of water, she'd drop the glass. Now was not the time to call attention to herself.

However, Bev would call Bernie as soon as she had a chance. Because if there was one person who would know how to get her out of the mess she suddenly found herself in, it was her aunt.

There was no question that Bernie could make a big mess herself. But she could also clean one up. The question was, would she?

Since Bev's distress was obvious to Sally, the older woman patted her editor's hand. Leaning close, she whispered, "Are you all right, dear?"

Across the table, Alex and Usha were looking at something on his phone. Giggling. Not paying the least bit of attention. Although Bev was flustered, she noticed something on the knuckles of Alex's right hand. A rash? Scrape? Bruise? When Alex caught her staring at it, he quickly moved his hand to his lap.

"Just a touch of intestinal distress," Bev lied, holding her stomach. "What have I missed?"

"Not a thing," said Sally. "We're waiting for Vic. Sunny and Del went to look for him, but they haven't come back."

Bev blanched.

Just then, everyone in the ballroom watched as a handsome middle-aged man and a striking young woman strode purposefully to the stage. Not visible to the audience were the nine-millimetre pistols holstered on their hips, nestled beneath their blazers.

At the reporters' table, Janice exclaimed, "What the hell are *they* doing here?"

Bob rubbed his chin thoughtfully. "It's not to announce the grand-prize winner, that's for sure. When those two show up, it can only mean one thing."

"What? Who are they?" asked Val, confused.

Bob and Janice turned away from the stage to face her.

"They're homicide detectives," said Janice, who had stopped covering crime after her first baby was born. "When they're invited to a party, it usually means someone has been…sent home early."

The reporters stared at each other. Simultaneously, all three said: "Vic."

As Detective Bourque approached the podium, a hush fell over the audience.

Speaking into the microphone, he introduced himself and Constable Slade. "We're sorry to interrupt your evening, but we're here to inform you that one of the hotel guests has been found deceased. And we believe it to be a suspicious death."

Janice and Bob looked at Val and mouthed *murder*. They pulled out their cellphones and started texting their assignment editors.

Shocked murmurs bubbled up from audience members. Bourque raised a hand to quiet them.

"Unfortunately, the ceremony to announce the winner will have to be rescheduled to a later date, after our investigation is complete," he continued.

Disappointed gasps filled the room. Emilie Craig looked close to tears.

When the hubbub quieted down, Bourque wrapped up. "We'll have to ask each of you not to leave the hotel until one of our officers has either taken your name and number in order to interview you at the station in the coming days or is able to take your statement while you're here. It'll be a long night, so if you have children or pets that need care at home, please contact someone who can look after them until you're free to go. Thank you for your co-operation."

A surge of adrenaline powered through Val's bloodstream, from the tips of her toes to the top of her head. Sitting up straighter in her seat, her cellphone buzzed. It was a text from Marianne at the *Post*.

Who popped their clogs at the hotel?

Val typed quickly: **How do you know?!**

From the office, working the night shift, Marianne snorted as she typed: **I am omnipresent. Like God. Ha. Also, we have a police scanner.**

Val replied: **Cops haven't said. Could be Vic Comeau. NOVA Prize nominee. He's missing.**

Val had to read Marianne's next message twice to be sure she wasn't hallucinating: **I need you to write a feature about the awards that ties in Comeau's murder as the story develops.**

Val's heart beat double-time: **What about Joel?**

Three dots swam, then stopped: **He's busy covering the mall-stabbing murder trial.**

For years, Val had been waiting for a chance to cover crime. To challenge herself. To prove, to both herself and to the higher-ups at the paper, that she could write about more than just books and entertainment. That she could dig. Flush out the truth. Ensure justice was served.

On it. Does Kevin know?

As Val read Marianne's reply, her eyes grew moist.

It was his idea. Texted from the hospital. He's down two toes but doing all right. And staying in the loop. He said to tell you: "Kick some criminal ass, Mary."

Smiling, Val typed: **I'll keep you posted. As soon as I can leave, I'll head to the office for a debrief. Mary Richards, over and out.**

Roger that, Marianne responded. **Keep it on the down-low while you're there. Might give you an edge. Let people talk. Listen. Eavesdrop. Sue Ann Nivens, over and out.**

Val laughed as the nickname Marianne had chosen for herself. The outspoken deputy managing editor couldn't be less like saccharine Sue Ann from the TV show.

Bob and Janice glanced up from their phones. Messaging their producers and their families, no doubt.

"What's so funny?" asked Bob, trying to peek at Val's phone.

Putting her phone back in her purse, Val replied, "That was Marianne. Kevin must be on some good meds, because she said he hasn't been making any sense."

"How's he doing?" asked Bob. At the beginning of his career, he'd been a reporter at the paper. Kevin had been a good boss.

"Okay," said Val, shrugging. "You know Kevin. He's tough."

Val was relieved when the detectives walked from the podium toward Emilie Craig. The poor woman looked like her dog had just died.

Janice noticed Val noticing Wade Bourque. "Tall drink of water, isn't he?"

"What? No…he just looks…um, familiar," said Val. Her pink cheeks betrayed her fib.

Janice winked. "He's single. Married and divorced young. No kids."

Thankfully, Val didn't have to answer because Bob grunted. "Jesus. Are we gonna get fed or starve in our seats? 'Cause if we're gonna starve, there'll be a lot more dead bodies to account for in here."

Janice made a face. Looking at Val, she said, "He goes from happy to hangry in two seconds flat."

Just then, tense-looking servers started trickling into the room pushing food trolleys.

"Thank Christ," said Bob, gripping his fork and knife like weapons. "I was gonna go all *Lord of the Flies* if they didn't feed us soon."

Standing up beside her chair, Janice stretched her arms overhead and rolled her shoulders a few times. "I could lead a chair yoga class while we're stuck here," she said. "Could be good for morale."

While Janice limbered up and Bob watched the trolleys approach like they were delivering manna from heaven, Val scanned the room, spying uniformed police officers stationed at both exits. Her eyes settled on Detective Bourque, who was doing his own crowd surveillance.

Val and Bourque locked eyes. For three full seconds.

When Bourque looked away to continue surveying the room, Val exhaled.

The tenth-anniversary NOVA Prize gala was not going according to plan.

And Val couldn't have been any happier.

Sunday evening
Lord Nelson Hotel

IN THE GEORGIAN LOUNGE, DETECTIVES BOURQUE AND Slade had completed their interview with Jamal Johnson. The kid was shaken, but he'd pull through, with the appropriate supports. He'd done everything right. They marked him off their list of potential suspects.

"Who's next?" asked Bourque, walking across the room to stretch his legs.

Slade consulted her notebook. "Sunil Patel. One of the judges."

Bourque nodded. "Okay. Let's bring him in."

When Slade returned with Sunny, Bourque introduced himself and gestured to the chair on the other side of the table. "We're investigating the suspicious death of Victor Comeau. For your information, we're making audio and video recordings of all of our interviews, which is standard procedure."

Bourque nodded at Slade, who was in charge of the equipment.

"Ready," she said.

"Mr. Patel, please tell us how you came to find Mr. Comeau's body in his hotel room," Bourque began. "Don't leave any details out, even if you think they aren't important."

Fiction writers are descriptive, detail-oriented, and dramatic. Sunny talked.

And talked.

And talked.

Sunny set the scene like a bad true-crime writer overdoing hackneyed metaphors. Bourque's favourites:

"Blood pooled under Vic's head like gasoline leaking from a cheap sedan."

"Vic's head was turned at such an unnatural angle he looked like that little girl in *The Exorcist*."

"The typewriter keys were more mangled and bloody than George Chuvalo's hands after a botched bout in the ring."

Until finally, Bourque held up his hand. "Thank you, Mr. Patel. That's an incredibly...vivid description of the crime scene. Did you happen to see anyone in the hallway before you entered the room?"

"I don't think so." Sunny closed his eyes to mentally review the moment. "I really wasn't paying attention to the hall."

"Could there have been someone there you didn't notice?" Bourque pressed.

Sunny paused to consider the question. "I suppose so. Maybe someone from housekeeping, but I can't say for certain. At that point, I was just focusing on finding Vic. And hoping he would open the door."

Bourque nodded. "Please tell us how you knew Mr. Comeau."

Sunny crossed his legs. Then uncrossed them. Even though he hadn't done anything wrong, he couldn't help feeling like he was in trouble.

"Well, I didn't know him personally." Sunny leaned forward and clasped his hands. "He is—sorry, *was*—a new author. I hadn't heard of him before I read his book as a NOVA juror. He kind of came out of nowhere."

Bourque glanced at his laptop screen. "You're a university professor, correct?"

Sunny nodded. "That's right. I teach part-time at the University of Cape Breton."

"Mr. Comeau was also a university professor. At Sainte-Anne. Did you know him in an academic capacity? Even peripherally."

Sunny shook his head. "No, he didn't teach in the English department, so our paths didn't cross."

"I see," said Bourque, while Slade made notes. Sunny wished he could peek at what she was writing. He hoped it was *Too nice to be a killer*.

"Do you know Mr. Comeau's wife, Simone Maillet?" asked Bourque, watching Sunny's facial expression. "She teaches English literature and creative writing at Sainte-Anne."

"No," said Sunny, removing his eyeglasses to rub his eyes, then readjusting them. "Sorry, I don't feel as though I'm being very helpful. As you know, our universities are at opposite ends of the province. And there isn't much of a budget to send us part-timers to conferences, which is where you usually meet other faculty members."

"I understand," said Bourque, then changed direction. "What was your impression of Mr. Comeau from your interactions with him on the jury, and from spending time with him this weekend?"

Crossing his arms, Sunny blinked. "What do you mean by 'impression'?"

Although Bourque had already heard rumblings, he had no intention of leading the witness. "I mean, did you like him? Was he a good guy?"

Sunny shrugged. "I didn't spend any time with him. As a judge, you need to be impartial. Del and I have been friends for years, so we've been hanging out this weekend."

"Have you been hanging out with the other judge, too?" asked Slade, glancing at her notes. "Steve Silver?"

At Steve's name, Sunny's armpits grew damp.

"Del and I had supper with Steve on Friday. Then tonight, the three of us were at the judges' table with Emilie Craig, the Westby Foundation chair."

"But you didn't spend time with Mr. Silver in between?" asked Bourque.

"No," said Sunny. Hoping the interview would wrap up soon. Before he soaked his shirt.

Bourque probed further. "Why not? Was Mr. Silver not a friend?"

"No, he was not a *friend*," said Sunny simply. "He was a… colleague." Sunny wondered if the detectives could tell how much he was sweating.

"Why wasn't he a friend?" questioned Slade.

Cracking under pressure, Sunny blurted out the truth: "Because he's an alcoholic who embarrasses himself, and everyone around him, when he's soused. He's a narcissist. A misogynist. He has no scruples or morals. For what it's worth, he's also a has-been, professionally. He used to be a talented writer. Now, he's a hack. He hasn't come up with an original idea in at least a decade. When he does write a book, it's…dreck. I don't think he has any friends, at least not in publishing. To be honest, I'm surprised it was Vic who was killed and not Steve."

Bourque and Slade remained poker-faced. They knew better than to trust statements that started with *To be honest*. Slade was taking copious notes.

"Let's return to Mr. Comeau," said Bourque. "Do you have any idea who might have wanted to kill him?"

Sunny paused. "Vic and Steve have—*had*—some sort of history," he said. "In a couple of our jury meetings, Steve made comments about Vic"—Sunny used air quotes—"owing his success to him."

"Really?" Now Bourque's eyebrows did lift. "How so?"

"No clue. This is pure speculation, but maybe Steve reviewed Vic's manuscript before he submitted it to publishers," said Sunny, his imagination working overtime. "That wouldn't be unusual. Lots of writers hire freelance editors to help polish their work before they submit it. But maybe Steve had to help Vic completely rework it because the first draft was garbage. Maybe he *rewrote* it."

"So, Mr. Comeau was a first-time author? Is this unusual for the NOVA Prize?" Bourque asked.

"Yes. I mean, it's just so strange that Vic had never written fiction before. Then, all of a sudden, he's nominated for the biggest prize in the province? It never sat right with Del and me. But it wasn't our place to question his publisher's submission."

"That *is* interesting," said Slade, looking up from her notes. "Would it be unusual for an editor to rewrite an author's manuscript?"

"To rewrite it, yes, highly unusual—and unprofessional," said Sunny. "Typically, after an editor reads the first draft, they provide a critique, several typed pages of suggestions they feel would strengthen the plot. Then the author makes the revisions and sends the amended draft to the editor to review. It usually takes several rounds of revisions before both of them feel satisfied that the draft can be considered final."

Slade frowned while pushing a loose bobby pin back into her bun. "So, if Mr. Silver *did* rewrite Mr. Comeau's manuscript, why do you think he would do so? If it was unusual and unprofessional."

Sunny held up his palms in surrender. "Beats me. You'd have to ask him."

"Of course," said Slade. Deciding not to press the point further. "Is there anything else you'd like to add?"

Sunny's shoulders slumped forward. He had to tell them. It was now or never.

"Yeah," he said. "Steve tried to bribe Del and me."

"Is that so?" said Bourque. Leaning forward, with his hands on the desk, he said, "Bribe you for what purpose?"

"He wanted Vic to win," Sunny replied.

Sunday night
Lord Nelson Hotel

BOURQUE AND SLADE HUNG UP THEIR RESPECTIVE calls. "Medical examiner has ruled homicide," said Bourque. "Blunt-force trauma to the back of the head. Toxicology report pending. He was right on with the time of death, approximately two hours. What's forensics saying?"

Slade referred to her notebook. "Forensics were thorough. No prints on the typewriter, probably wiped off with the bloody towel found in the bathtub full of water. Facecloths there, too, probably used to wipe prints elsewhere in the room. Assailant likely took one with them to clean the door handles on the way out."

"What does all of that tell us?" asked Bourque, crossing his arms.

Slade closed her notebook and placed it in her lap. "Mr. Comeau knew his killer. He would have had to open the door to let them in. Friend, family, colleague. There might have been an argument, and the killer snapped. In which case, it was a crime of passion. Not premeditated."

"Why *couldn't* it have been premeditated?" pressed Bourque.

Slade considered the question. "If it was, why kill Mr. Comeau here, with so many potential witnesses? And right before the gala ceremony, where he was expected to appear soon after. He'd be missed too quickly. Which, it turns out, he was. It doesn't leave the killer a lot of time to get away. Also, if it was premeditated, the killer would have been wearing gloves. And wouldn't have needed to stick around to clean up afterward."

"All good points," said Bourque. He glanced at his watch. "Who's next on our list?"

After Sunny was cleared to leave, Slade brought Del in. His story of finding Vic and his impressions of both Vic and Steve were similar to his friend's, and he was sent home. Alex was also dismissed after he was questioned. Since Del and Alex lived in the city, the detectives could summon them if they had further questions.

Sonya and Sally had also been interviewed and given the green light to leave. During the two-hour time frame in which Vic was killed, they were each other's alibis. Sonya had been in Sally's room, helping her choose an outfit for the gala. The kitchen staff confirmed that Sonya had ordered a cheese-and-fruit plate from room service to snack on. Since it was now after midnight and both women lived out of town, they had chosen to spend one more night at the hotel. Video surveillance showed Booth King striding into the Lord Nelson's front door just in time for the gala dinner, so he only had to provide his name and phone number.

After their statements were taken, the Kings helped Sally get settled in her room and saw that she took her medications, along with a sleep aid. Then they retreated to their room to discuss the astonishing turn of events.

No one had mentioned it to the detectives, but there was a question lurking behind the obvious—*Who killed Vic Comeau?*—in the back of everyone's minds:

Who had won the NOVA Prize?

For the time being, there would be no answer.

Sunday night
Alex's house, Halifax

IN HIS LUXURIOUS ENSUITE BATHROOM, ALEX STOOD IN front of the sink in a pair of silk leopard-print pajamas. After washing and moisturizing his face, and cleaning his teeth on autopilot, he stared at himself in the mirror. Unhappy with his reflection.

Sickly pallor.

Dark under-eye circles.

What a clusterfuck, he thought, rubbing the stubble on his chin and cheeks. *Vic ruined everything*.

After plugging his toothbrush into the charger, Alex opened the cupboard beneath the sink and pulled out a wicker basket of first-aid supplies. Placing it on the counter, he rummaged around until he found antibiotic ointment and a gauze bandage.

The knuckles on Alex's right hand looked angry. Which was how he felt about being robbed of the NOVA Prize. He had dreamt about approaching the podium with an air of grace and humility after *Cape Breton Calls Him* was announced. At this rate, who knew when they'd find out the winner.

Gently applying the ointment with a cotton swab, Alex winced at the sting. A dark bruise was blooming. To keep the cut from getting infected, he'd stay home from the fitness centre tomorrow. He'd be too tired to work out, anyway. Taking a sick day might be just what the doctor ordered. His students were away for the summer. Usha would understand—it had been a late night for her, too. No one would notice if he hid in bed all day. Tending his wound. Soothing his shattered nerves. Reflecting on the shameful thing he had done.

Early Monday morning
Lord Nelson Hotel

AT 1:00 A.M., DETECTIVES BOURQUE AND SLADE MADE a beeline to the coffee urn the hotel kitchen staff kept generously refilling. Bourque took his black. Slade added almond milk. Standing in front of Nelson's portrait, they sipped their fortifying beverages.

"Let's review what we've got so far," said Bourque, setting his mug down so he could stretch his stiff arms. In between interviews, Slade had done restorative yoga poses to keep her muscles from cramping. The two settled into neighbouring armchairs.

Slade took off her shoes, pulled a footstool closer, and propped her feet up on it. "Ah, that's better," she said, opening her notebook. "Okay. We've interviewed the three men who found Comeau: Jamal Johnson, Delmore Davis, and Sunil Patel. The hotel's on-duty manager and two of the three authors who were on the jury panel. Their stories all appear to check out."

"As do the stories of the two women authors," said Bourque. "Sally MacPhee has terminal cancer and couldn't lift a Chihuahua let alone a fifty-pound typewriter. Although she could have had an accomplice, of course. Sonya King appears to have appointed herself as MacPhee's caregiver for the time being."

"King's a retired physician, so that makes sense," Slade pointed out.

"Yes, it would be in her DNA to help," agreed Bourque. "What about Alexander Fitzgerald?"

Slade shrugged. "Seems to check out. Not sure, though. Did you notice him trying to hide a gash on the back of his right hand?"

Bourque nodded. "I did. Let's call him in tomorrow to press him further on how he got it. We'll give him tonight to rest and ruminate."

Slade made a note. "And I'll speak with Comeau's wife."

Draining his coffee, Bourque got up to put his empty mug next to the coffee urn. "What about the portrait Patel painted of Silver?"

"Well, it sounds like Silver had a beef with Comeau," said Slade, cradling her half-finished cup of coffee. "That could mean motive. But are there grounds to do a search?"

"Not at this point," said Bourque. "We need to talk to him first."

Slade suppressed a sigh. She was tired, and she missed Daphne, but sleep deprivation came with the job. And so did the occasional night away from your spouse. "Shall I bring him down?"

Wade glanced at his watch. "No. According to witness statements, he was drunk before they served the meal. Let's let him sleep it off and hope he's sober in the morning. We'll interview him first thing."

As Wade closed his laptop and shuffled papers into his briefcase, he added, "Good work today, Slade. Go home and get some sleep. See you back here at 06:00."

"Thanks, Sarge," said Slade, gathering up her things.

Just as Bourque reached the door, Slade called out, "Sarge? I had a thought."

Turning in his tracks, Bourque said, "Yes?"

"I think we should call Val Jenkins in for a conversation," said Slade, slipping her shoes back on. "The book columnist. If anyone has any intel on this crowd, it's her."

"Good idea," said Bourque. "Let's get her in tomorrow. 'Night."

"Goodnight." As soon as Detective Sarah Slade was alone, she released her hair from her bun and massaged her scalp. Wondering what secrets Val Jenkins might be safeguarding.

Early Monday morning
Val's apartment

WHEN VAL RETURNED TO HER APARTMENT JUST BEFORE midnight, she was shocked to discover another murder had occurred.

Mouse Number Twelve lay dead on her bed. Next to the poor stiff creature sat Sherlock Holmes.

"Holy shit! You finally caught one," said Val. "You look mighty proud of yourself. I know I've been encouraging you to kill them, but did you have to deposit it there?"

Sherlock meowed a plaintive *Don't be so picky, peasant.*

After Val disposed of the body in the dumpster behind the building, she lay on her back in bed, a clean blanket covering the sheets, stroking Sherlock's scalp. The comforting vibrations from his purring on her ribs helped her relax. Yet sleep wouldn't come. Her mind was racing. The police had taken her information before she left the scene, but hadn't seemed interested in speaking to her.

One question kept spinning in her mind.

Who killed Vic?

She felt like she was back on the Mad Tea Party ride at Disneyland. Although this was no twirling oversized teacup. She was finally covering a murder investigation.

Since sleep was elusive, and Val was now on the crime beat, she might as well do some research.

Bumping Sherlock off her chest, she reached over to turn on her bedside lamp and picked up her laptop from the floor. She decided to draft a document with a list of suspects. Fingers moving quickly, she jotted down her thoughts.

WHO KILLED VICTOR COMEAU?

Fellow NOVA Prize nominees:

Alex Fitzgerald (possibly)

Sonya King (unlikely)

Sally MacPhee (unlikely/possibly?)

"Okay, Sherlock, let's think this through," said Val, placing her laptop on a pillow so she could type more comfortably. "The award is a lot of money, but we don't know who the winner is. If someone wanted to get their hands on the prize, wouldn't it make more sense to murder the winner *after* the money was in the bank—not before the winner was even announced? So, the motive can't be the money. Can it?"

In response, Sherlock snored.

Val continued theorizing silently. Someone could have had a grudge against Vic. Big enough to want to kill him. Or a secret Vic was threatening to expose. Blackmail? Could it be Alex? If so, for what? Did they have a history in academic circles? Surely it wasn't Sonya, who was successful and wealthy. She wouldn't risk breaking a perfectly polished fingernail to hurl a typewriter. No, Sonya's method of murder would be something ladylike and clean. Poison in a teacup.

Val also ruled out Sally, who didn't look like she was strong enough to have done the deed herself. Maybe she was the mastermind, and someone else had done the heavy lifting. Bev, perhaps? The author and editor seemed close. But what would be their motive? To eliminate the competition? Sure, Sally had never won an award, but if Vic *was* the winner, he'd still receive the NOVA Prize posthumously. Wouldn't he?

Sighing, Val typed *Sally MacPhee author* into the search box. The results revealed an array of articles about her novels being nominated for (but never winning) awards. Skimming Q&As and profiles, a different sort of headline stopped her short.

LOCAL AUTHOR'S SECOND HUSBAND DEAD AFTER TRAGIC FALL

Sitting bolt upright, Val's eyes widened as she raced through the thirty-year-old news report.

> On Tuesday, August 25, Sherman Sponagle of Wolfville was discovered dead at the foot of the basement stairs by his wife, local author Sally MacPhee, in the home they shared on Chestnut Street. According to MacPhee, her husband, a meat cutter at the IGA, had been on his way to his basement workshop to build a birdhouse when he tripped on a

loose board he'd been meaning to fix and fell, hitting his head on the cement floor. Police have ruled it an accidental death.

"Talk about run-on sentences," muttered Val. "Needs an edit."

Skipping the details about the funeral, she tried to process what she had just read. First, she didn't know Sally had been married twice. What happened to her first husband? Second, it seemed Sally hadn't taken her husband's last name. Why not? That practice was unusual for a woman of Sally's generation, especially in small-town Nova Scotia. Was MacPhee her birth name? Or her first husband's surname?

Could the police have gotten Sponagle's death wrong? Might there had been foul play after all? At the time of Sponagle's death, Sally would have been in her mid-forties. Would she have been strong enough to push a man down a flight of stairs? If so, why would she have wanted to?

Val needed to know what had become of Sally's first husband. It didn't take long for her to find out. When Sally had been in her early thirties, an editorial had been published in a community newspaper.

Staff members at *The Valley Examiner* offer heartfelt sympathy and condolences to our volunteer proofreader, Sally MacPhee, on the recent loss of her husband, Everett Melanson. We were saddened to learn of Everett's tragic sudden death from ingesting toxic cyanobacteria (blue-algae bloom) after swimming in Reservoir Park Ponds. You'll find funeral details in our obituary listings. In lieu of flowers, Sally has asked that donations be made to a charity of your choice.

"Jesus," Val said softly. So MacPhee *was* her birth name.

Two husbands, two tragic deaths. "Is Sally a black widow?" mused Val, rubbing her dry eyes. "Or were her husbands just unlucky?"

It wasn't until much later that Val would discover Sonya King knew the answer to those questions.

Even though it was close to two o'clock in the morning. Val decided to reach out to the one person she knew could help. She composed a text: **Hey Lou, how are you? I need a sounding board. Could I come see you tomorrow?**

Five minutes later, Kevin replied: **Mary. Let me check my social calendar. Yes, I have a brief unit of free time. Your visit will be a refreshing**

break from the therapists trying to fix me: OT, PT, social worker. The chaplain even paid a visit. Christ. Text me after breakfast re: timing. Be a pal and bring me a smoke. And a nail file in a cake.

Val snorted so loudly, Sherlock jumped off the bed. She replied: **You're in hospital, not jail! Happy to hear you haven't lost your sense of humour. Get some sleep, okay?**

Three dots danced on Val's phone's screen: **You try sleeping when your cellmate snores like a hibernating bear. Smells like one too.**

Shaking her head in affectionate exasperation, Val sent one last note before putting her phone away: **I'll put together a care package: smokes, cake, file, earplugs. Goodnight.**

Up until that moment, Val had been feeling out of her depths. Tomorrow, she'd bounce some ideas off Kevin. Somewhat reassured, she turned off the light and soon fell asleep.

It was a good thing Val didn't know what news would break the next morning, or she wouldn't have slept at all.

Monday morning

Big Bernie Brown's penthouse suite

"I SUPPOSE YOU WANT TEA OR COFFEE," SAID BERNIE. All bluster, no charm. "Just so you know, this ain't a restaurant."

"No, I'm fine, thanks," said Bev, sitting in a roomy armchair. All of the furniture in Bernie's suite was oversized. "I need your help," she whispered. Palms sweaty, mouth dry. Tea would have been nice.

Sitting on the sectional across from her frightened niece, Bernie learned forward and cupped an ear. "Come again?"

"I need your help," Bev repeated, louder.

"Heard you the first time," said Bernie, settling back on the sofa. "I'm just messin' with ya."

When visiting Bernie, patience wasn't a virtue. It was a prerequisite.

Picking up a reusable bottle with a straw in it, Bernie sucked hard. "Damn doctor says I gotta stay hydrated if I want to stay off dialysis," she said. "Problem with that is I always gotta piss."

Bev cringed. If she wasn't desperate, she wouldn't be here. In fact, she'd be more comfortable letting a tarantula crawl across her hand than asking Bernie for a favour.

"Okay, let's talk shop." Bernie drained the last drop of water from her bottle and then trumpeted a belch like an elephant in distress. "Exactly what kind of trouble are you in?"

Drawing a big breath, Bev began to explain.

About being at the Lord Nelson for the NOVA Prize gala.

About going to see Vic in his room before the ceremony started.

About why she had gone to see Vic.

About a knock at the door while she and Vic were talking. And how Bev had stepped into the bathroom when someone else entered the room.

About overhearing angry voices.

About a crash, followed by silence. Then the door opening and closing.

About what Bev had discovered when she came out of hiding. And what she had done.

"Is that the story you're going to tell the police?" asked Bernie, when Bev was finished.

"It's the truth," said Bev. A bit too earnestly.

"I didn't ask if it was the truth." Bernie's eyes locked on her niece's. "I asked if it was the story you're going to tell the police."

"Yes," said Bev.

"Then that's the story we're sticking with," said Bernie. "I don't need to hear any more."

"But..." Bev began.

Shaking her head, Bernie held up a hand. "No buts. Buts can land you in the clink. If you didn't commit a crime—which, according to your *story*, you didn't—then why do you think you're in trouble? Besides owing me a shit ton of money."

Lowering her voice, Bev whispered, "Because..."

"For God's sake, girl, this time I really *can't* hear you," said Bernie, exasperated. "And I can't find my goddamn hearing aids."

Bev burst into tears.

Bernie rolled her eyes. "All right, kid. Spill it."

So, Bev did. The truth, along with decades of repressed emotions, tumbled out.

Bev said she blamed her gambling addiction on her aunt; she'd introduced her to betting when she was young and impressionable. That while Bernie had disliked her youngest brother, Bev's father, she'd always had a soft spot for Bev's mother, her sister-in-law. That if her aunt had any compassion, she'd bury the past and put family first.

Bernie looked at Bev blankly. Remembering that fateful day at the track when she'd handed her young niece a ten-dollar bill. She felt a strange sensation building in her chest. Unpleasant, painful. And for once, it wasn't indigestion. She felt guilty.

After Vinnie The Vulture's untimely demise during a mafia takedown, Bernie had married twice more, but she'd never had children. She knew early on she wasn't mother material.

Throughout Bernie's life, there had been no one for her to do right by. Until now.

Monday morning
The Post's *office*

WHEN VAL ARRIVED AT WORK, SHE FOUND MARIANNE sitting at Kevin's desk. It was strange to see someone using all of their fingers to type on her boss's keyboard. Leaning in the doorway, bike helmet in hand, Val smiled at Marianne's unruly hair. Her curls, the colour and texture of steel wool, refused to be tamed into submission. Val wasn't sure Marianne even owned a hairbrush.

Turning to face her coworker, Marianne noticed Val's grin. "What? You laughing at my lid? The back of my head is none of my business. Or anyone else's, for that matter."

Chuckling, Val said, "Of course. And good morning to you, too."

Marianne grunted. "Sorry. Sometimes I forget the pleasantries. Good morning. What's your plan for the feature?"

"I thought I'd talk to the nominees to suss things out," said Val, dropping into the visitor's chair. "See how they feel about waiting to find out who won. Their thoughts about Vic. That kind of thing."

"Okay, but don't be surprised if they're tight-lipped," said Marianne. "People tend to clam up in tense situations. First, I'd like you to file a short piece on what happened for the website. Just bare bones. You can tease the feature at the end."

"No problem," said Val. "That won't take long. I can write it while I'm here."

Pulling a tissue from a box, Marianne blew her nose. "Fuckin' hay fever. I hate winter, I'm allergic to summer, and your shoulder seasons are too damn short."

Marianne was from Vancouver, and she never let them forget it. Tossing the tissue with a smooth free throw aimed at the garbage can, she shouted, "Two points!" Followed by, "You look like hell. Did you get any sleep?"

"What I look like is none of my business," said Val, trying to sound disgruntled. "Or anyone else's, for that matter." She knew that

Marianne's coarseness was her way of showing concern. If she was polite, you'd better watch your back.

Tapping an index finger on the side of her nose, Marianne said, "Touché."

Val briefed the acting managing editor on her theory of Sally as a black widow.

Marianne frowned. "Okay, so let's say MacPhee offed at least one of her hubbies. Most likely the one who fell down the stairs. Maybe he beat her, and it was self-defense. Or self-preservation. That makes sense, but it also means she covered up a felony. But how does that lead to her killing Vic? What's her motive? She's ill, right? So, she's old *and* frail. My dad had an antique typewriter. It was a sonofabitch to lift. Which means MacPhee couldn't have done the dirty work herself."

"It's a weak theory, I know," said Val, scratching her head. "I'm just spitballing ideas at this point."

Marianne thought back to her days as a young beat reporter, sniffing out leads. Although that early chapter in her career was decades ago, she would never forget the adrenaline that had coursed through her veins. When she chased down a source. Or got someone to speak to her on the record, when they wouldn't talk to anyone else. Or dug up an obscure yet revealing detail that hadn't been reported elsewhere.

"You do realize that you don't actually have to *solve* the murder," Marianne pointed out. "That's what the cops get paid for. You just have to report on the case."

"Yeah, I know," said Val, fiddling with her bike helmet's strap. "But I feel like if I can help solve the case, it'll look good for both me *and* the paper."

Maybe I'll win a journalism award, Val had fantasized while she had tossed and turned in the night. *But I'll skip the ceremony and have them courier it to me. Better safe than sorry.*

Marianne's next "achoo!" registered about a seven on the Richter scale. Pulling a clean tissue from the box, she honked like a goose. "I'm pretty sure there are medicated creams for crime-curiosity rashes," said Marianne, scoring another two points with the tissue. "So, let's entertain your theory for a second. If MacPhee *is* the mastermind behind Victor Comeau's death, who's her accomplice? Can you think of anyone she's close to?"

"Hmm. Maybe Bev Clarke? Her editor. She's fit enough to hurl a heavy object. I just don't know what their motive would be."

Marianne slapped her palms on the desk. "Tell ya what. Keep digging on the interweb. Check out Clarke's past. But talk to people too. In person, if you can. Ask questions. Look 'em in the eyes so you can decide whether they're telling the truth. Then report back."

"Will do," said Val, standing up. "I'm going to visit Kevin now. He always has good ideas."

"Please pass my regards along to the old coot," said Marianne, scribbling in her notebook for a minute. Tearing the page out, she handed it to Val, adding, "And give him this."

Roses are red
Violets are blue
Your office stinks
And so do you

I hate poetry. Get well soon, you miserable bastard.
MP

"I will," said Val, smiling as she tucked the note in her backpack. "Do you know when he's coming back to work?"

Marianne hesitated. "That's a question for Kevin," she replied, refusing to meet Val's eyes. "Now scram, Nancy Drew."

Monday morning
Lord Nelson Hotel

AT 08:00 A.M. THE DAY AFTER VICTOR COMEAU'S MURder, Detective Constables Wade Bourque and Sarah Slade were sitting in the Georgian Lounge, drinking coffee and reviewing their case notes. They had decided to conduct interviews in the incident command room they'd set up at the hotel for a few more days. There were advantages to speaking to potential suspects near the murder scene. Being so close to where the crime occurred often unnerved people, which in turn loosened their lips. Officers at the station would take the statements of everyone else who had been at the hotel the night before.

Bourque inhaled the rich dark roast, lingering on that first sip. "All right, Slade. Who are we bringing in first?"

Slade glanced at her notes. "Steven Silver. The third judge."

Bourque nodded. "Very good. He stayed here overnight, didn't he?"

"Yeah. Hopefully he'll be sober enough to answer questions," said Slade, standing up. "I'll go get him. Might have to wake him up."

"Good luck with that." Bourque opened his laptop. While he waited, he'd catch up on emails.

Fifteen minutes later, Slade returned. Alone.

"You'd better come with me, Sarge," she said. "Silver's not talking."

In the elevator, Slade briefed her boss on what she had discovered when the on-duty manager let her into Steve's room. The detectives both wore nitrile gloves. Because Wade had been briefed, he knew what to expect when they opened the door.

On the floor next to the desk, Steve lay spread-eagled on his stomach.

Skull smashed.

Hair covered in blood.

Next to him lay a beautiful antique typewriter, its keys mangled and bloody.

"Déjà vu," said Bourque, taking out his phone to take photos.

"Same killer, do you think?" wondered Slade, walking carefully around the body. Checking the top of the desk, bureau, and bedside tables for clues. In the closet and dresser drawers. Under the bed.

"Too soon to tell," said Bourque, heading to the bathroom. "It's clean in here. No towels in the tub this time."

"Possibly premeditated, then, if the killer was wearing gloves and didn't need to wipe off prints," said Slade, pulling out her phone. "Unlike Comeau's murder. Interesting distinction. I'll call forensics to check for prints. And get the medical examiner back here. Comeau's tox report came back clean, by the way. We'll see about this guy's."

"Good," said Bourque. "You handle things here. I'll call Val Jenkins in. She might have some intel."

Monday morning
Halifax Infirmary

AT THAT VERY MOMENT, VAL WAS CYCLING THE SHORT distance from the newspaper office to the Halifax Infirmary to visit her bedridden boss. On the way, she had stopped at a pharmacy to buy a get-well card and a big plush teddy bear, which was tucked into her pannier. After she locked her bike to a rack, she checked her phone. Two urgent voice mails were waiting for her.

The first was from Sunny Patel. Asking if she could meet with him and Del Davis to talk about Vic Comeau's murder.

The second was from Detective Constable Wade Bourque. Asking if she could meet with him to talk about Vic Comeau's murder.

"What the...," said Val out loud. Staring at her phone in disbelief. When her return call to the detective went unanswered, she left a voice mail of her own and walked briskly toward the hospital entrance. If there was ever a time that she needed her boss's guidance, it was now.

Monday morning
Alex's house

BY THE TIME ALEX WOKE UP, JUST BEFORE NOON THE next morning, the story was breaking news.

A second author had been murdered at the Lord Nelson Hotel.

This time, it was Steve Silver.

Lying in bed, Alex put his phone on his stomach after scanning the article. He removed his glasses and set them on the bedside table.

No great loss to publishing, he thought. *Or to society*.

The cut on Alex's right hand still stung. He had been careless. Stupid, even. Which wasn't like him. Normally, he was the model of restraint. When he got up, he'd change the bandage. For now, he closed his eyes and tried to settle his mind. It had been a rough night.

The phone's ringtone startled him. Holding it close to his face, he squinted at the screen.

Unknown number.

Alex let the call go to voice mail.

When he checked the message, bile rose in his throat.

The cops wanted to speak with him again.

Turning on his side, Alex curled into the fetal position. Hugging the spare pillow to his chest, he buried his face in it and sobbed.

Monday morning
Big Bernie Brown's penthouse suite

THE COPS WEREN'T THE ONLY ONES WHO WANTED TO have a private word with Alex Fitzgerald.

Big Bernie Brown did, too.

"Quit your bawling, girl, and buck up," Bernie scolded her niece. Her initial guilt was frittering away with every tear. She couldn't stand a crybaby.

"I can always count on you for a pep talk," said Bev, wiping her eyes and blowing her nose.

"That's more like it," said Bernie, nodding. "A little sass means you've got some fight in you. Sounds like you're gonna need it. Now, the first rule when you're in trouble is to figure out who else you can finger who might be in more trouble than you. Thoughts?"

"I don't want to snitch on anyone," said Bev, sniffing. Truth be told, she *did* want to snitch. She just wasn't sure if snitching would end up making her situation even worse.

"Better to snitch on the outside than have someone hear something they don't like in the big house. You know the saying about what happens to snitches in prison?" With an index finger, Bernie mimed slicing a knife across her throat. "Snitches get stitches."

Bev shuddered. Of course she knew what happened to snitches in prison. Like most of the free world, she had binged *Orange Is the New Black*. After she read the book, of course.

"Okay, we're gonna walk through your story again," said Bernie, sucking water from her bottle. "From the beginning. With a watered-down bombshell. Exactly like you plan to tell it to the police."

Taking a deep breath, Bev began.

Before the gala started, Bev went to the front desk. On a lanyard around her neck, she wore an old book-festival pass that didn't have her name on it. She told the clerk she was a volunteer with the Westby Foundation, and that she had something important to give

Vic. Looking behind Bev at the long lineup of impatient guests waiting to check in, the harried clerk gave her Vic's room number.

Bev planned to talk to Vic about the money he still owed her for the work she had done on his manuscript. The previous year, Vic had paid Bev a modest installment before she got started. Partway through, he had sent another small payment. When he landed a publisher, he assured her, he would pony up the rest.

It turned out that Vic's promise was as flimsy as a sheet of airmail paper.

Months passed. Bev's messages to Vic asking about the outstanding payment went unanswered. She really needed the money. To pay Bernie back. And to clear her other debts, once and for all.

So, Bev decided to surprise Vic by confronting him in person.

Privately.

In his room at the Lord Nelson.

To say their meeting hadn't gone well was a bigger understatement than saying Vic didn't mind the look of himself.

Vic downplayed Bev's work. Said it didn't warrant further payment.

He added that he'd notified his legal team, and their contract was now null and void. But the NDA still stood.

That in the end, Vic's wife had done the final edit.

That Bev wasn't to contact him again. Or she would hear from his lawyer.

Just as their conversation was heating up, there was a knock on the door. Vic said he'd get rid of whoever it was.

Not wanting to be discovered, Bev beat it to the bathroom.

(Bernie had suggested saying she hid behind a drape, to which Bev said, *Don't be ridiculous*, that only happened in bad horror movies. Her feet would be sticking out, for Pete's sake.)

Then the angry voices, the crash, the silence, the door opening and closing. And then, how she'd tiptoed back into the room, only to find…

"Yeah, yeah, I know what you found," said Bernie, waving a hand in circles to speed up the story. "Then what did you do? This is more gripping than *Murder on the Orient Express*."

There was no question that Vic was dead. Bev knew she should have called the police. But she was in shock. And scared. So, she bolted. Removing her lanyard and tucking it in her purse, she hurried to the Imperial Ballroom. To slip into her seat next to Sally.

Bernie started clapping. "Brava! A five-star performance. I'd give you a standing ovation if I didn't need new hips. Now, for our purposes, let's get to the juicy part. Who was in the room when you came out of hiding?"

Bev looked miserable. "Alex Fitzgerald."

"And why didn't you rat the murderous weasel out right away?" Bernie prompted.

"Because he…threatened me?" said Bev.

Sighing, Bernie shook her head. "Don't say it like it's a question. Try again."

"Because he threatened me," said Bev, with some conviction.

"Better," said Bernie, fully embracing her new role as acting coach. "We'll work on his threat later. Now, back to the crime scene. When you left the room, the bathtub was empty. Right?"

"That's right," said Bev, nodding. "When I left the room, the bathtub was empty."

"So, Alex must have killed Vic in a fit of rage while they were arguing." Leaning back against the sofa cushions, Bernie smiled. "I love a happy ending."

"Well, I'm not happy," said Bev. "I'm scared. Because that's not *exactly* what happened."

"It *is* exactly what happened," said Bernie, glaring at her niece. "Alex looked at you like a deer-jacker spotting a doe. You noticed he had a cut on his right hand. He threatened to kill you if you called the police. Shaken, you took off, while he stayed to clean up the mess."

Bev's intestines were roiling. *I'm headed to the big house*, she thought.

"You should really write fiction," Bev told her aunt. "But…"

Bernie raised her hand to silence her. "What part of 'I don't want to hear the truth' do you not understand? This is the story you're telling the police. If you want me to clean up this mess, we do it my way."

On the verge of crying again, Bev said, "Okay."

Bernie's glare caused Bev's tears to instantly retract into their ducts.

Rummaging in the voluminous purse next to her, Bernie pulled out a tube of bright-pink lipstick. Her generous reapplication signalled their meeting was over.

When Bernie's lips were well coated, she slipped the tube back into the abyss, next to tissues, eyeglass cleaner and cloth, cough drops, keys, and a Smith & Wesson LadySmith double-action revolver.

"Last item on the agenda," said Bernie, before dismissing her niece. "Invite that putz Fitzgerald over here for tea."

Monday morning
Halifax Infirmary

"HOW'D YOU SNAG A PRIVATE ROOM?" ASKED VAL, standing at the foot of Kevin's hospital bed. She dropped her bike helmet and backpack on the floor, shocked at how pale and grim her boss's face appeared. Like Casper the Unfriendly Ghost in a johnny shirt.

"Won a poker game and swapped my semi-private with the schmuck who lost," said Kevin, grunting. "Oh, and health insurance. Got an upgrade. Pretty sure whoever was in here before me croaked. Hope it's not an omen."

Val held out the bear. "This is Ted Baxter."

Kevin snorted. "That bozo! Great, I can boss him around. I gotta be nice to the nurses so they don't pull the plug while I'm asleep."

"You aren't on life support," Val pointed out, tucking Ted in beside Kevin. "You just had two toes amputated. You'll be right as rain and back to work in no time."

"What's so right about rain, anyway?" Kevin muttered. "It's wet. Sometimes it's cold and smacks you in the face sideways. Or it's frozen and feels like bees are stinging you. And hey, easy for you to say 'just' two toes. You've got all of yours."

"Well, Sherlock Holmes has extra toes, and he's never done anything with them."

Kevin frowned. "Not helpful."

"I see the drugs they're giving you haven't improved your disposition," said Val, taking a seat in the visitor's chair.

"I don't know what you're talking about," said Kevin, squeezing Ted and knuckling his head. "In my last performance review, I was told that I have the temperament of a choirboy and the soft skills of a social worker."

Val snorted. "Who doctored *that* report? Anyway, I'm happy the surgeon didn't remove your charm along with your toes. Oh yeah, before I forget..." Opening her backpack, Val took out her get-well card and Marianne's note.

"Where are my damn glasses?" Kevin mumbled.

Val pointed at the top of his head.

"Oh, yeah, right," said Kevin, looking sheepish. "Sorry. I'm all out of sorts."

After reading Marianne's note, Kevin sniffled and wiped fake tears from his eyes. "Please tell the old battleaxe her concern is touching," he said. "You can quote me verbatim. Now, what are you doing here pestering a sick old man who's prostrate on his hospital bed?"

"You're sitting up, actually," said Val. "First, I want to thank you for putting my name forward to write about the NOVA Prize murder. I *really* appreciate it. Seriously, Kevin."

Her boss shrugged, but a hint of pink warmed his wan cheeks. "No skin off my toes. I know you can handle it. Wanna run through what you've got so far? I can only take so much sudoku."

Val relayed what she had unearthed about Sally and her husbands.

Stroking his stubbly chin (because he hollered at the nurses if they tried to shave him), he said, "Nah. I don't peg her for Comeau's murderer."

Val leaned forward. "Why not?"

"I'm not saying the old broad didn't commit a crime," said Kevin. "Maybe she did push Sponagle down the stairs. I'm just not convinced she committed *this* crime. We can circle back to her later. For now, let's focus on Comeau. Who would want him dead?"

"Everyone, apparently," said Val, running her fingers through her curls. "He wasn't winning any popularity contests, that's for sure."

"If that was a motive for murder, I'da been iced decades ago," said Kevin, putting Ted in a chokehold. "What you've gotta remember is the motive is almost always going to be money, love, lust, jealousy, or revenge. Unless it's gangs. Then it's drugs."

"It's not gangs and drugs," said Val.

"Who's on the case? Bourque and Slade?" asked Kevin. "And what's the matter? Ants in your pants? There's probably a nurse who can give you a pill for that. Want me to buzz for one?"

Laughing, Val said, "Yes, Bourque and Slade. And don't pester the nurses, but these chairs are like sitting on concrete. I can't get comfortable."

"It ain't the Hilton," said Kevin, sighing. "You should try the food. Pig slop. Those detectives are thorough. Play nice. You'll want them as allies. Before you go, tell me this. Why do you wanna solve this? Why not just report on it?"

"Yeah, Marianne made the same point." Val paused. "I guess it's two-fold. I want to prove my worth at the *Post*. And also, in a way, these authors are my tribe. I've known most of them for years. I feel... protective of them. So, it's like this is my story on multiple levels."

"Fair enough," said Kevin. "But given the pitiful state of print publishing, I'd update my CV if I were you. Maybe the universities are hiring. They always need writers, except they call them 'communicators.' Buncha commies. You know I'll give you a good reference."

"Thanks, boss," said Val softly.

Propping Ted Baxter on top of his rounded belly, Kevin lifted one of the bear's arms to make it wave at Val. "See ya, Mary," he said in a high-pitched voice. In his normal voice, he added, "Stay away from old typewriters. And come see me again soon."

Val grew serious. "When do you think you'll be back to work, Lou?"

Kevin went quiet. "Not sure if I will, Mary."

Val raised her eyebrows. "What? Are you thinking about staying on medical leave until your pension kicks in?"

"Don't know," said Kevin, grunting. "Maybe. Depends on how my foot heals. *If* my foot heals."

"Just be a good patient so you can get out of here faster," said Val. "And try not to pick up a superbug. I hear that's a lousy way to go."

Kevin guffawed, then looked serious. "Listen, be careful, okay? This isn't one of your murder-mystery books. And you aren't Nancy Drew. This is real life. There's someone dangerous out there who doesn't want to be found."

"Yes, Dad," said Val, picking up her stuff. "I'll check in regularly with reports."

It wasn't until Val went to unlock her bike that she saw a missed text from Marianne.

Steve Silver was dead.

While she waited for Detective Bourque to call her back, she texted Sunny and Del to arrange a meeting.

Monday afternoon
Val's apartment

SUNNY AND DEL CONVENED AT VAL'S PLACE AFTER lunch. They all agreed it was best to meet in private.

This might be as close as I'll ever come to having a date with her, thought Del, silently cursing his lack of confidence. *Except Sunny's crashing it. And we're here to discuss murder.*

Val didn't waste any time. As soon as she closed the door behind them, she asked, "Just throwing this out there, but could you tell me who the NOVA Prize winner is? I can't stand the suspense. I'll keep it locked down."

Del looked at Sunny, then replied, "We'd really like to, Val, but we can't. It would compromise our integrity as judges."

Val nodded. "No problem, I get it. Had to ask, though. The curiosity is killing me. I mean…not *actually* killing me. Like, with a giant old typewriter." Then Val grimaced. "Oh gosh, do I sound insensitive?"

"It's been a weird trip, Val," said Sunny, waving it off. "Don't sweat it."

Just then Sunny spotted Sherlock Holmes slinking into the living room. "Holy shit! Is that a dwarf bobcat?"

"Looks more like a lynx," said Del, squinting. "But I'm no wildcat expert."

"Calm down, you don't have to report me to the Department of Natural Resources," said Val, laughing. "This is Sherlock Holmes. He's a domestic Maine coon cat. I got him as a kitten three years ago."

"The poor guy is cross-eyed," said Sunny, sitting on the floor in Lotus Pose. "Was he on sale?"

"Hush, you'll hurt his feelings," Val called over her shoulder on her way to the kitchen for treats. "It's unkind to point out his shortcomings."

Handing Sunny the bag of Temptations, Val flopped into an armchair. "What a night, eh? I'm beat. So, what's up?"

From his spot on the couch, Del said, “We thought if anyone knew anything about why Vic was killed, it would be you. Maybe something secret slipped out during your interviews?”

Val looked at them. “How do I know one of you didn’t do it? Or maybe you were in on it together.”

Sunny’s jaw dropped. “I’m a Buddhist,” he said, appalled. “One of the precepts is to abstain from killing living beings.”

“And I have anxiety,” said Del. “I lose sleep if I kill a mosquito.”

“Fair points,” said Val, nodding. “I’m just eliminating suspects.”

Despite the fatigue fogging her brain, it occurred to her that Sunny and Del hadn’t heard about Steve.

“What?!” the friends said simultaneously, after she told them.

“This is bad,” said Sunny, removing his glasses and rubbing his eyes. While he did, Sherlock crept closer, following the trail of treats leading to Sunny’s lap.

“Really bad,” said Del, placing a palm on his chest. “I’m having heart palpitations.”

“It’s not great,” admitted Val. “Something sinister is going on. A pattern developing. And authors are clearly the target. You should know that I’ve been asked to write a feature for the paper. A combo NOVA Prize-slash-murder story.”

“Wow, good for you,” said Sunny. “What’s your plan? Do you think it’s a serial killer?”

“I’m not sure about a serial killer, and I don’t have much of a plan yet,” Val replied. “Detective Bourque wants to speak with me. I’m meeting him when we’re done here.”

“Do you have any preliminary thoughts about suspects?” asked Del, pressing the point. “Now that you’ve ruled us out, I mean.”

By this time, Sherlock was sitting in Sunny’s lap, purring.

“Wow, he rarely socializes with strangers,” said Val, impressed. “You must have special cat-whispering powers.”

“Animals know who their friends are,” said Sunny with a smile.

Val had decided to keep Sally’s background to herself. She was still mulling it over, and Kevin didn’t think it was relevant. So she led them in a different direction, “Back to your question about suspects. I know that Vic and Steve had a contentious history. Someone who worked with both of them once told me, in confidence, that Vic wouldn't have gotten his book published without Steve's help. What that 'help' entailed, he wouldn't say. But maybe their rivalry ran even deeper than that."

"We heard something similar," said Sunny, wincing as Sherlock's paws kneaded his thin cotton T-shirt, sharp claws scratching his stomach. "Maybe Steve was Vic's ghostwriter? I mean, let's be real—there's no way Vic wrote that book by himself. But regardless of motive, if Steve murdered Vic over whatever was between them, then who killed Steve?"

"Do you mind if I get a glass of water?" asked Del.

Val noticed he was looking weak. "Sorry, I'll get it," she said. "I'm a terrible host, but I'm so tired I'm not thinking straight. Sunny?"

"Thanks," he said. "I don't want to disturb Sherlock." Stretched across Sunny's lap, the cat was purring loudly over his head massage.

Val delivered glasses of water to them both and sat back down. Hoping Mouse Number Thirteen wouldn't choose this time to appear.

After sipping his drink, Sunny added, "Didn't something happen to Steve's wife?"

Val nodded. "Yeah. That's a really sad story. She died by suicide a decade or so ago. Overdosed. Depression, I think. Their only child, a daughter, was in her early twenties at the time. She must have been devastated. To lose her mom, and then to be left with a dad like Steve."

"God, that *is* awful," said Del. Val knew from interviewing him how close he was with his own parents.

"I hate to break things up, but I really need to shove a sandwich into my system, then head to the Lord Nelson to see Detective Bourque," said Val, hoisting Sherlock from Sunny's lap. "I'm too beat to bike. I'm gonna grab a Communauto."

Val kissed her cat's head as she lifted him off Sunny's lap. "God, you're a heifer."

"Hush, he can hear you," said Sunny, brushing fur off his shorts and shirt.

"Thanks for having us over," said Del, who was reluctant to leave. "If you learn anything new, will you keep us in the loop?"

"As long as it doesn't compromise my inquiries, then yeah, no problem," said Val. "And please let me know if you hear anything helpful. As soon as the winner is announced, my feature goes to print."

"Will do," Del promised. "And…be careful, okay?"

"I will," said Val, seeing the pair to the door. Touched by the younger man's concern.

Could he…? Val thought, as she closed the door behind them. *Nah.*

Val couldn't have known then just how careful she'd have to be.

Monday afternoon
Lord Nelson Hotel

FROM HIS VANTAGE POINT ON THE GEORGIAN LOUNGE'S wall, Admiral Horatio Nelson continued to oversee Detectives Wade Bourque and Sarah Slade while they worked on cracking the case.

Correction. Cases.

Nelson's beady blue eyes watched the detectives drink copious cups of coffee. Type on laptops. Make calls. Review notes. Stare at surveillance video. Interview witnesses and suspects. Stand. Stretch. Sit. Repeat. He was invested now, couldn't look away even if he wanted to. Mostly because he was a portrait.

"What's the status on Comeau's wife?" asked Bourque, clasping his hands behind his head.

"Her alibi checks out," said Slade, looking up from her laptop. "It sounds like they really did have an open marriage. Personally, I don't get it, but…no judgement." Shrugging, she added, "She appears to have had no malice toward him. Or motive."

"Okay," said Bourque, drumming his fingers on the desk. "We can eliminate her from our suspect list, for now. What about the other nominated authors?"

Looking at her notes, Slade summarized.

Sally MacPhee and Sonya King were each other's alibis, and neither had an obvious motive.

Alex Fitzgerald had a cut on his hand they would ask him about when he came in. A possible motive was currently unclear.

"Do you think the prize money plays a role in either murder?" asked Slade. Standing on one leg, she raised her arms above her head to balance in Tree Pose.

Bourque thought it over. "Not Silver's, but maybe Comeau's. It's a lot of money. Someone might have been blackmailing him, hoping for a big payout. But at the time of his death, the killer wouldn't have known if Comeau was the winner."

"Silver knew," Slade pointed out.

"True," said Bourque, nodding. "But we can't ask him. We need to find someone who was familiar with both of them, well enough to know their history. To see if Silver had motive."

"I'll start digging," said Slade, shifting from one leg to the other. "Is it okay if I head to the station for the rest of the afternoon, or do you need me here?"

"Go ahead," said Bourque. "Val Jenkins will be here soon. I'll grab something to eat before she arrives."

Slade closed her laptop and stuffed papers in her briefcase. "She's cute, eh?"

Eyebrows raised to his hairline, Bourque looked up from his screen. "Is she? Hadn't noticed."

"Hmm," said Slade. She couldn't help wishing her boss had someone special in his life, like she did. Someone to share his day with when he got home. Bourque didn't have anyone to greet him when he walked in the door. Even sadder, the poor man's cat had just died. He could really use some companionship. "Whatever you say, Sarge. See you later."

Monday afternoon
Lord Nelson Hotel

BEFORE VAL MET WITH DETECTIVE BOURQUE, SHE WENT to the hotel washroom to pat her sweaty face with paper towels. The late June afternoon was hazy and humid. Inspecting herself in the mirror, Val saw that despite the sunblock she had applied, her face was flushed. Just walking over from the Public Gardens was a hot workout.

She imagined herself in an interrogation: *Is it the atmospheric pressure causing your cheeks to redden, Ms. Jenkins? Or is it the thought of sitting near Detective Bourque?*

"Don't be ridiculous," Val said aloud. Running her hands through her damp curls did nothing to tame them. "Be professional."

"Come again?" said a voice from one of the stalls.

"Sorry! Just talking to myself," said Val, peering at a pair of black pumps below the door.

"No worries," said the stranger, mid-tinkle. "I do it too. A gal's gotta give herself a pep talk every now and then."

"Have a nice day," said Val, grabbing her purse and hightailing it to the Georgian Lounge.

Well, at least Constable Slade would be there, too, thought Val. So, she wouldn't be alone with Bourque. The thought made her the tiniest bit less nervous.

Val soon learned that, in fact, she *would* be alone with Bourque. Slade was nowhere in sight. Sitting at the table across from the detective, Val took the hand he offered and shook it firmly.

"Thanks for coming in," said Bourque, leaning forward in his chair. "I'm hoping you might have some information that could be helpful in our investigation. Would you like a glass of water?"

"Yes, please. And I'm happy to help if I can," said Val. Crossing her legs, one of her feet hit the desk. "Ow. Sorry."

"It's normal to be anxious," said Bourque, smiling. "Most people are when they talk to me. Occupational hazard."

"Ha, thanks," said Val, her shoulders relaxing. "I bet you're a real hit at parties."

"I'm not much of a party person," said Bourque, setting the water glass in front of Val.

Me either, Val thought.

"I was hoping you could tell me if you know anything about the key players at the gala," Wade continued. "Anyone who might have held a grudge against Mr. Comeau and Mr. Silver. Something serious enough to motivate them to kill."

Val hesitated. "Well, I have been told a few things in interviews over the years, but strictly off the record." She wasn't sure where to start. Or how she'd feel betraying confidences.

"For our purposes, the record is on," said Bourque. "Although I'm not recording this interview. I am going to take notes, though."

Val settled back in her chair. "I know that Vic and Steve were good friends a long time ago. When Steve's wife, Elaine, died by suicide, their friendship soured. I don't know why. But there were rumours that Steve...got physical with Elaine when he was drunk. And that Vic tried, but failed, to help her leave him."

Bourque's pen stopped moving. "That's interesting. Do you think Vic had a romantic relationship with Elaine?"

Val paused. "I really couldn't say. But I guess if he did, Steve might have been angry enough to kill him. Why now, though? Elaine died almost ten years ago. And then who would have killed Steve?"

Ignoring her questions, Bourque asked, "What can you tell me about Alex Fitzgerald?"

"Well, he gets more grant funding than any other author I know," said Val, crossing her other leg and kicking the desk again. "Ow. It pisses off people whose applications regularly get declined. There's more jealousy and resentment in the local author community than you might think."

"Jealousy is a complex emotion," said Bourque, head lowered, scribbling in his notebook. Val wondered if he was speaking from personal or professional experience.

Changing the topic again, Bourque asked, "What can you tell me about Bev Clarke?"

Val closed her eyes to consider the question. What *could* she tell him about Bev? She opened her eyes slowly. "I've always gotten the impression that Bev would rather be a writer than an editor. She said something to that effect to me once. And…I've heard through the grapevine that she gambles and owes a lot of money to some not-very-nice people."

Bourque looked surprised. "How do you know that?"

Val smiled. "Trusted reporters are kind of like bartenders," she said. "People confess stuff to me. In confidence. Mostly it's a secret they're dying to tell someone. If I promise to keep it off the record, they let fly." She felt her face flush. Trying to balance her journalistic integrity and her duty to help solve the case. "Until this very moment, I've kept everyone's secrets."

"There's a time to keep secrets and a time to…*let fly*," said Bourque. Mimicking her, but not unkindly. "Go on."

He's cute when his dimples flash, Val thought. *He should smile more often.* She decided to trust him. For now.

"Did you know that the notorious Big Bernie Brown is Bev's aunt?" asked Val.

"Yes," said Bourque, putting his pen down. "Although I wouldn't describe her as notorious."

"Come on, she's a *little* notorious," said Val, pressing. "Biggest bookie and loan shark in Atlantic Canada. Former bootlegger. Serial monogamist. Widow of Vinnie 'The Vulture' Capello. Those aren't an ordinary octogenarian's achievements."

"Hmm," murmured Bourque, conceding nothing. "Do you think she's somehow mixed up in the murders?"

"I don't know, but she's a good place to start," said Val. Leaning forward, she added, "I was thinking about having a chat with her."

"You'll do no such thing," said Bourque. Anger passed over his smooth features like a storm cloud. "You aren't Jessica Fletcher."

"Oh, I love *Murder, She Wrote*," said Val, looking wistful. "I've watched all twelve seasons. Several times. My favourite episode is the one where Jessica teaches a writing class at a women's prison. Season two, episode nine, if you're interested."

Bourque frowned. The interview was going sideways. "I'm trying to tell you to leave the investigation to the police, Ms. Jenkins. This isn't a game. And it isn't for amateurs who think they're being helpful but end up making things worse by sticking their noses into hornets' nests, then get surprised when they're stung. Murder is dangerous business. Understood?"

Val felt like he'd thrown the glass of water in her face. "Understood, Detective."

He'd make a good bad cop, she thought. *So much for those dimples*.

Recovering quickly, Bourque said more pleasantly, "What about Ms. MacPhee and Ms. King? Do they have any deep, dark secrets?"

Since Bourque had basically told her to butt out, Val had no intention on sharing her suspicions about Sally.

"Nope," she said, attempting a convincing poker face. "Both squeaky clean. No skeletons in their closets. That an *amateur* would know about, anyway."

Ignoring the dig, Bourque seemed to sense that Val was withholding something, but he didn't press. Not this time.

"I *have* wondered if Sally and Sonya took their vintage typewriters home," said Val, attempting to lighten the atmosphere. "They were gifts from the Westbys. I mean, would you want to keep something that had been used as a murder weapon? I sure wouldn't. I'd never be able to see it without thinking of dead bodies."

Bourque looked at Val. He guessed there was no harm in telling her. "They didn't," he said. "All of the typewriters are secured in our evidence lockers at the station."

"Do you know who won the NOVA Prize?" asked Val. *Couldn't hurt to ask*.

"Yes," Bourque replied.

"You aren't going to tell me, are you?" said Val.

"I am not," said Bourque. "And I'm the one asking the questions."

"Fine. But I have one more. Am I free to go?" asked Val. Uncrossing her legs carefully so she wouldn't ding the desk again.

Closing his notebook, Bourque handed Val his business card. "Yes, you're free to go. Thanks, Ms. Jenkins, for your time and insight. If you hear anything that we need to know, please get in touch."

As Val reached out to take the card, their fingers touched. And, for a brief second, lingered.

That's the closest I've had to a date in months, thought Val, as she walked out the front door of the air-conditioned hotel into what felt like a coke oven.

Detective Bourque had told Val not to contact Big Bernie Brown. And she planned to obey that order. If nothing else, she would be respectful of police procedure and protocol.

However, he hadn't said anything about not speaking to Bev. Which is exactly what Val planned to do next.

Monday afternoon
Sally's apartment

SALLY HAD NEVER BEEN SO EAGER TO LIE DOWN ON HER own bed. Before unpacking her suitcase, she turtled toward the bedroom. Leaning heavily on her cane, she lowered herself onto the quilt, and then covered herself with an afghan.

It's good to be home, she thought. *But it won't be home for much longer*.

Casting her eyes around the room, Sally let her gaze rest on the antique chest of drawers with its oval mirror that had been her mother's. On top sat her nearly threadbare childhood teddy bear. Above it, a framed cross-stitch featuring a ruby-red cardinal that read *Bless This House*.

When Sonya had offered to pay for a private limousine to drive Sally from Halifax to her apartment in Wolfville, the older woman had swallowed her pride and accepted. The limo had practically purred, and the driver had been skilled at skirting the potholes pitting the pavement. It was much more comfortable than being squeezed in shoulder-to-shoulder with several other passengers in the shuttle van the hotel had offered.

If Sally had won the NOVA Prize that night, she would have had enough money to rent a helicopter to whisk her home in a jiffy. Well, close to home, anyway. Where would it land? A foolish thought. But it was nice to dream.

Throughout her life, Sally had imagined what she'd do if she won a big lottery jackpot. Always spending the winnings the same way in her mind. A cute bungalow with an attached garage in town. A reliable car. Diamond drop earrings, and a few nice outfits for special occasions. What was left she'd invest so she wouldn't have to pinch pennies anymore. Like she had done all of her life, in the end.

There was only one problem with that dream. Sally never bought lottery tickets. Because she never felt lucky. Or deserving of all the good things life had to offer.

Luck certainly hadn't been at play during the awards weekend. No matter how Sally looked at it, the gala had been a bust of epic proportions.

Two dead authors. And the NOVA Prize winner hadn't been revealed.

There was little time left for Sally to get the rest of her affairs in order. Probably not long enough for the police to catch the killers. And only then would the Westby Foundation announce the winning book.

If it wasn't *Alex Cage*, Sally would meet her maker unable to call herself an award-winning author.

Sally sighed. Moving onto the mattress to get more comfortable, she wasn't sure she even cared anymore. The anticipation and excitement had dissipated alongside the ruined gala.

It was all a disastrous disappointment.

And yet.

Something positive *had* emerged from the spoiled weekend. Like a phoenix rising from the proverbial ashes. And that was confessing her sins to Sonya.

Sonya, who hadn't batted so much as a single tinted eyelash.

Sonya, who had (almost) convinced Sally that God would forgive her.

Sonya, who had agreed to sit with Sally as she left this world for the next one. To hold her hand on that journey.

If, after Sally died, the Westby Foundation announced that *Alex Cage* was the winner, Sonya was aware of Sally's wishes for the prize money. That thought served as a reminder to call her lawyer in the morning. To add another codicil to her will.

For now, Sally pulled the afghan up under her chin. Closed her eyes. And dreamt of a salvation that was free of pain, shame, and guilt.

Monday afternoon
Big Bernie Brown's penthouse suite

ALEX FELT LIKE ALICE IN WONDERLAND. OR DOROTHY in Oz. Or most of the characters in *The Twilight Zone*. Completely and utterly out of place. That's because he was sitting in an oversized armchair in the penthouse suite of an upscale seniors' home.

With no idea why he was there.

Across from him on the sofa was a very big, very scary old lady wearing a multicoloured floral muumuu, blue fuzzy slippers, and bright-pink lipstick. Next to her sat Bev Clarke. Who, Alex had just learned, was the woman's niece.

Lady being an incredibly loose term for Bernice Alice Brown.

Bev was chewing a hangnail on her thumb. Refusing to meet Alex's eyes.

"Apologies if my head of security startled you when you came out of your house," said Bernie. "Boris was an MMA fighter back in Russia, and he can be a bit rough. He's working on that in therapy."

"Mrs. Brown..." Alex began.

"Please, dear, call me Bernie," she said, sucking water through a straw in a reusable bottle. "All of my *friends* do." Patting her broad bosom, Bernie belched. "Goodness, pardon me. *What* a relief. I've been trying to move that since lunchtime. Too much cucumber in the Greek salad. And the dressing was overly onioned. I love onions, but they don't love me! Must have a word with Chef. Now, let's get down to business, shall we?"

Alex's mind was whirling. His left arm throbbed where Boris had wrapped his massive paw around it to escort him to the back seat of a black Escalade with tinted windows.

"You may be wondering why you're here," said Bernie, dabbing her generous décolletage with a tissue. "Understandable. I'll explain. You see, my dear niece, Beverly, has gotten herself into a spot of trouble. And we're hoping you can help us out."

Although it was cool in the temperature-controlled suite thanks to three perfectly positioned heat pumps, sweat dampened Alex's armpits. "How can *I* help?" he asked. Biting his lower lip, he tasted blood.

Bev remained silent, hands clasped on her lap. Alex noticed her hangnail was bleeding.

"I'm so glad you asked," said Bernie pleasantly. "I'm going to pitch the situation to you as I see it. What is it you writers call that? An escalator something?"

Alex and Bev replied simultaneously: "An elevator pitch."

Bernie slapped her thigh. "That's right! An elevator pitch. Here we go. An editor—that's Bev—goes to see an author—that's Victor—in his hotel room, to ask him to cough up the cash he owes her for editing his manuscript."

"You were his editor?" said Alex, looking at Bev in surprise.

Bev sat as still as a statue.

Bernie raised a hand. "Please hold your questions until I'm done. Pitches are supposed to be brief, so I'll nutshell the rest. While Bev was hiding in the bathroom, she heard someone argue with Victor, then bash him over the head with a typewriter. When she felt the coast was clear, she bolted—and saw you in the room with a nasty cut on your hand."

Alex's eyes widened. He could see where Bernie was heading. "I *was* in the room, and I *did* hurt myself, but—"

Bernie's hand went up again. "Zip it. I'm almost done. So, when the police question Bev, she's going to tell them that there were no bloody towels in the bathtub when she was in there. That's because you cleaned up your mess after realizing your fingerprints were all over the place. Am I right? Of course I'm right. I'm always right. Now you can talk." She motioned to the giant Russian. "Boris, our guest looks parched. Please fetch him a glass of water."

"That isn't really an elevator pitch," said Alex, frowning. "It's more of a summary. And a fictional one at that."

Bernie shrugged. "You say po*tay*to, I say po*tah*to. So. I want to make sure that when you talk to the police, you're clear on the facts."

"No one says po*tah*to," said Bev under her breath. Low enough that Bernie didn't hear.

"What facts? There *are* no facts," cried Alex. "Your summary is pure fiction."

"Elevator pitch," Bernie corrected, incorrectly. "I was thinking more along the lines of non-fiction. Or memoir. Not to boast, but mine would be a bestseller."

Alex caught Boris's glare as the giant man placed a glass of water on the coffee table in front of him. Although Alex's throat felt like sandpaper, there was no way was he drinking anything Big Bernie Brown offered him.

"Let me get this straight," said Alex, bewildered. "You want me to confess to killing Vic?"

"Bingo!" Bernie shouted. "I like you. You're smart."

"But I didn't!" Alex cried. "I'm not going to confess to something I didn't do."

"Well, you might want to have a little think about that," said Bernie. "I mean, you have *such* a lovely house. Victorian, isn't it? Two storeys? Needs a lick of paint? You really must maintain your investment. Curb appeal is so important in today's market. Anyhoo, it'd be a real shame if something happened to it. Boris has a terrible habit of dropping lit matches in the worst possible places. Especially if those places have been doused with kerosene first."

Alex jumped up, face flushed in anger. "You're threatening me? Who do you think you are? I'll *tell* you who you are. You're a bored, lonely old woman with a god complex who is long past her best-before date and who gets her jollies making up stories that will get innocent people in trouble."

Clapping her hands, Bernie hooted and gestured for Boris to stand down. "You've got spunk! I like spunk. But hey, it's your funeral, putz."

Alex saw red. "I'm not a putz or a patsy. And did it ever occur to you that Steve Silver might have killed Vic? There was some kind of bad blood between them."

Bernie titled her head, considering. "Yeah, that would be a good story, too. But Silver's dead, so he's of no use to me. I prefer a patsy with a pulse."

Boris laughed. At least, that's what Alex thought he heard coming from the man who was blocking the door. Maybe he was just clearing phlegm from his massive throat.

Turning to Bev, Alex asked point-blank: "Did *you* have anything to do with Vic's death?"

Making eye contact for the first time, Bev slowly shook her head from side to side. *No.*

"Did you really edit Vic's novel?" was Alex's next question. If Bev had, he couldn't begin to consider the implications for the NOVA Prize. The submissions guidelines expressly stated that it was a conflict of interest for an editor to have worked on more than one nominated novel. And Bev had very publicly worked with Sally on hers.

Before Bev could answer, Bernie said, "We're done here. I would encourage you to go home and consider our little chat before you talk to the police. It really *would* be in everyone's best interests. Just like it's in my best interest to look out for my family. Now, Boris will see you out."

A short while later, Alex would find himself in the Lord Nelson's Georgian Lounge having a tête-à-tête with Detective Bourque. At the same time, Val would be engrossed in a private conversation with Bev. Off the record. Of course.

Monday afternoon
Sonya's house

SONYA'S TWO CLOSEST FRIENDS WERE SEATED AT HER breakfast banquette, sipping almond-milk lattes and nibbling ricciarellis. Rose had made the chewy almond cookies after watching an Italian-week episode of *The Great British Bake Off*. She'd had to hide a container of them or her partner, Allan, would have eaten them all.

"So, what the hell happened?" asked Wendy. "We've been following the news reports, but there hasn't been much detail."

"I still can't believe it," said Rose, disbelief flooding her face. "What a disaster. If I were in your shoes, I'd be so disappointed. I'm disappointed *for* you, Sonya."

A few months earlier, Rose's debut book—a heart-wrenching, heartwarming memoir about her first year of midlife widowhood—had been published. She knew better than any of Sonya's friends how the disaster of the NOVA reception would feel.

"Yes, it's unfortunate, but it isn't a tragedy," said Sonya, cupping her hands around the mug. "The tragedy is that two people were murdered. Brutally. And the killer, or killers, is still at large."

"It hasn't even been twenty-four hours," Wendy pointed out. "The police need to do their due diligence. I'm sure they have to interview a lot of people."

"What can you tell us about the victims?" asked Rose, reaching for another cookie.

Sonya sighed. "Well, both men were unpleasant. I hesitate to speak ill of the dead, but if the dead had behaved themselves better when they were alive, I wouldn't have to. Steve Silver had a long history of harassing women. Mostly physically, but emotionally, too. There were whispers that he abused his wife. She died by suicide several years ago."

"The poor woman," said Wendy. After selling the Fishnets & Fantasies sex shop to Rose, she had found fulfilling work as a death doula. She'd met many women who'd overcome difficult relationships.

Who'd taken their lives, and deaths, into their own hands. "There are so many resources to help women now, but even so..."

"It's hard to reach out for help," admitted Rose, twisting a strand of her straight, shoulder-length brown hair. "If Jean Joudrey hadn't pushed me to attend her grief-support group after Jim died, I might have become a hermit."

"Instead, you hooked up with the hottest single man in town," said Wendy, smiling.

"Lucky me," said Rose, with a laugh.

"And the other author? Victor Comeau?" prompted Wendy, reaching for the dessert plate.

"I don't know too much about Vic," said Sonya, taking one of the rapidly disappearing cookies. "He's a new author, and I'd certainly never heard of him before. He really came out of nowhere. On Friday night I had supper with my fellow nominees, and I can tell you that I found Vic...well, to be frank, he was vile."

"How so?" asked Wendy, sliding off the padded bench to put their cups in the dishwasher.

"He was loud, rude to the server, and full of himself," said Sonya. "Big ego."

"He probably has a small penis," said Rose. "Or should I say *had*." Her friends groaned.

"Actually, I heard he was quite the playboy," said Sonya. "One of the pretty young front-desk clerks at the hotel broke down sobbing when the police announced his death. She had to leave the ballroom. Let's just say it was clear she wasn't his daughter."

"So, Vic was single? No kids?" asked Wendy.

"No, he was married," said Sonya, frowning in disapproval. "Don't know about kids."

"Any theories on who killed them?" asked Wendy, slipping back onto the bench. "Same killer? Or copycat? If this were a novel, how would you write it?"

Sonya laughed. "Since I don't write murder mysteries, I haven't a clue. And while I'm sure both men had made a few enemies over the years, given their *charming* personalities, I can't imagine what they might have done to warrant being murdered."

"Well, I'm glad you write the kind of the books you do," said Wendy. "What's in the news is bad enough."

"Thanks," said Sonya. Reaching across the table, she squeezed her friend's hand.

"How's Sally?" asked Rose. Eyeing the empty cookie platter, she regretted not making a double batch.

Wendy had briefed her friends on Sally's prognosis.

"She's palliative," said Sonya, her forehead wrinkling in concern. "She has a date set for MAID, and I told her I'd be there with her when the time comes. But I think she might move the date if she can hang on a bit longer. All of us want to know who won the NOVA Prize, but Sally wants to know most of all. If anyone deserves it, she does."

Sonya thought of her own secret plan for the prize money. Even if *Frances Coleman Carries On* didn't win, she could still go through with it, she supposed.

Just then, a cellphone buzzed. All three women picked theirs up.

"It's mine," said Sonya. Donning a pair of designer reading glasses, she peered at the screen. Re-reading the message, she looked perplexed. "The newspaper book columnist from the city wants to speak with me. In person. Tomorrow. Here."

Monday afternoon
Halifax Central Library

AFTER A BRIEF STOP AT HER APARTMENT FOR A SNACK and snuggles with Sherlock, Val parked her Communauto and cycled the short distance to the library. Halifax Central was Val's local branch, and she loved it. She had attended several book events there. Cafés on the first and fifth floors came and went, depending on the state of the economy. None were operating there currently. Val missed her green tea and pain au chocolat.

Because she was bone-weary, Val opted for the elevator instead of the steep, criss-crossing flights of stairs. She located Bev standing on the rooftop patio, looking not at the harbour vista but at her cellphone. When Bev turned, Val noticed she looked drawn. Dark shadows lay beneath red-rimmed eyes.

Choosing a table in the shade near the almost floor-to-ceiling windows, Val set down her helmet and backpack. "Thanks for agreeing to meet me. That was a rough night. How are you holding up?"

Bev drew a big breath in, then exhaled slowly. "Not that well, to be honest. I'm pretty shaken up."

Val nodded. "I get it. Me too. I think everyone is. Two murders. Shocking."

Bev didn't respond. Val waited. Eventually, sources tended to fill in silences.

After a few seconds, Bev asked, "Are you writing a story for the paper?"

"I will be, but not until the winner is announced," Val lied, wanting to safeguard her new role covering the murders. "Another reporter covers crime."

Bev tilted her head, confused. "Why did you want to meet with me? I'm not one of the nominees."

Luckily, Val had anticipated this question. "When I *do* write the story, I'd like to include a few quotes from authors and editors who knew Vic and Steve," she said. "The main story will be about the

NOVA Prize winner and runners-up, but I'll write a separate, shorter tribute sidebar for…the deceased. I wanted to catch you before you left for Hantsport. Interviews are always more fulsome in person than on the phone or over email. And, I wanted to see how you were doing. Our authors' community is small. We all need to support each other."

"I'm not an author," Bev pointed out. Somewhat bitterly, Val thought.

"True, but editors are an important part of the book-publishing community," Val pointed out. "I consider myself part of it, and I'm not an author."

"You're a writer, though," said Bev.

"Well, yeah, but writing a newspaper column about books isn't the same as writing a book," said Val.

Val only knew Bev peripherally, from sharing small talk at Sally's events. Each time Sally launched a new novel, Val conducted a phone interview with Bev about the author's talent. Val had always gotten the impression that Bev respected her. Val's profiles of Sally, and her reviews of her novels, had been positive, if not five-star. As Sally's editor, that reflected well on Bev.

"I don't really know anything about Vic or Steve," said Bev, shrugging. Eyes darting like a hummingbird. Finally alighting on her bloody hangnail. Refusing to meet Val's sympathetic gaze.

Val hadn't forgotten Marianne's advice: *Look 'em in the eyes so you can decide whether they're telling the truth.*

There was no question in Val's mind that Bev had just told a whopper of a lie.

Because Bev was buttoned up tighter than Lady Catherine de Bourgh in *Pride and Prejudice*, Val decided to redirect her line of questioning, recalling the conversation she'd had with Sunny and Del about ghostwriting.

"You freelance sometimes, right?"

Finally looking up, Bev replied, "Yes…why?"

Val put her notebook and pen on the table. "I just wondered if you knew whether there was any conflict of interest if a staff editor at a publishing house freelance-edited a novel that ended up being nominated for an award alongside a novel that same editor had worked on in-house. I know the NOVA Prize sets parameters around that."

It was a stab in the dark. But a stab nonetheless. And the knife must have nicked an artery.

Glancing at her watch, Bev frowned. "I really should get going. I haven't been home for a couple of days."

"Oh, sorry, I don't want to keep you. And I really do appreciate you meeting me under such trying times. I guess what I mean is—and this is *totally* hypothetical—if one editor had worked on two of the NOVA Prize nominees' manuscripts, that would be a conflict of interest, right?"

Val already knew the answer. She had read the guidelines.

Bev looked like she was going to be sick. "You'd have to ask the judges. Where is this interview going, anyway?" she asked, annoyance marring her smooth features. "I thought you wanted a quote about Steve and Vic."

"I do, but if you don't know them well enough, that's okay, I'll find someone else," said Val, putting her notebook and pen in her backpack. Recognizing it was time to stop pushing. "I should get going, too."

A warm wind blew Bev's bob into her face. On the other side of the patio's glass fencing, she watched two fluffy baby seagulls pecking in the green roof's water-storing sedum plants. Perched nearby were their protective parents.

"Can I tell you something off the record?" asked Bev, tucking her hair behind her ears.

Here we go, thought Val. Aloud, she said, "Of course. You know I never record my interviews. Whatever you say stays here."

Bev exhaled. "All right. Just let me run to the washroom first."

As Bev hurried away, Val knew she didn't have much time. The washroom was only a few feet away from the patio door.

Bev's cellphone was lying face-up on the table.

Picking it up, Val prayed, *Please don't ask for a password.*

Swiping left, the phone sprang to life.

Bingo! thought Val. It was an old smartphone, like hers. Quickly locating the texts, she scanned. Scrolled. Stopped. Read. Then returned the phone to where she'd found it.

Just in time, too. Seconds later, Bev returned. She grabbed her phone and tucked it in her purse.

Val tried to calm her pounding heart. "So, what was it you were going to tell me?"

Bev inspected her hangnail. Was that a tell?

"Oh, it wasn't important. Just that if you want a quote about Steve, you should ask Del and Sunny. They probably knew him better than anyone."

"Good idea, I'll do that," said Val. Not letting on that she already had spoken with the pair. "Well, thanks again for coming. I'm going to head back to the office. Safe drive home."

"Thanks," said Bev. And then the skittish woman was gone.

Gazing at the seagulls, Val thought about the texts she had scanned. Pulling out her notebook and pen, she scribbled furiously. So she wouldn't forget.

Right before Vic died, Bev had texted him.

The kicker?

Bev hadn't edited Vic's manuscript.

She had *written* it.

What's more, Bev was demanding overdue payment for her services. A big payment. If she hadn't received it by the gala, she planned to expose him as a fraud.

Monday afternoon
Lord Nelson Hotel

DETECTIVE CONSTABLE SARAH SLADE SHOWED ALEX Fitzgerald to his seat in the Georgian Lounge.

The interview would be recorded.

Admiral Horatio Nelson was all ears.

Bourque didn't beat around the bush. "I'd shake your hand, but it looks painful. What happened?"

"It was an accident," replied Alex, flustered.

"Would you care to elaborate?" asked Bourque, leaning forward. Elbows on the desk. Hands clasped. Slade's pen was poised above her notebook.

Alex weighed his options.

If he went along with Bernie's mad scheme, he'd likely end up in jail.

If he ended up in jail, he'd likely end up dead.

If he told the truth, he'd likely end up dead. Boris would see to it.

"You know," said Slade conversationally, "the truth really *is* the easiest option. If you tell the truth, you won't fuck up the details when we ask the same questions again later. Lying takes a lot of forethought and planning."

Bourque nodded. "And a memory like a steel trap."

"Yes, that too," replied Slade. "I'm going to write that down, so I don't forget it. A good memory is key, or the whole house of cards collapses."

Alex slumped in his chair. "All right, fine. I'm damned if I do and damned if I don't."

Bourque's eyebrows lifted. "Explain."

Alex told them about his visit with Bernie, Bev, and Boris.

"Okay, we'll come back to that in a bit," said Bourque. "First, give us an overview of your activities on Sunday afternoon, from after lunch until you showed up for the gala."

With his left hand, Alex removed his glasses and rubbed his bloodshot eyes. When they were back in place, he started talking.

After lunch, he had gone back to his hotel room to reply to emails, texts, and social media messages. Most were from people congratulating him on his nomination and wishing him good luck at the gala.

One text stood out from the others. It was from Vic. Asking if Alex could meet him in his room before the dinner. To tell him something important.

"How did he get your cellphone number?" asked Slade, looking up from her notepad.

"When the nominees were announced, the Westby Foundation chair asked if we were okay with having each other's contact information," Alex replied. "So we could plan shared events, like Friday night's supper, on our own."

"Okay, continue," she said, making a note to confirm that fact with Emilie Craig.

Instead of going to see Vic right away ("When he said jump, I didn't say how high"), Alex lay down for a nap. After awakening an hour later, he made his way to Vic's room.

"What was the important 'something' he wanted to share with you?" asked Bourque.

"This is where the house of cards collapses," said Alex, chewing his bottom lip. "Vic told me that Steve had been blackmailing him. That Vic owed Steve hush money, but he couldn't pay him unless he won the NOVA Prize. That Steve had tried to bribe the other judges, more than once, to ensure that Vic won, but Sunny and Del had shut him down."

Slade interrupted: "Why was Mr. Silver blackmailing Mr. Comeau? And why confess to you?"

Alex shrugged. "He didn't say why, and I didn't ask. I was stunned the whole time he was talking. I mean, we weren't friends. So, yeah, why me? I guess he felt desperate and wanted an ally. He told me he thought Sally was going to win. And that if she did, he'd have to find another way to pay Steve, or else..."

"Or else what?" asked Slade.

Alex's face paled. "He said he was in a lot of trouble financially. And not just with Steve. If he didn't pay his debts, he was scared someone was going to try to kill him. He must have been out of his mind with desperation, because he asked me to give him *my* prize money if I won."

"But why would someone kill Vic *before* the winner was announced?" asked Bourque. "That makes no sense."

"Mr. Silver knew who the winner was," Slade pointed out.

"Do you know?" asked Alex. Hoping they'd throw him a bone, if not the whole piece of meat.

"Yes," the detectives said simultaneously.

"I don't suppose you could..." Alex ventured, hopefully.

"We're asking the questions here," said Bourque. "Let's back up. Why don't you tell us how you hurt your hand?"

"Oh, yeah, sorry. I got sidetracked. I'm pretty sleep deprived," said Alex, growing more agitated by the minute. "Well, I'm not proud of myself. When it became apparent that I couldn't do anything to help Vic, even if I'd wanted to, he told me he'd read my novel. And that he thought it was 'trite.' *Trite*!" Spittle flew out of Alex's mouth. "After Friday's supper, I already thought he was an arrogant asshole, but that was the last straw. I blew up."

"Did you hit him?" asked Slade. Given the state of Vic's crushed skull, the postmortem wouldn't have picked up bruising from a fist to his face.

Alex's face crumpled. "I tried to, but I've never been a fighter. I mean, I was bullied in school. I never wanted to embarrass my parents. My dad was a judge, for Chrissake. So, I learned to walk away from taunts, and I got beaten up a lot. But I was furious with Vic, so I threw a punch. Vic ducked. I missed and hit the wall. Then he laughed and called me a pussy."

Bourque's lower back was sore. Standing, he said, "Let us get this straight. Mr. Comeau owed Mr. Silver money, but you don't know why. If Mr. Comeau didn't win the NOVA Prize, he wouldn't be able to pay Mr. Silver back. He also owed money to someone else. As a result, he was afraid for his life. So, he asked you to meet him, hoping you'd be some sort of ally. And that you might give him your prize money if you won? Then, when you refused, he insulted you and your book. Those don't sound like the actions of a reasonable man."

Alex shook his head. "Vic wasn't a reasonable man."

"Did you kill him?" asked Slade. She didn't beat around the bush, either. "Maybe you were so angry at Mr. Comeau, you picked up the typewriter and threw it at him. You look like you work out. Those old typewriters are heavy, but I bet you could manage it. Especially in a fit of rage."

"No! That's not what happened," cried Alex. "After Vic called me that…awful name, I told him he could go fuck himself. Then I left and went back to my room to calm down. I ran cold water over my hand in the bathroom to wash off the blood, but there were no first-aid supplies. When I was ready, I pulled myself together and went to the ballroom to wait for the gala to start. The graduate student I'm supervising had come with me. I didn't want her to know I was upset, or why. I carried on as though nothing had happened. Fake it till you make it, right?"

Taking a deep breath in, then letting it out, Alex looked at his bandaged hand. "That's what happened, no matter what Bernice Brown or Bev Clarke tell you. Do I need to call my lawyer?"

"That won't be necessary," said Bourque. "We're done for now. You can go."

"You know I'm a dead man walking," said Alex, standing up. Voice trembling.

"We'll have a plainclothes detective keep an eye on you," said Slade. "And we'll have a chat with Mrs. Brown."

"Terrific," said Alex bitterly. He didn't look reassured. "Please give Boris my regards."

After Alex had gone, Slade said, "He had motive for Vic's murder, if not Steve's."

"He did," said Bourque, heading for the coffee urn with both cups. "And now we know Mr. Fitzgerald has a temper."

Slade got up, kicked off her shoes, and assumed Eagle Pose. "My shoulders are killing me. I'd kill for a massage."

Bourque laughed. "That's a lot of killing."

In the South End, Bernice Alice Brown was anticipating Detective Constable Wade Bourque's visit the next day. It was always a treat when the handsome cop came calling.

Tuesday morning
Val's apartment

VAL HAD A BEE IN HER BONNET. TWO DEAD BEES, IN FACT: Sally MacPhee's husbands. Something was still niggling her about their deaths. After breakfast, she was heading to the South Shore to meet with Sonya King. Before leaving her apartment to pick up a Communauto, she texted Kevin.

Val: **Mary here. Where are you?**

Kevin: **Rehab centre. Not to dry out. Been there, done that. To learn how to walk with eight toes.**

Val: **How's it going?**

Kevin: **I'm spinning in circles. Solved the murders yet?**

Val: **No. Still investigating. On my way to talk to Sonya about Sally's husbands.**

Kevin: **Ah, the black widow theory. No stone left unturned.**

Val: **Spoke with Bev. BIG bombshell there. Tell you in person.**

Kevin: **Come see me when you get back. Still waiting for the nail file.**

After sending a thumbs-up, Val picked up Sherlock, gave him a hug, kiss, and treats, then left to get her car. Just over an hour later, she was sitting in Sonya's sunny kitchen banquette, sipping a soy latte.

Over the years, Val had interviewed Sonya on the phone or via video call every time she had launched a new novel. And every time she was nominated for, or won, an award. In other words, often. The two women were comfortable with each other and shared a mutual respect. Still, Val decided to proceed cautiously with her line of questioning.

"Thanks for agreeing to meet with me in person," said Val. "Your house is beautiful. And this is such a great location."

"Thank you," said Sonya, slipping into the chair across from Val. "Booth and I love it here. It's an oasis after the rat race." Sonya spent her career as an anesthesiologist at a big Toronto hospital. Booth had been a partner at one the city's most prestigious law firms. "Retiring in our hometown was the best decision for us on so many levels," continued Sonya. "I would never have become an author if we hadn't moved back. But I don't think you're here to talk about our house and its harbour views."

"No, I'm not," admitted Val. "I'm working on a feature story about the NOVA Prize. I don't know the winner yet, of course, so I'll add that after the announcement."

When Val explained about the sidebar she wanted to include as a tribute to Vic and Steve, Sonya raised her salon-sculpted eyebrows. "I suppose that's a good idea," she said neutrally, sipping her frothy homemade latte. Val was trying not to slurp hers.

Val took her notebook and pen from her purse. "Could I ask you a few questions for the article?"

Sonya shrugged, then smiled. "Sure. You know I'm always happy to chat with you."

"Okay, great," said Val, flipping to a fresh notebook page. "I was hoping you could give me a couple of quotes about Vic and Steve. Something about their writing and their roles in the provincial author community."

There was silence as Sonya gathered her thoughts. Finally, she said, "I think the best comment to that question is *no comment*."

"Really? Why?" Val was surprised. The question had been a simple diversion before she asked about Sally's past.

"Off the record?" asked Sonya.

Here we go, thought Val. Putting her pen down, she said, "Of course."

"Personally, I can't think of one kind thing to say about either man," said Sonya, frowning. "Professionally, I only knew Vic marginally from our NOVA Prize meetings, which until last weekend were all on Zoom. Steve's been around for decades. Everyone knows what he was like."

"What about Vic's novel?" pressed Val. "Did you read it?"

"I read all of the nominated novels," said Sonya.

She's not going to give anything up easily, thought Val. *She's learned a lot, being married to a politician.*

"Did you like Vic's?" Val asked.

"I liked all three well enough," said Sonya. "That's really all I'm prepared to say."

Val could see that it was time to change tactics.

"All right. How's Sally?"

Sonya blinked. "Well, it's clear to anyone who saw her last weekend that she's ill."

"Yes, she looked frail," said Val, her tone tinged with sympathy. "You know, I learned only recently that Sally has been widowed twice. She has never referenced her late husbands when I've spoken with her. I don't believe it's common knowledge. Has she mentioned them to you?"

Sonya looked wary. "Why do you ask? What does this have to do with your story?"

Val was prepared for that question. "If Sally's illness is serious, I'll have to draft an obituary for her ahead of time, given that she's such a well-regarded regional author. I wondered if you knew anything about her husbands that I could include?"

Sighing, Sonya looked out the window behind Val at the calm waters of Back Harbour. When she replied, her gaze didn't shift from the view. "I understand. But I'm afraid I can't help you. I don't know anything."

She's lying, thought Val.

"No problem, I just thought I'd ask," said Val, hiding her frustration. "I hope Sally is getting good care. I might give her a call to wish her well."

Turning her head to make eye contact with Val, Sonya narrowed her eyes. "I don't know what you're fishing for, Val, but I'd advise you to drop it. Leave Sally in peace."

Val felt like she'd been slapped.

Standing, Sonya glanced at her watch. "Good luck with your story. I have a call with my editor in ten minutes, so I'll show you out."

Val had hit a brick wall. Hard. In the car, as she buckled her seat belt, she worried that she was in over her head. Maybe she *should* leave the investigation to the police. She didn't have a clue what she was doing. Except pissing off all of her reliable sources.

Maybe she was only cut out to be a book columnist, after all.

Val decided she'd console herself the best way she knew how: by stopping in Mahone Bay for tea and a cinnamon bun.

If she'd had known then about the anonymous notes waiting for her at the office, she would have sped straight back to the city.

Tuesday morning
Big Bernie Brown's penthouse suite

BIG BERNIE BROWN'S HOUSEKEEPER HAD LAID OUT A TEA service fit for a king. On the living-room coffee table, a tiered tray held scones with clotted cream and strawberry jam, lemon meringue slices, raspberry cheesecake macarons, and lavender cupcakes with buttercream frosting. A bone china pot of English breakfast tea was steeping, matching cups and saucers nestled nearby.

When an important guest paid a visit, Bernie pulled out all the stops.

In the lobby, Boris waited for Detective Bourque to sign in at reception. They rode the elevator to the top floor in silence. Bourque was mentally reviewing his strategy for the meeting. Boris was recalling his previous night's work waterboarding a weasel. It had been a pleasant evening. The weasel, a delinquent debtor named Jimmy the Greek, had been chopped into little pieces in the back of his restaurant and fed into the meat grinder, then stuffed into sausage casings that were now feeding seagulls in the harbour.

Bourque had been to visit Bernie before. She was a worthy adversary. He knew he had to be sharp.

Boris punched in the code to open the apartment door, then held it open for Bourque.

"Detective, it's *so* nice to see you again," said Bernie from her spot on the sofa. "I'd get up to greet you properly, but these old hips ain't what they used to be."

Bourque went to shake Bernie's hand. "No problem, Mrs. Brown. I won't keep you long."

Placing a hand on her broad bosom, Bernie tried her best to look bashful. "Mrs. Brown, so formal! I wish you'd call me Bernie. And you can stay as long as you like. It's not often a handsome young man comes to call. Would you like tea and a treat?"

"No, thanks, I had a big breakfast," said Bourque, lowering himself into the armchair across from his hostess. "But you go ahead."

"Yes, I think I will indulge, if you don't mind," said Bernie, nodding at Boris. The beefy Russian piled a plate with sweets and poured a cup of tea for his boss, then resumed his position in front of the door.

"Hell of a waiter you've got there," said Bourque, crossing his legs.

"Boris has many useful skills," said Bernie, smiling. Swallowing a mouthful of cupcake, she licked frosting off her fingers. "Now, how can I help you this morning?"

"I'm assuming you've heard that two authors were murdered at the Lord Nelson over the weekend," Bourque began.

Bernie was a picture of wide-eyed innocence. "Why would you assume that?" she asked.

"Because your niece, Beverly Clarke, was there," said Bourque.

Bernie waved a hand in dismissal. "It's no secret that Bev and I aren't close. I couldn't stand her father. As you well know, he was a horse's ass."

"I don't disagree with you on that point," said Bourque. Years ago, he had helped put Dougie Clarke in prison for fatally shooting the driver of a cash-filled armoured truck. "However, your niece was seen coming into your residence yesterday morning."

Batting her eyelashes, Bernie said, "Why, Detective! Are you spying on me?"

Bourque smiled. "Not on you, no. But we're keeping an eye on some of the guests who attended the gala dinner. For their own safety, of course. We don't want another author to be murdered."

Bernie sipped her tea loudly. "Well, you needn't worry about Bev. She's an editor, not an author. And as meek as a church mouse. No one's interested in that girl."

"Several witnesses at the dinner told us that Ms. Clarke showed up at her table late, after everyone else was seated," said Bourque. "Which puts her whereabouts in question right around the time of the first murder."

Bernie shrugged. "Bev was late for her own birthday parties when she was a kid," she said. "Did you know she has an irritable bowel? Maybe she had diarrhea."

Uncrossing his legs, Bourque leaned forward, placed his elbows on his knees, and clasped his hands. "We're going to interview Ms. Clarke this afternoon. Before we do, I wanted to ask *you* why she came to see you yesterday."

To stall for time, Bernie popped the last piece of cupcake in her mouth and chewed it slowly. Suddenly, her gaze turned steely. "Bev came to me for advice," she said, stopping to sip her tea. Even though the detective could see that her cup was empty.

"Advice on what?" asked Bourque.

"Advice on what to do if she felt she was being framed," said Bernie.

Bourque held Bernie's gaze. "If you aren't close, why would Bev come to you for advice?"

Bernie shrugged. "My niece and I may not be touchy-feely types, but…what's that old saying? Blood is thicker than water. Even if it's bad blood. Now, detective, do you have any other questions? Or are we done here? My Lax-A-Day is kicking in."

Bourque remained in his chair. "One more question. What advice did you give Alex Fitzgerald when *he* visited you?"

Blinking, Bernie didn't miss a beat. "What a lovely man. So stylish! He wants to start a book club in my building. The widows will adore him. I told him we'd read his novel first. I'll ask Boris to pick up several copies at that nice independent bookstore down the road. I like to support local small businesses whenever I can."

Standing up, Bourque nodded. "Now we're done. Thanks for your time. I can see myself out."

Bev shook her head. "Boris will take you down. Don't forget to sign out. The receptionists get their panties in a twist if people don't follow protocol. They don't like it when the riffraff try to sneak in."

In the parking lot, when Bourque was back in his Prius, he thought about what his meeting with Bernie had revealed.

Bernie was lying about Bev. And about Alex.

Tuesday afternoon
The Post's *office*

WHEN VAL APPROACHED HER DESK AT THE OFFICE, she noticed two envelopes lying on her keyboard. One was white and smooth, with her name typed neatly on the front. The other was bigger and brown; it had been folded in half and crumpled, as though it had been stuffed in someone's pocket, and had her name printed in small capital letters in blue ink.

When readers wanted to reach her, they usually emailed or sent messages through social media. Senior citizens who weren't tech savvy sometimes mailed letters. These envelopes didn't have stamps or addresses, so they must have been dropped off.

Val picked up the white envelope and opened it. Scanning the short note, she sucked in a sharp breath.

STOP SNOOPING OR YOU VILL DIE

"Jesus," said Val, her voice strained.

Was *VILL* a typo? A sticky keyboard button? Looking at her own keyboard, she saw that the *W* was two lines up and a couple of letters to the left of the *V*. It could have been a mistake.

Good grief, thought Val. *I can't believe I'm proofreading a threatening note.*

With trembling fingers, Val opened the second envelope.

STEVE SILVER GOT WHAT HE DESERVED. JUSTICE WAS SERVED.
DIG DEEPER AND YOU'LL FIND OUT WHY.

Bile rose in Val's throat.

The notes proved that at least two interested parties knew she was asking questions.

One wanted her to stop.

The other wanted her to continue.

Putting the notes back in their envelopes, Val walked to the reception desk. Robert was the newspaper's gatekeeper. Headset always in place, he was a multitasker with a photographic memory.

"Hey, can I ask you something?" said Val, skipping the small talk.

Robert held up a hand. "One sec." After he finished listening to a voice mail and scribbling a note, he turned to her and said, "What's up?"

Val showed him the envelopes. "Did you see who dropped these off for me?"

Robert closed his eyes for a few seconds. When he opened them, he said, "The white envelope was brought in by a bike courier named Lex just after ten o'clock."

Val waited for Robert to finish. She knew better than to stop him midstream.

"They were wearing a grey Thrush Hermit T-shirt, black shorts, and black clipless mountain bike shoes. No helmet. Their hair was in serious need of a shampoo. They're one of our regular couriers. Very reliable."

"Okay, great. But there was no address on the envelope. How did they know where to deliver it?"

"There was a yellow sticky note stapled to the envelope with our address on it," said Robert. "I removed it before I put it on your desk." Rummaging under his desk in the recycling bin, he handed the sticky note to Val.

"And the second envelope? Did Lex bring that in, too?"

Robert shrugged. "Don't know. I was on lunch. It was here when I got back. William was filling in, but he went home with a migraine, so you can't ask him. He might not remember, anyway. Memory like a sieve. You could ask security to show you the CCTV footage from between twelve and one."

"Good idea, thanks," said Val.

Robert raised his eyebrows. "Why the twenty questions?"

Val paused. "The contents of the notes are…odd."

"As long as they aren't hate mail," said Robert, frowning. "We've had a fair bit of it lately. Readers pissed off at the shrinking content and all the advertorials. They miss their Monday delivery, too. If we stop printing obits, there'll be anarchy. My mother will be at the head of the picket line. If the notes are vicious, you should send them to the police."

"No, no…it's nothing like that," said Val, protesting a bit too intently. "They're just…unusual. Thanks again for your help."

Back at her desk, Val scrutinized the sticky note with the paper's address written on it. There was nothing remarkable about the penmanship. Black ink. All caps.

At the end of her workday, after sitting with the security guard and examining the CCTV footage, Val was no further ahead. She had watched as someone of medium height in a navy hoodie, grey track pants, black ballcap, and dirty white sneakers pulled a crumpled brown envelope from the hoodie's pocket, placed it on the counter, and hurried off. All while William was looking in the other direction, talking to one of the reporters.

As the person turned away from the counter, Val caught a brief glimpse of a face mostly covered by a black surgical mask. When the security guard paused and enlarged the image, Val leaned forward to get a closer look. She didn't recognize what she could see of the face. But she was captivated by a pair of beautiful green eyes.

Tuesday afternoon
Lord Nelson Hotel

BEV CLARKE WAS SHITTING HER PANTS. FIGURATIVELY speaking, of course. Literally, it had been a close call. Currently, her bowels were erupting with volcanic velocity into a toilet in a washroom at the Lord Nelson. Three "mercy flushes" couldn't disguise the sounds that were blowing out of her backside.

Bernie hadn't lied to Detective Bourque about one fact. Bev really did have an irritable bowel. Stress was a contributing factor. In this case, the thought of being interviewed by the police in ten minutes had brought it on.

After meeting with Bernie and Alex, Bev had driven home to Hantsport to spend a night in her own bed. Where she tossed. Turned. And worried. When sleep finally did overtake her, she awoke in a cold sweat from a nightmare in which she was bound, gagged, and tied to a chair. Unable to move or speak. Barely able to breathe. Trapped.

Now, in the hotel bathroom, Bev washed her hands, then pulled a bottle of water and a box of Imodium from her purse. She palmed two pills and washed them down. Staring at the mirror, her reflection frightened her. Bloodshot eyes with dark circles beneath them. Pale pallor. Lifeless hair.

Rummaging in her purse, Bev found a compact of pressed powder and a tube of cherry lip gloss. Patting her face with the powder did nothing to quell the butterflies in her belly. After applying a coat of gloss to her lips, she glanced at her watch.

It was time.

In the Georgian Lounge, Detective Slade led Bev to a chair in front of a desk. On the other side sat Detective Bourque. He reached across to shake her hand. "Thanks for coming in, Ms. Clarke," he said. Sitting down, he indicated that Bev should do the same.

Like I have a choice, thought Bev. She felt like she was about to write an exam for which she hadn't studied. Aloud, she said, "I'm happy to help."

Lie number one.

After explaining that their interview would be recorded, Bourque began. "In your own words, please tell us the series of events that occurred between noon last Sunday and when you arrived to sit next to Ms. MacPhee in the Imperial Ballroom that evening," he said.

Bev was skilled in the art of parsing language, of reading between the lines. *In your own words* was a red flag. Bernie had warned her niece that the detective had visited her. And she had insisted that Bev stick to the script.

Bev told the story as she had rehearsed it with Bernie. Now and then, Bourque nodded and wrote in his notepad.

"Just so I'm clear," said the detective, putting his pen down, "when you came out of the bathroom, you saw Mr. Comeau lying on the floor of his room with a crushed skull and the bloody typewriter next to him. He appeared to be dead, but instead of calling the police or the front desk—or anyone—you left to take your seat in the ballroom. As you came out of Mr. Comeau's bathroom, you saw Alex Fitzgerald in the room with a cut on his right hand. Does all of that sound right?"

Nodding, Bev answered, "Yes. I think so."

Detective Slade spoke up. "Yes? Or you think so?"

Looking flustered, Bev said, "Yes."

Just then, her guts gurgled loudly. "Excuse me," said Bev, blushing.

"No problem," said Bourque. "Interviews can be stressful. Now, you said that when you left the bathroom, the bathtub was empty. There were no bloody towels in it. Correct?"

"Yes, that's right," said Bev, trying not to pick at her hangnail, which was now twice its original size.

"And you believe that Alex returned to Mr. Comeau's room after killing him in a fit of rage when he realized he had left his fingerprints on the typewriter and the door handles. Also correct?"

Bev nodded. "That's what I think, yes."

"But you have no proof?" asked Slade. "No actual evidence?"

"Well, no, I guess not…" Bev looked unsure. "But I didn't see anyone else in the hall or on my way to the ballroom. Just Alex."

Bourque leaned back in his chair and crossed his arms. "Maybe Mr. Fitzgerald didn't kill Mr. Comeau. Maybe *you* killed Mr. Comeau."

"No," said Bev quickly. "I didn't."

He carried on as though she hadn't spoken. "Maybe you were so angry that he hadn't paid you the rest of what he owed you for writing his novel for him, it pushed you over the edge. Maybe you didn't go meet him intending to kill him, but when he refused to pay you, the situation spun out of control."

Bev was flummoxed. *How do they know?* This wasn't part of the script. She had to improvise quickly.

"Why would you think I wrote Vic's book?" asked Bev, trying to keep her voice from shaking.

Slade answered, "Because we found Mr. Comeau's cellphone on him. And your texts. That's pretty strong evidence for motive."

Silence.

Bourque filled it. "It's against NOVA Prize policy for a nominated novel to be ghostwritten. Did you know that?"

Bev's eyes filled with tears. "Yes."

"Then why did you write it?" asked Slade, already knowing the answer. They had reviewed Bev's bank statements. The editor was deeply in the red.

Bev exhaled slowly. "I needed the money to pay off some debts. And I was praying no one would find out."

"How did Mr. Comeau come to contact you?" asked Slade.

"He had asked around for a freelance editor, and he told me that someone had recommended me," said Bev. "It wasn't until our first phone call that he confessed he really wanted a ghostwriter. That he had a great idea for a novel, but he wasn't a good enough writer. He said he'd act like a research and story-development consultant. But only he would get author credit. He offered me good money. Really good. I signed an NDA. I thought the arrangement was above board."

"Except for the part about scamming the Westby Foundation by ghostwriting," Slade pointed out.

Bev slumped in her chair. "Except for that, yes. It's just that I was desperate for the money. I didn't know what else to do. It was against the regulations, but it wasn't an actual crime."

Bourque stood up. "Couldn't you have asked your aunt for a loan?"

"I already had," said Bev, grimacing. "I owe her money, too."

"Are you still gambling?" asked Slade.

This time, Bev wasn't surprised. She supposed she couldn't keep any secrets from the police. "No," she said firmly. "That chapter's finished. For a long time, it was the only thing that brought me close to Bernie. It doesn't anymore. Now it just causes grief and pain."

Bev's guts gurgled again.

"Do you need to take a break?" asked Bourque. "We aren't finished, but we could reconvene in ten or fifteen minutes."

"That would be great," said Bev, relief written all over her face. Getting up from her chair, she said, "Thank you."

Even later, Bev couldn't explain what happened next.

As she made her way to the nearest washroom, she pivoted. Suddenly, she found herself running down a stairwell, heading to her car in the underground parkade.

Tuesday evening
Nova Scotia Rehabilitation Centre

AT THE REHAB CENTRE, VAL FOUND KEVIN IN THE communal games room. Walker parked next to his chair—Ted Baxter tied to the seat with a shoelace—he was complaining loudly that his opponent, a young man in a wheelchair, was cheating at checkers.

From the door, Val watched as Kevin threw up his hands in resignation. "That's three in a row!" he grumbled, collecting the red stones.

"You're a sore loser," said his opponent, grinning while picking up the black pieces. "Pay up."

Val saw her boss hand over a twenty-dollar bill.

Looking up, Kevin spotted Val in the doorway. He waved her over.

"Hey, I could use your help with the next game," said Kevin. "Pull up a chair. Mary Richards, this is my buddy Haruto Shimoki. He goes by Harry."

Val shook Harry's extended hand. "Nice to meet you. I'm Val Jenkins. Mary is Kevin's nickname for me."

Harry grinned. "Yeah, he told me. He said you're like a daughter."

Kevin grunted. "Did not."

"Did too. You're a terrible liar. And a worse cheater. I'm outta here. I have chemistry homework. See ya, sucker."

The two men bumped fists.

Val picked up a chair from a nearby table and set it down next to Kevin's. "What's his story?"

Shaking his head, Kevin sighed. "Spinal cord injury. Dove headfirst into the shallow end of a friend's swimming pool. Broke his back. Great kid. Good attitude. Second-year science student at Dal. Wants to be a pharmacologist."

"Wow," said Val.

"Yeah," said Kevin. His voice cracked. "Pretty humbling."

"How are *you* doing?" asked Val, setting up the checkerboard.

"No complaints," said Kevin, shrugging. "I can walk. Not well, but my legs work. Which is more than Harry can say. And he doesn't complain. So." Her boss's voice broke.

"Buck up, Lou," said Val, making the first move on the board. "You're letting your soft side show."

"Soft side, my ass," said Kevin, looking at the board to devise his strategy. Composing himself. "I only got two sides. Front and back. Both ugly. But enough small talk. How goes the sleuthing?"

Reaching into her backpack, Val pulled out the two envelopes and handed them to Kevin.

"More love poems from Marianne?" he asked.

"No," said Val, cracking her knuckles.

"Quit that," said Kevin. "You know it sends shivers straight into my sinuses."

"Sorry," said Val, sitting on her hands. "I don't realize I'm doing it."

After reading both notes, Kevin got quiet.

"Fuck," he said, handing them back to her.

"Yeah." Val returned the notes to her backpack.

Kevin frowned. "There's a typo in one of them."

"I know."

"Could be a clue."

Val sighed. "I thought of that, but I'm not sure how..."

"Well, you've certainly stirred the pot," Kevin said, checkers game momentarily forgotten. "At least two people are on to you. Has anyone else seen these? Sunny and Del? You've been sharing information with them, haven't you?"

"I have been, but they're leaving for a Banff residency in a week, and I don't want to distract them," said Val, chewing her lower lip.

"What about Bourque?"

"No," Val admitted. "You're the first person to see the notes."

"You need his help, Mary. He has resources you can't access."

Val sighed. "I'm pretty sure he wants me to butt out of his investigation."

"Those notes take the investigation to a whole new level," said Kevin, fiddling with a checker stone. "We're talking serious shit. You got good locks on your doors and windows?"

"Yeah," said Val. "And an alarm system. My landlord upped security a couple years ago when that creep was sneaking into women's apartments in my neighbourhood and staring at them while they slept."

"Good. Got any pepper spray?"

"You know that's illegal, right?"

Kevin feigned innocence. “Bear spray, then.”

“Same thing.”

“Stun gun?”

“Also illegal. It’s sweet that you’re worried about me, Lou.”

Kevin met Val’s eyes. “I wouldn’t want anything bad to happen to you.”

“Aw,” said Val, smiling. “Is it because I’m like a daughter?”

Kevin grunted. “I never said that.”

“Harry says you did,” Val teased. “My bets are on the kid.”

Just then, both of their cellphones buzzed. It was a text from Marianne.

Bev Clarke took a bathroom break during an interview with the Bobbsey Twins and bolted. She’s MIA. Cops issued an APB. She’s officially a person of interest in Comeau’s death.

Kevin and Val stared at their phones. Then at each other.

“The plot thickens,” said Kevin.

Leaning forward, he hopped over several of Val’s checker stones. Sweeping them to the side of the board, he sat back. The next move was hers.

Tuesday evening
On the run

UNTIL SHE HIT THE HIGHWAY, BEV HADN'T KNOWN where she was headed. Just that she had to get away. The walls were closing in on her. Like that scene in *Star Wars* where Luke Skywalker, Han Solo, Princess Leia, and Chewbacca are trapped in a garbage compactor. Terrified of being crushed. Fighting for their lives.

Sadly, there was no C-3PO to save her.

While at the hotel, the skies had clouded over and opened. Bev hadn't been paying attention to the forecast. She had no idea a severe weather alert had been posted. Even if she had, it didn't matter. A summer storm was the least of her worries.

The wind and rain were whipping wildly. Tempestuous and tormented, just like Bev's conscience. Turning on her wipers, she pointed her car in the direction of Bayers Road. A few minutes later, she was travelling east on Highway 101. She passed Exit 8, which led to her house in Hantsport. Instead, she continued on to Exit 10 and Wolfville.

Passing vehicles sprayed waves onto her windshield. Her heart was racing, and she was sweating. The air conditioning was broken, and she couldn't afford to fix it. It was all she could do to stick to the speed limit. Under the circumstances, she didn't want to draw attention to herself. She was already in enough trouble.

Bev had decided to do the right thing, Bernie be damned. The truth was torturing her. It was time for atonement. But she wouldn't make a move until she had seen Sally.

Fifteen minutes later, Bev drove into the parking lot of the elderly author's apartment building. Glancing at the clock on the dash, she saw that it was 7:05 P.M. Pulling her cellphone from her purse, she found Sally in her contact list, then hit the call button.

Three rings. Four.

Please answer, Bev begged silently.

Five rings. Six.

Please.

"Hello?"

Bev exhaled in relief. "Hi, Sally. It's Bev. Can I come in?"

"Bev! What a nice surprise." Sally's voice was faint. "Call from the lobby, and I'll buzz you in."

Holding her purse over her head to shield herself from the rain, Bev dashed to the front door. When she got to Sally's apartment, she knocked twice.

"Come in," called Sally. "It's unlocked."

After taking off her damp shoes and dropping her sodden purse in the tiny entryway, Bev found Sally sitting on the loveseat in the living room. A colourful afghan covered her thin legs. A walker was parked in front of her. On a small side table, several pill bottles sat next to a glass of water, along with a crossword-puzzle book, a tissue box, a bible, a rosary, and a remote control.

"It's good of you to come," said Sally. A smile lit up her gaunt face.

Bev sat in the armchair across from Sally. "I'm sorry for dropping in without any notice," she said. "I just really wanted to see you."

Sally waved her hand. "That's all right. I have home care workers from the VON arriving morning, noon, and night. It's like Grand Central Station in here. They take good care of me, though, so I don't mind. It's comforting to have the company."

In fact, Sonya had paid for a private home care business to take care of Sally while she was palliative. Sally hadn't wanted to accept what she felt was an overly generous offer, but Sonya had insisted and promised it would be their secret.

"Can I get you anything?" asked Bev.

"No, thank you," said Sally. "Faith will be here in an hour to help me get into bed. She's lovely. From Jamaica. A devout Catholic. She's praying that her husband and children will be able to join her here in a few months."

"I won't keep you long, then," said Bev. Pausing. Not knowing where to begin.

Sally could sense her long-time editor's distress. "What's wrong, dear?"

Bev burst into tears.

Tuesday evening
Lord Nelson Hotel

AFTER TWENTY MINUTES, IT BECAME EVIDENT TO THE detectives that Bev Clarke had left the building. Security cameras in the underground parking lot showed her climbing into her car and driving away. Thanks to the APB, they knew it wouldn't take long to locate her. It was hard to hide in a province as small as Nova Scotia. Especially if you weren't a career criminal.

Bourque stood in front of the portrait of Admiral Nelson. "I'd love to hear your theories on this case," he said to the dead man. He sighed and turned to Slade. "While the team is searching for Clarke, let's review what we have on Silver."

Slade pulled up the notes she'd typed on her laptop. "Alcoholic. Widowed. Wife died by suicide ten years ago. Neighbours called in domestic disturbances to 911 on several occasions, but she never pressed charges. One daughter, Elizabeth, age thirty-one. The team is working on locating her."

"Good. Tox screen?"

"Positive for a lethal dose of ketamine, given that he also had hypertension and coronary artery disease," said Slade. Eyes on the screen, fingers moving on the keyboard's trackpad. "There was one empty glass in Silver's room, on his desk. He had ordered a Caesar from room service. It tested positive for ketamine. The combination of the drug and alcohol without the health conditions would have rendered him unconscious. So, someone drugged him, which caused heart failure. *Then* he was struck over the head with the typewriter."

"Interesting," said Bourque, crossing his legs. "Comeau's tox screen was clean. What does that tell us?"

Tapping two fingers on her keyboard, Slade said, "That Comeau's murder was a crime of passion. If Silver was drugged first, that's premeditation. Which could mean we have a copycat who wants us to think it's a serial killer."

Bourque nodded. "That means for Silver's killer, we're looking at someone with knowledge, opportunity, and access."

Slade's eyebrows raised. "Inside job?"

"Possibly," said Bourque, standing up to fetch two glasses of water. "Who would know the details about the first murder, have easy access to Silver's room, and be able to deliver a doctored drink?"

Slade didn't hesitate. "A hotel staff member. Maybe a room service attendant."

"Right," said Bourque. "If we pursue that theory, the question then is, why would an employee want Silver dead? Let's get the team to take a closer look at staff, starting with the room-service attendants."

"I'll take care of it," said Slade, trying to stifle a yawn.

Bourque glanced at his watch. "Tomorrow morning is fine. Let's call it a night."

"Sounds good, Sarge." Slade started packing up. "When are we moving back to the station?"

"Let's finish the week out here," said Bourque, running a hand through his hair. "I'm getting pressure from the chief to make an arrest. The Westby Foundation is leaning on him. I guess the optics of an unsolved murder aren't good for business. Who knew?" He shook his head. "I keep reiterating that our resources are stretched to the limit."

"We're doing our best, Sarge," said Slade. "Have a good night. See you tomorrow."

"Good work today, detective," said Bourque, packing his briefcase with paperwork.

Tuesday night
Big Bernie Brown's penthouse suite

BERNIE WAS HAVING A HARD TIME STAYING ANGRY AT Bev for bailing on her interview with the cops. That's because as soon as she heard the news, she started gasping for air.

Her breaths were rapid and shallow. Each time she coughed, it felt like someone was stabbing her chest with a butcher's blade. The digital thermometer showed a fever of 104°. Up two degrees from an hour earlier. Sweating and shivering simultaneously, she leaned over the side of the bed and threw up her evening snack—a box of garlic fingers and two litres of root beer—into an empty garbage can.

That's when the hallucinations started.

First, Bernie's former husbands showed up at the foot of her bed. All three of them. Howling like deranged hyenas.

Threatening to smother her.

Shoot her.

Drown her.

Stab her.

Strangle her.

Then Bernie's mother was there. Berating her ten-year-old self. Shouting that she was a worthless piece of crap. Beating her bare bottom with a wooden spoon until her skin burned and bled.

After that, her brother Dougie made an appearance. Skinny and shackled, in an orange jumpsuit. Eyes wild. Spittle flying from his mouth. Accusing her of letting him rot in jail.

Bernie tossed, turned, and moaned. And screamed silently.

Help.

Help.

Help.

One final relative showed up to the Bash Bernie Party. Teenaged Bev. Sweet smile. Infinite potential. Loved horses. Good heart. Kind mother who died too soon. Lousy dad, just like Bernie's had been.

Corrupt, selfish aunt. How could you?

As Bernie's breathing became more laboured, she felt the strangest sensation, like she was levitating off the bed. Hands slid underneath her bulk, supporting her. She was floating in space. Weightless, for the first time in her life. As she felt the lid closing on her coffin, she chose to surrender to the feeling.

It was a great shock, then, when Bernice Alice Brown woke up hazy in a hospital bed with oxygen tubes in her nostrils.

"Pneumonia," said a brusque young doctor with no bedside manner.

The nurses in the intensive care unit were efficient, but far too busy to comfort their patient who had been one breath away from dying.

When Bernie was more alert, she would learn that during Boris's regular night patrol, he had heard his boss moaning. The Russian had placed a call for an ambulance. In doing so, he had saved Bernie's life.

Her first thought upon waking—right after a full-body ache for a cigarette—was of Bev.

Her niece, who'd loved her once. Who she'd let down so many times.

Bernie was eighty-two. Her organs had nearly shut down. Her expiration date was within sight. She'd been given this second chance for one reason only. It was time to atone for her sins. To set things right between her and Bev.

Boris had brought his boss's purse (minus the gun) to her hospital room. Bernie pressed the call button, and a nurse gave it to her. She was so weak she could barely lift her arms.

When Bernie was alone again, she picked up the phone. Found Bev in her contact list. And hit dial.

Tuesday night
Val's apartment

JUST BEFORE MIDNIGHT, VAL WOKE UP TO THE SOUND of soft squealing. When she turned on the bedside lamp, she spotted Sherlock Holmes in the doorway.

Passing Mouse Number Thirteen back and forth between his paws like a hockey puck.

"Sheesh," said Val, feeling queasy. "I know you're just doing your job—but seriously? Do you have to do it right now?"

Val switched the light off and covered her head with her pillow.

She could still hear it.

Worried that Sherlock would deposit his bounty on her bed again—this time with her in it—Val moved the pillow and turned the light back on. Now, she had a dilemma. Should she leave Sherlock to finish off the poor creature? Or take care of it herself, to ease its suffering? And if so, how would she do it?

Val had watched every episode of *The Nature of Things*. She knew that predators play a crucial role in the natural cycle. If Sherlock were an outdoor cat, he could be killed by any number of them. Owls. Raccoons. Dogs. Cars. So, Val kept him inside. Where he was safe. Wild mice didn't have someone to make that choice for them. They were risking their lives both in the great outdoors *and* inside her cozy apartment. Where cracker crumbs on the floor were a feast.

Because Val was squeamish, she couldn't bear the thought of directly exterminating a living creature. After a few minutes of deliberation, she decided to go full David Suzuki and let nature run its course, without her interference. However, that didn't mean she wanted a front-row seat at the show.

In the time it had taken Val to make her decision, the mouse had gone quiet. Sherlock picked it up in his mouth, turned around, and padded away.

"That's for keeping me awake," Val grumbled, getting up to close the door.

Tossing and turning, she tried to block out the image of Sherlock playing mouse hockey. It was then that she heard the faint sound of footsteps on the porch.

Her bedroom window faced the street. To the left of the front steps. Day or night, she kept the blind drawn. After the creep who stared at women in their bedrooms was caught last year, she kept her windows and doors shut and locked. Even during the days when she was home.

Val held her breath and strained to listen.

A mailbox lid opened and closed.

Footsteps receded.

In the dark, she peeked behind the blind. Squinting, all Val could see was someone running away in the rain wearing jeans, sneakers, and a hoodie. Slight build. Average height. Brisk pace. The hood was pulled up, so Val couldn't see hair colour.

"Should I call the police?" she worried aloud. It was one o'clock in the morning. Who was dropping something off at such an ungodly hour? Not even delivery drivers worked this late.

Pulling on her robe and slippers, Val tiptoed to her apartment door. She knew the young married couple in the flat above hers were on vacation in Prince Edward Island. They had asked her to collect their mail and water their plants. It was just the two apartments in the house. The landlord lived in Bedford.

As far as Val knew, she was all alone. Although it was warm in the hallway, she shivered.

Maybe she *should* call the cops.

Setting aside caution, Val decided to be brave and channel her inner sleuth. She'd just step onto the porch to check the mailboxes. It would only take two seconds. Then she'd scurry back to the safety of her place.

Ten seconds later, Val was back in bed. Breathless. In her trembling hands, she held a brown envelope. With her name printed in capital letters in blue ink. Just like the note about Steve Silver. She'd had the foresight to use a tissue to take the envelope out of her mailbox. In her kitchen, she donned a pair of the disposable gloves she wore to clean the kitty litter. If the envelope and its contents had fingerprints on it, they wouldn't be hers.

Taking a deep breath, Val opened the envelope and pulled out a piece of paper.

STEVE SILVER WAS A MAGGOT. EXPOSE HIS CRIME SO JUSTICE CAN BE SERVED.

Val blew out a sigh. She supposed it was good news that the message was from the person who wanted her to keep investigating, not from whoever wanted her to stop. The bad news was that whoever it was knew not only where she worked, but also where she lived.

After checking all of the locks and ensuring the security system was armed, Val went to the kitchen to make chamomile tea. Sitting at the table waiting for the kettle to boil, she composed a text to Kevin.

Hey. I got another anonymous note. At home this time.

Val loosened her grip on the phone when she saw three dots appear. Knowing that she was connected to someone in that moment made her feel less afraid.

Huh. From which secret admirer?

Val's thumbs flew.

The one who wants me to keep digging. What should I do?

Three dots again.

Tell Marianne. And show the notes to Bourque.

Val breathed a sigh of relief. She agreed that she couldn't put off showing the notes to Bourque any longer.

Val: **Okay. First thing in the morning. Thanks.**

Kevin: **Get some sleep, kid. Keep me posted. Still waiting for my nail file.**

When Val finished her tea, she triple-checked the locks and alarm. Returning to her bedroom, she crawled under the covers. Checked her messages. There was a text from Del, asking for an update. She'd reply in the morning. Before she turned out the light, Sherlock hopped onto the bed. No mouse in sight. Curling up next to her, the cat soon fell asleep. Eventually, Val did, too.

Tuesday night
Sally's apartment

IN SALLY'S BATHROOM, BEV DRIED HER TEARS, BLEW HER nose, and splashed cold water on her face. Back in the living room, she felt lighter.

"Sorry about that," said Bev, returning to her chair. "I was overdue a meltdown. The past few days have been stressful."

"No need to apologize," said Sally, pulling the afghan higher up on her lap. "Everyone who attended the gala is feeling the strain, I'm sure."

"Are you?" asked Bev, tucking her legs under her. "I don't know how you can bear waiting to find out who won."

Sally's smile didn't reach her eyes. "I don't have any choice *but* to be patient. It's disappointing, certainly. But I have…other things on my mind."

Bev knew there wasn't time to be coy. Sally was dying, the police were likely searching for her, and her conscience was weighing on her.

"Sally, I have a confession to make," said Bev, folding her hands in her lap. "It's why I came."

Raising her eyebrows in surprise, Sally said, "Oh? Shouldn't you go to church to confess?"

Untucking her legs, Bev put her feet on the floor and leaned forward. Her hands were clasped, elbows on knees.

"You know I'm not religious, Sally," said Bev. "Not like you. In fact, I'm not even a good person. But I do have a conscience. And this confession is only for you."

"All right, dear," said Sally, eyebrows knitted in concern. "Go ahead. I'm listening."

Bev looked into Sally's eyes. They were warm and kind. Her loving gaze gave her courage.

"Remember when Sonya helped you to your room at the hotel on Friday?" she began.

"Of course," said Sally. "It was gracious of her. She has been a godsend."

Taking a deep breath, Bev continued. "Well, I followed you. I was planning to check on you, to make sure you were all right. To see if there was anything I could do to help. The door was just about to close when I got there, so I stuck my foot in it. I was planning to knock and call out when I heard you talking."

Realization showed on Sally's face.

"Ah," she said, nodding. "I see. I was telling Sonya about Sherman."

Bev nodded. "You know, of course, that I didn't come in. But…I stayed in the doorway until you finished your story."

"Well, that's hardly worth driving here in a rainstorm to confess," said Sally. "Eavesdropping is neither a sin nor a crime. Nor is keeping a secret. But I appreciate that you told me. You know, I wouldn't have minded if you'd come into my room. I trust you."

Bev's eyes filled with tears. "Thank you," she said, her voice breaking. "But I don't deserve your trust."

"Don't fret, dear," said Sally, looking wistful. "What happened was a very long time ago. You heard that Sherman was abusive. But smart, too. My bruises were always covered by my clothes. If it wasn't for Frank, my next-door neighbour, Sherman would have killed me that night."

Sally leaned back, like she always did when she told a story. Bev knew what was coming, but prepared herself to hear it first-hand.

"When Frank heard Sherman screaming and dishes breaking, he ran over. I was lying on the floor, half conscious. Frank tried to help me up, and Sherman lunged at him with a sharp knife. The door to the basement was in the kitchen. It was open. Frank pushed Sherman in self-defence. I didn't want to go to the hospital for my injuries, where the doctor would ask questions. When Frank was sure I'd be all right, I cleaned myself up as best I could, then called an ambulance for Sherman."

"I'm so sorry," said Bev. Hating that Sally had been hurt, repeatedly. "Was your first husband abusive, too?"

Sally shook her head. "No, but Everett was an alcoholic. On hot summer nights, he'd go for a swim at the pond to cool off. One evening, he swam after he'd had too much to drink. He drowned, but the water was also full of blue-algae bloom. The coroner said if he hadn't drowned, the bacteria would have killed him eventually."

Sally sipped her water. Sighing, she said, "It was a blessing for me when Everett died. It was no picnic being married to him. He drank all of his money. My money, too. I never knew if he'd come home at night. It was a constant worry, day and night. But he had a quiet kindness when he was sober. After he was gone, believe it or not, I was lonely. Then I made another poor choice with Sherman. Oh, he was handsome and charming at first. I didn't find out that he was manipulative until it was too late. Back then, there were no resources in rural areas to help women leave bad marriages."

"What happened to Frank?" asked Bev. In the twenty years she had worked with Sally, she'd had no clue about the secrets the author had been safeguarding.

Now Sally's eyes welled with tears. "Once the coroner had ruled it an accidental death, Frank lived next door to me for another year. Until he knew I'd be all right on my own. We never spoke about what happened. Then he moved away. We didn't stay in touch. A few years ago, a church friend told me he had died of a heart attack in Sudbury."

Pulling a tissue from the box, Sally dabbed at her eyes. "Frank was my guardian angel. I tortured myself for years, thinking maybe we should have called the police and told them the truth. I felt such guilt keeping that secret. But what good would it have done? It was only when my cancer began to spread that I could accept the truth, that Frank and I had done nothing wrong in the eyes of the law *and* in God's eyes. I'm hoping to meet my guardian angel on the other side. To thank him."

Bev gave Sally a moment to compose herself. Then she said, "You mentioned 'the other side'…"

Sally guessed what was coming next. "Yes?"

"At the hotel, I stayed in your doorway long enough to hear about the appointment you've made," said Bev.

"Ah," said Sally, nodding. "I wondered."

"Were you going to tell me?" asked Bev, her voice cracking.

Sally shook her head. "I wasn't going to tell anyone. Somehow, Sonya knew."

"I'd offer to be there, but..." Bev paused.

"It's all right," said Sally quickly. "I wouldn't ask you to bear witness to..."

"It isn't that," Bev reassured her. "It's just...I don't know where I'll be. Or what's going to happen to me. I guess I just wanted to tell you...to say...goodbye."

Sally looked confused. "What are you talking about?"

In the distance, sirens were wailing. Growing louder. Coming closer.

"I don't have much time," said Bev, getting up to look out the window. Rain pummelled the pane relentlessly. Turning back to Sally, she said, "I came here to tell you what really happened to Vic."

Wednesday morning
Val's apartment

WHEN VAL LOOKED IN THE MIRROR, SHE WAS MORTIFIED at her reflection. She took a mental inventory.

Hair a rat's nest.

Eyes bloodshot. Dark circles as deep as moon craters beneath them.

Perimenopausal pimple poking up on her chin.

Stress-induced cold sore on her lower lip.

Horizontal wrinkle stretching from one side of her neck to the other. More like a crease. Maybe a crinkle?

Was *crinkle* even a word?

Val looked it up online.

It was. A synonym for *wrinkle*.

A Wrinkle in Time could have been *A Crinkle in Time*. Val wondered if Madeleine L'Engle would have had the same success with the latter title.

In October, Val would turn forty-five. Maybe it was time to start using a moisturizer with a more potent active ingredient than vitamin E. Sighing, she turned away to get dressed. Then she walked around her apartment to check the locks. Satisfied that everything was still secure, she fed Sherlock his breakfast, then ate a bowl of granola with yogurt, local strawberries, and maple syrup.

The late-night delivery had rattled her. She had slept, but fitfully. Rummaging around in her backpack, she fished out Detective Bourque's business card. It was almost 8:00 A.M. Surely he'd be at work by now. She composed a text.

Val Jenkins here. I have some information that might help your investigation. Could I meet you this morning?

Crickets.

While she was brushing her teeth, her cellphone buzzed.

Free for a few minutes in half an hour. Still at the hotel.

Putting her toothbrush back in its holder, Val replied that she'd meet him there. After covering her pimple with concealer and applying ointment with a cotton swab to her cold sore, she sat on the sofa with Sherlock on her lap for a few minutes. Her cat's purring calmed her. When she got up, she tucked all three notes in her backpack.

The rain had ceased at dawn, so Val decided to cycle to the Lord Nelson. When she was almost there, a muddy pickup truck hit a pothole puddle, splashing dirty water all over her. Her cotton capris and T-shirt were drenched.

"Shit," she said, gritting her teeth. Stopping herself from raising a middle finger. All she needed right now was to incite road rage.

After locking her bike in front of the hotel, Val headed to the bathroom to pat herself down with paper towels. Still damp but no longer dripping, she was grateful she hadn't worn mascara.

Looking in the mirror, she said out loud, "I'm a hot mess."

"Life is messy," said a familiar voice from one of the stalls. Followed by a steam of urine hitting the bowl.

Ohmigod, thought Val. *Not the tinkling philosopher again.*

"You have no idea," said Val, attempting to fluff up her curls with her fingers.

Detective Bourque was on the phone when Val arrived at the Georgian Lounge. Looking up, he waved her in, pointing to the same chair as before. When his call ended, he looked at Val, observing but ignoring her rumpled appearance.

"So, Ms. Jenkins, what can you tell me?"

"It's more what I can show you," said Val, pulling the notes from her backpack and placing them on the desk.

"Why is only one envelope bagged?" asked Bourque.

"I didn't touch that one with bare hands," said Val, explaining how the notes were delivered. "The other two will have multiple fingerprints."

Pulling on a pair of nitrile gloves, Bourque carefully removed the notes from their envelopes and read them.

"There's a typo in one of them," said Bourque.

Val sighed. "I know. Do you think it's clue?"

Bourque shrugged. "I don't know what to think at this point. I'll share these with my team."

"Good," said Val. Crossing her right leg over her left, she smacked her foot into the corner of the desk. "Ow. God. Sorry."

"So," said Bourque, crossing his arms. Looking annoyed. Like a teacher about to dole out detention. "Why don't you tell me what's been going on since we last met."

Wednesday morning
Alex's office, Dalhousie University

AFTER HIS MEETING WITH BIG BERNIE BROWN, ALEX HAD become a shell of his former flamboyant self. Instead of wearing his regular uniform of brightly coloured paisleys and florals, he was opting for neutrals. Beige. Black. Tan. All monochrome. It was his way of trying to fade into the background.

It helped some that a plainclothes detective was assigned to follow him in an unmarked vehicle when he left his house. Only from Point A to Point B. After that, he was on his own. This morning, she had tailed him to his office. But police resources were stretched thin, he'd been reminded. He couldn't have a police presence forever. He prayed the killer, or killers, would be caught soon.

Alex felt safer on campus than in his house. There were other people at the office. Not many, because it was summer, so most of the faculty were working at home or on vacation, but graduate students, research assistants, and secretaries were still around. Usha was across the hall, toiling away in her cubbyhole. That was reassuring. If he screamed for help, she would hear him. She couldn't overtake Boris, of course, but she could call the cops.

Unless Boris eliminated Usha first. Alex shuddered at the thought.

It didn't help that the scary Russian hulk kept popping up in unexpected places.

In the grocery store, across from the lemons.

In line behind him at the pharmacy counter.

In the parking lot of the liquor store.

To help keep his senses sharp, Alex decided to stop drinking. Along with cutting out alcohol, he also cut down on his outside movements. He started ordering everything he could online. When he was running errands, he felt as though he had a bull's-eye on his back.

At home, he was afraid to step into his own shower.

He couldn't eat. He couldn't sleep. In his office, he would nod off briefly, leaning back in his computer chair. Only to jerk awake from a nightmare. Of the burly man's hands wrapped around his throat, squeezing the breath out of him.

Now, Alex awoke to a timid knock on his locked door. He tipped back in his swivel chair, almost falling onto the floor.

"Who is it?"

"Usha," came the reply. He could tell she'd noticed he was acting strange.

"Hold on," he said, getting up to unlock and open the door. Knocking over a stack of books on the floor on his way.

Alex gestured for Usha to sit in his visitor's chair. When she hesitated, he swept the pile of books from it onto the floor.

Usha frowned. "Dr. Fitzgerald, are you all right?"

Alex sighed. "Sorry. I'm not myself. The murders are taking a toll on me. I can't focus."

"Maybe you should go somewhere on vacation?"

"No!" Alex practically yelled. "Sorry. Sorry. I know you're just trying to be helpful."

The truth was that here at home, he at least had some police protection. If he went away, he'd be on his own.

Vulnerable.

Defenseless.

A sitting duck.

"Is there anything I can do to help?" asked Usha.

Hire an assassin to neutralize a Russian mobster and an old bookie, thought Alex.

Out loud, he said, "No. Thank you. I'll manage. Is there anything *you* need help with?"

"Not right now, but I'm hoping by Friday I'll have finished writing the social commentary portion of my thesis," said Usha, standing. "Would you take a look at it?"

"Yes, yes, of course," said Alex, nodding. "Happy to." *If I'm still alive.*

Usha smiled. "Thank you. I'll close the door on my way out. And if you need anything, please let me know."

"Thanks, I will," Alex said, faking a smile. "Don't worry about me. Just concentrate on your paper." He locked the door behind her.

After Usha left, Alex went to the window, which overlooked the parking lot. And watched in horror as his BMW Roadster burst into flames.

Wednesday afternoon
Halifax Infirmary

BERNIE'S IV ANTIBIOTICS WERE KICKING IN. AS THE drugs dripped into her body, she felt as though the Holy Spirit was moving through her. She was experiencing a rebirth, of both her physical and spiritual selves. The hospital chaplain had even been in to visit. What a badass she was, with a hell of a story. Previously, she had been an army chaplain. They had talked about the importance of reconciling with relatives. Before it was too late.

Bernie wished Bev would answer her calls. She would send Boris to find her, but today he was busy blowing up Alex Fitzgerald's car. Her niece would surface sooner or later. Like a homing pigeon. Even when she was young and in trouble, she had never flown far.

That morning, Bernie had been moved from the ICU to a step-down unit. She was still hooked up to oxygen around the clock, but she was making progress. Except for Boris, no one had visited. So when she looked up from her crossword puzzle, she was surprised to see someone standing at the foot of her bed.

Closing the door, her dishevelled visitor said, "What the FUCK is wrong with you?"

Alex Fitzgerald's hair was a mess. His clothes were wrinkled. And he smelled like he hadn't showered in days.

Bernie sniffed the air. "Good afternoon to you, too. I have pneumonia. What's that odour? Smells like sewage. Is it you?"

Alex plopped down in the chair next to the bed. "Listen, you old crone. Your lackey blew up my car this morning," he said, scratching his scalp. Flakes of dandruff fell like snowflakes onto his shoulders. "I'm not in the mood for insults."

"Now that's the pot calling the kettle black," said Bernie, who loved nothing better than to argue with the enemy. A battle of wits was better than sex. Especially at her age. "Besides, what Boris lacks in brains, he makes up for in brawn. *And* his skill around explosives."

"So you admit he blew up my car?" asked Alex, sliding his right hand into his pants pocket.

"I admit nothing," replied Bernie with wide-eyed innocence. "I'm a sick old woman. I'll have you know that I almost died. I don't have any idea what's happening outside the hospital. Oh, and by the way, you might want to think twice about recording this conversation on your phone."

Alex looked defeated. Sighing, he pulled out his phone and hit the stop button.

"What will it take for you to leave me alone?" asked Alex.

"Tell the police you killed Victor Comeau," said Bernie.

"I didn't, and I won't," said Alex. "I get that you're trying to protect Bev. But if she did the crime, she has to do the time."

Bernie snorted, then adjusted one of the tubes in her nostrils. "I can't believe you just said that. So trite. I thought you were a writer."

Why do people keep calling my work trite? thought Alex, trying to tamp down his simmering rage.

"My poetry is better than that," said Bernie, rubbing salt in the wound.

Sighing, Alex let go of his anger. "You write poetry?" he asked, looking doubtful.

"What, you don't think I can? I've been writing it since I was a kid," said Bernie. Hesitating, she added, "Until I found horses, it was my sole escape from an abusive childhood."

Alex absorbed this unexpected information, then shook his head. "Spare me the sob story! You aren't the only one who had a rough childhood, and you don't see me threatening people and torching cars. This harassment has to stop."

"Tell you what," said Bernie. "I'll make you a deal. If you read my poems, I'll call off the big guy."

Alex considered her offer. "I wouldn't mind reading *some* of them," he admitted. "Actually, I'm looking for contributions to an anthology I'm editing. I got a grant to publish it. If your submissions are good, I could even pay you for them."

"I don't need the money," said Bernie, blushing. "But I'd be pleased to send you a few poems. They've really helped me work through my PTSD."

Alex's eyebrows hit his receding hairline. "Seriously?"

"Cross my heart," said Bernie, a hand flopping in front of her chest. "And anyway, I'm a changed woman since my near-death experience. It's the least I can do for what I've put you through."

Alex was skeptical. "What about Bev?"

"Don't worry about Bev," said Bernie. "I'll take care of her."

She could see Alex trying to figure out what she meant by her vague phrasing. She loved making men squirm.

"So we have a deal?" asked Alex.

Bernie held out her right hand. "We have a deal."

Alex shook it.

"I admire your hutzpah," said Bernie, squirting sanitizer into her palms. "It takes a brave soul to go toe-to-toe with me."

Alex shrugged. "You didn't give me much of a choice, Bernie. I'll keep an eye out for those poems." Then he left.

Lying back on her pillow, Bernie closed her eyes. Before drifting off to sleep, she smiled and whispered, "What a putz."

Wednesday afternoon
Lord Nelson Hotel

AFTER VAL BROUGHT DETECTIVE BOURQUE UP TO SPEED, he positioned himself in front of Admiral Nelson's portrait. Silent. Hands clasped behind his back.

One minute passed.

Val waited for the detective to say something.

Two minutes.

Three.

Val knew at four minutes, she'd crack.

Four.

"Is everything all right?" she asked.

At the sound of Val's voice, Bourque turned around sharply. He had been so lost in his thoughts, he seemed surprised to see her sitting there.

"No, Ms. Jenkins, everything is *not* all right," he replied. "We have two murders and no arrests. My chief is breathing down my neck. The Westby Foundation chair is having panic attacks. And the icing on the cake is that you've been secretly investigating on your own, and now you're being threatened, which compromises, and complicates, *my* investigation."

"What's your favourite kind of cake?" asked Val.

Bourque looked confused, and mildly charmed. "Excuse me?"

"Your favourite kind of cake. What is it?"

Without hesitation Bourque replied, "Carrot."

Val's face broke into a smile. "Mine too! With cream-cheese frosting. Yum."

"Could we please stay on topic?" asked Bourque, leaning on the end of his desk.

"Of course," said Val, carefully crossing her leg. "I just thought it might be nice to think of something pleasant for a second."

A tiny smile played around Bourque's lips. "Yes, I suppose. Except now I want carrot cake. And for the record, I prefer mine without frosting."

Val cocked her head. "Raisins and walnuts?"

"No to both. Now, would you please describe to me one more time the person you saw dropping off the notes about Mr. Silver."

Although the details were vague, Val went over them again.

Bourque made notes. When Val stopped talking, he said, "Thanks. Next, we'll have forensics check for fingerprints."

"Will you let me know what you find?" Val looked hopeful.

Bourque closed his notebook. "Once again, please leave the police work to us. If you get any more notes, don't touch them with your bare hands. And bring them to me right away."

Val barely stopped herself from saluting. "Yes, sir."

Just then, Detective Sarah Slade rushed into the room, briefcase in hand. She stopped short when she spotted Val.

"Oops, sorry," Slade said, dropping her briefcase on an armchair. "Didn't mean to interrupt. Hi, Val."

"Hey," said Val. The two women had attended a few of the same book launches. Plus, Slade was a fan of *Book Briefs*.

"Is your column coming out on Friday?" asked Slade.

"Shit! I don't know," said Val, gathering her things. "Nothing is normal about this week. I have to check in with my editor. Thanks for the reminder."

"No problem," said Slade.

Backpack and helmet in hand, Val looked at Bourque. "Are we done here?"

Bourque nodded. "For now."

After Val was gone, Slade shared some startling news.

There was a good reason the team had been having trouble finding Steve Silver's daughter.

Immediately after Elaine's suicide, Elizabeth had disappeared. The last known sighting of her had been at a surf school in Tofino, where she had worked. Not long after that, her digital footprint disintegrated.

Until now. The tech team had unearthed her. Elizabeth Silver was now legally Jackie Oulton. She'd taken her late mother's middle name, Jacqueline, and her maiden name.

Even more surprising, Jackie had been working at the Lord Nelson Hotel for a few months. On Monday, she hadn't shown up for her shift. No one had seen or her heard from her since.

Wednesday afternoon
Sally's apartment

JUST AFTER 2:00 P.M., SONYA PULLED HER RED MIATA into Sally's parking lot. The drive north from Lunenburg to Wolfville was beautiful at this time of year. Tall stalks of pink, purple, and white lupins dotted the ditches along the highway. Farm fields were green and lush. Bald eagles soared overhead. Maple, birch, and willow trees were in full leaf. Blomidon posed, postcard-perfect, beyond the ebbing-and-flowing Minas Basin tides.

Today, Sonya wasn't focused on the scenery. Instead, she was thinking about Sally's MAID appointment. The date was growing closer. Turning off the ignition, she sat quietly in the car for a few minutes. When she'd worked as an anesthesiologist, despite the surgeons' best efforts, she'd lost patients on the operating table. Dealing with death was part of a doctor's life.

Sally was ready. Her date was firm. The following Sunday morning, Sonya would return.

Holding Sally's hand when she took her final breath didn't frighten Sonya. She believed it took great courage for someone to make that decision. And then to follow through on it. She hoped her presence would be a comfort.

Breaking her reverie, Sonya stepped out of her car, locked it, and buzzed Sally from the lobby. The apartment door was unlocked, so Sonya let herself in.

"I'm in the living room," said Sally, her voice weaker than it was a few days ago.

Sally was sitting on the loveseat, bible open on her lap.

"How are you feeling?" asked Sonya. Crouching next to the older woman, she put two fingers to Sally's wrist, checking her pulse.

Smiling, Sally closed her eyes at her friend's gentle touch. "Better, now that you're here."

"How's the pain?" Sonya patted Sally's hand as she let it go.

"Tolerable," said Sally, opening her eyes. "The home care workers make sure I take my medication."

"Good. Can I get you anything?"

Sally shook her head. "No, dear. Just sit a spell so we can chat. If you'd like a glass of water or iced tea, please help yourself."

Sonya settled into the armchair. "Thanks, maybe in a bit," she said. Then, "Has Val Jenkins from the *Post* been in touch?"

Sally tried to recall those who had reached out to ask after her health. There hadn't been many. A few church friends and neighbours in her building.

"No. Why?"

Sonya frowned. "She came to see me yesterday morning. Asking questions for a story she's working on about the NOVA Prize, for when they finally announce the winner. She asked after you."

"Do you think there *will* be a winner? After everything that's happened?"

"I don't see how the foundation can't name one," said Sonya. "It would be extremely poor optics."

Sally paused. "What if it's Victor?"

Sonya took a deep breath, then exhaled her frustration. "In that case, I guess he'd receive the prize posthumously. I suppose his widow could accept it on his behalf."

"Well, it's out of our hands, so there's no sense in fretting over it," said Sally. "I don't think it'll be me. But if by God's good grace it is, you know my wishes."

Sonya nodded. "I do. And I promise to honour them."

"Thank you," said Sally. "Now, for a bit of business. Everything is in place for this Sunday. The doctor will be here at nine o'clock in the morning. I didn't want to wait around all day, thinking about it. You'll contact my lawyer when it's…over, and he'll take care of everything after that. In the meantime, Father Marcellus is coming here on Thursday morning to hear my confession. And to give me Communion and the last rites."

Sonya crossed her legs. "And you still don't want a funeral, just a memorial mass? And for your urn to be interred in the columbarium at Holy Cross?"

Sally had chosen Holy Cross in nearby Kentville as her final resting place because she didn't want to lie next to her husbands for eternity.

"That's right. Father Marcellus and my lawyer will see to all of that."

Sonya looked around the living room. "What will happen to the contents of your apartment?"

"I don't have much. I've asked my lawyer to donate whatever is useful to charity. Whatever's left can go in a dumpster." Sally's gaze landed on the middle shelf of her grandparents' mahogany cabinet. "Sonya, do you see the Old Country Roses teacup and saucer in the cabinet?"

"I do," said Sonya, smiling. "My mother had the full set. Such a beautiful pattern."

"That cup and saucer belonged to *my* mother," said Sally, tearing up. "I'd like you to have it. You can take it after I'm gone."

"Thank you," said Sonya, her voice thick with emotion. "I'll treasure it."

Sally dabbed her eyes with a tissue. "Now, I'm ready for a rest before Faith arrives to make my supper and give me my pills."

Picking up her purse, Sonya went to place a pillow behind Sally's head. "I'll see you on Sunday, but I'll call you before then to check in."

Leaning back against the pillow, Sally closed her eyes. "You're a good soul, dear."

When Sally was alone again, she fingered her rosary until she fell asleep. Then she dreamt of unburdening all that was weighing on her to Father Marcellus. Including what Bev had confessed.

Wednesday afternoon
Lord Nelson Hotel

ADMIRAL HORATIO NELSON WAS BATTLING A monstrous migraine. Since the murders had occurred, there had been far more activity than he would normally tolerate in the Georgian Lounge. To be clear, he wasn't opposed to the occasional gathering. A crush of warm bodies and intelligent conversation livened things up a little. The events would be followed by a few days of quiet, allowing him to recover. He had long ago accepted that a gentleman born in 1758 could no longer celebrate quite like he used to.

But lately, people were coming and going morning, noon, and night. Interviews were being conducted. Calls were being made. Detectives were talking, typing, and pacing. Drinking coffee. So much coffee! Putting their dirty feet up on his footstools. Sitting on his desk and in his chairs, like they owned the place. Staring at him. *Talking* to him.

Two dead authors didn't compare in the faintest to the countless men he'd lost in bloody naval battles. Never mind that he'd had more than his own share of near-death experiences. At any rate, from what he'd overheard, the dead men had been imbeciles. No loss to general society, or otherwise. In fact, his only real query in the case was why someone hadn't killed them sooner.

The admiral, himself, had died at sea at age forty-seven. Such a memorable moment. He was on his flagship, HMS *Victory*. Lying in the arms of his loyal flag captain, Thomas Hardy (not to be confused with the poet and author of the same name, who had yet to be born). Nelson's final words were immortalized: "Now I am satisfied. Thank God, I have done my duty."

The admiral supposed the detectives were also doing their duty. He just wished they would pick up the pace. All the to-ing and fro-ing was tiresome. Right now, he would kill for a catnap.

"I'd kill for a massage," said Detective Slade, digging a thumb into a knot in her neck.

"I thought you booked one?" said Detective Bourque, looking up from his laptop screen.

"I did, but her first available appointment is Saturday," said Slade. "I hope I don't have to cancel."

"We're closing in," said Bourque. "Did forensics lift any prints off the notes?"

"Yes, but only from the one Val bagged," said Slade, arching her neck from side to side. "Hold on—I just got an email." She scanned it. "Prints belong to Jackie Oulton."

Bourque stopped typing. "Steve Silver's daughter. The same daughter who was working in this hotel the night of the murders. That's interesting."

"What's even more interesting is the team can't find her," said Slade. "She's disappeared. We're on it." She started typing furiously.

Bourque went to refill their coffee cups. "Any luck tracking down Bev Clarke?"

"Thanks," said Slade, taking her cup. "She hasn't been home, but she used her credit card this morning to buy gas at the Irving station in New Minas. So, she's close to home. She really only has two options in either direction, the highway or the old road. It's just a matter of time. And we have eyes on her house."

"Has anyone checked to see if she went to see Sally MacPhee?" Bourque wondered.

"I was planning to pay Sally a visit myself." Slade glanced at her watch, adding, "I can be there in an hour."

Bourque nodded. "Good idea. I'll deal with Alex Fitzgerald's allegation that Bernice Brown's bodyguard blew up his car."

Snorting, Slade picked up her briefcase. "Never a dull moment."

"You got that right," said Bourque, lifting his cup of coffee to his lips.

Jackie: The Daughter

Wednesday afternoon

Dartmouth

JACKIE OULTON WAS HOLED UP IN A FRIEND'S DAMP, dingy basement in Dartmouth trying to figure out her next move. She knew the cops would be looking for her soon, if they hadn't started already. She couldn't return to her sublet in Halifax's North End. One way or another, the ugly truth about Steve Silver had to come out. Since she had "buried" Elizabeth Silver on the West Coast, she'd stopped referring to Steve as her father. She told anyone who asked that her parents were dead.

It was the truth. Her mother *was* dead. And up until Sunday, her father had been dead to her.

Now, Steve Silver was dead for real.

Jackie was sick and tired of hiding. And not just in the dank basement, where she'd been squatting for the last few hours. She was sick and tired of hiding Steve's cruel secret from the world.

Several months earlier, when Jackie saw on social media where Steve would be attending the NOVA Prize gala, she set in motion a plan to move from Tofino back to Halifax. Once settled there, she took a job cleaning rooms at the Lord Nelson, quickly moving her way up to room-service attendant. She hadn't thought beyond the fact that she needed to confront Steve, to solicit an apology, for her own peace of mind. And that it was bound to be an unpleasant encounter.

Best-case scenario now? Val Jenkins would work out what Steve had done to Jackie's mother, then write an exposé for the newspaper. Nothing would make Jackie happier than to see her father disgraced and shamed publicly. And in the process, Elaine would be vindicated.

Worst-case scenario?

Jackie shuddered to think of it. Time was running out.

Wednesday afternoon
Highway 101

BEFORE BEV CLARKE DROVE OUT OF THE CITY, SHE'D turned off her cellphone. She couldn't risk the police pinging her location. She didn't know much about technology except that phones were easy to track, unless you knew how to properly disable them.

Unfortunately, Bev had no clue what she was doing. Or where she was going, after she left Sally's. That night, she checked into a motel off the highway under a fake name, paying with cash.

All Bev knew for sure was that she needed time alone. To think. And to plan.

Lying on the cheap thin bedspread, drapes drawn against the twilight, a light bulb flashed in her brain. In the morning, she would head to an old haunt she hadn't visited in decades: a dilapidated cottage in Morden that belonged to her mother's side of the family. A small, single-storey, white-clapboard structure nestled next to a cliff on the North Mountain, overlooking the Bay of Fundy.

The cottage was really no more than a glorified shed with a couple of cots. As a child, Bev had spent many happy summer holidays there. Whale watching from the clifftop. Wind whipping through her hair. Salty ocean breezes tickling her nose.

As far as Bev knew, the place was derelict. It had electricity (the wiring was most certainly not up to code) but no running water. No insulation. A space heater. A two-burner hot plate. An outhouse. A propane barbecue on the wooden picnic table. It had been an adventure to camp out there when she was a kid, but it was too rustic for adults requiring creature comforts. Over the years, it had been bequeathed more than once, but she had no clue who owned it now.

Bev would drive by the cottage. If it looked abandoned, she'd stop. The mostly seasonal residents in the area wouldn't recognize her car. Wi-Fi was spotty in those parts. People didn't go there to listen to news reports. They went to escape them.

Bev hoped Bernie wouldn't think to send her goon to look for her at the cottage.

Only time would tell.

Wednesday evening
Sally's apartment

VAL'S COMMUNAUTO ROLLED INTO WOLFVILLE JUST AS her favourite true-crime podcast was wrapping up. Her stomach rumbled and she glanced at her watch: 5:30 P.M. No wonder she was famished. There had been an accident on Highway 101 eastbound, slowing traffic to almost a standstill near the Windsor exit. A toasted bagel with cream cheese and an apple juice from Tim Hortons would tide her over for now. She picked up her food, returned to her car, and devoured it in three minutes flat.

Val had ignored Sonya's warning to not contact Sally. Five minutes later, she pulled into Sally's parking lot. Before leaving Halifax, she'd called to confirm that the author was home and available to talk.

After buzzing up, Val settled in an armchair and pulled a notebook and pen from her backpack. Smiling at the elderly woman, she said, "Thanks again for agreeing to see me. I'm going to take notes for my story, if you don't mind. My memory isn't what it used to be."

Sally chuckled. "You're still young, dear. Wait till you're my age. The short-term memory goes but the long-term doesn't. I still remember the white dress and shoes I wore to my church confirmation. And the smell of my mother's perfume and my father's aftershave."

"Those are lovely memories," said Val, crossing her legs. "I won't keep you long. I'd also like to ask Bev Clarke a few questions, but she isn't replying to my messages. Has she come to see you, by any chance?"

Sally hesitated. It was a sin to lie. *Thou shalt not bear false witness to thy neighbour* was one of the ten commandments. *The devil is the father of lies* was in John 8:44.

"Is Bev in trouble?" asked Sally, eyebrows knitted in concern. Her arthritic knuckles nervously kneaded the afghan on her lap.

"Not that I know of," Val lied. "Has she been here?"

"If I tell you the truth, I'll feel like I'm betraying her," whispered Sally.

That's a yes, thought Val.

"You know I've always kept confidences," said Val.

Sally stared at the reporter's pen, poised over a clean notebook page.

Val put the pen down.

"Bev came to say goodbye to me," said Sally. "I have a MAID appointment on Sunday morning."

"I'm so sorry to hear that," said Val. Wanting to hug Sally, but for some reason, stopping herself. "I didn't know. I'm sure it gives you some peace, and a sense of control, to have made that decision."

Sally nodded. "Yes. It does."

Now wasn't the time to be coy. Val chose to press on. "Did you and Bev talk about anything else?"

Sally thought about Father Marcellus's upcoming visit. She decided to add one more item to the list of her transgressions.

"No, dear, we didn't. We've worked together for twenty years. We talked about our journey together as author and editor. I never had a daughter, but if I did, I'd want her to be like Bev. Smart. Independent. Strong. Loyal."

"You're right," said Val. "Bev *is* strong. Strong enough to pick up a heavy typewriter and kill Victor Comeau with it. Maybe she killed Steve Silver, too. In which case, she *would* be in a lot of trouble."

Sally shrugged but didn't appear shocked. "I don't know anything about that."

"Maybe Bev murdered Mr. Comeau for *you*," said Val. "Because she wanted you to win the award. You just said she was loyal."

"That's ridiculous," said Sally, spots of pink flushing her cheeks. "If I win, it'll be because my novel deserves it."

Although she felt terrible pushing Sally, Val decided to play her ace. "Did you know that Bev wrote Vic's novel? That he *paid* her to ghostwrite it?"

Shock showed on Sally's face. "No. I don't believe it. She wouldn't…she couldn't…"

"I'm sorry," said Val gently. "But there is evidence that she did. Did Bev say where she was going when she left here?"

"No, she didn't," said Sally, looking dazed. "I don't think she knew. You might want to check with her aunt."

I don't think so, thought Val. *Bourque wouldn't be happy about that.*

Out loud, Val said, "I'm sorry if I upset you," putting away her pen and notebook. "And I'm sorry about...Sunday. You're a wonderful writer, Sally. It has been an honour to get to know you over the years, and to read your novels. NOVA Prize aside, *Alex Cage* is a winner to me."

Sally's eyes grew moist. "Thank you. I'm very proud of it."

Val closed the door softly on her way out. When she was back in her vehicle, she checked her phone. There were messages from Kevin and Sunny. Both asking for an update. Marianne had texted to say she planned to run the profile of last year's NOVA Prize winner in Saturday's *Book Briefs*. She wanted Val focused on the bigger story. And to show her a rough draft by noon the next day.

Just then, Val's cellphone rang.

Unknown number.

Val answered. Then listened in stunned silence as the caller identified herself.

Wednesday evening
North End Halifax

UNDER A TALL MAPLE TREE AT FAIRVIEW LAWN CEMETERY, a lone figure sat cross-legged on the grass in front of a granite gravestone. The spacious grounds were located near Halifax's busy Windsor Street Exchange. The final resting place of more than one hundred victims of the *Titanic*. And Elaine Silver.

"I'm so sorry I couldn't save you," said Jackie, laying a bouquet of carnations in front of the stone. "I've thought about you every day since you died. But I think about you today most of all. Happy birthday, Mom."

Clouds covered the sun, casting shadows on the ground. Wiping her cheeks, Jackie tried to recall only happy memories of her beloved mother. Instead, flashbacks of her father punishing his wife for imagined transgressions pushed their way into her mind.

Steve stumbling around drunk in the living room.

Elaine cowering.

Elizabeth, screaming at Steve to stop.

Elaine crawling up the stairs to bed.

Steve passing out on the sofa.

When Elizabeth had gone to check on her mother that last morning, she found her lying on the bathroom floor. Unresponsive. Pill bottles strewn around her. Her right hand clutched an empty bottle of Steve's vodka.

Elizabeth called an ambulance. The coroner called it a suicide, in spite of the bruises on Elaine's arms.

After that, Elizabeth lost faith in the police. Once her mother was buried, she packed her bags. Left home. And never spoke to or saw Steve again.

Soon after, in Tofino, Elizabeth Silver became Jackie Oulton.

Standing up, Jackie brushed off the bad memories along with the blades of grass from her jeans. Then she bent to kiss the cool stone. Looked at it lovingly one last time.

"I'm sorry I couldn't save you," she said. "But I'm not sorry about what I did."

Wednesday evening
Lord Nelson Hotel

"ONLINE TIP CAME IN THROUGH CRIME STOPPERS, Sarge," said Detective Slade. Plucking a piece of paper from the printer, she passed it to Bourque. "Someone thinks they saw Bev Clarke's vehicle parked at a residence in Morden this afternoon."

"We could use a break," said Bourque, frowning as he read the tip. "This case is killing me."

It was an old joke. Despite the strain of the past several days, a smile played around Slade's lips. "Pun intended?"

"Of course," said Bourque, checking his watch. "Let's head to Morden. We should get there just before dark."

"Separate vehicles?" asked Slade. Pulling her gun from her hip, she checked to make sure it was loaded.

Bourque followed suit. "Yes, in case we have to split up." He holstered his weapon. "Let's meet at the French Cross."

"Ten-four," Slade said. "Race ya."

"No racing," said Bourque, fully aware of Slade's love of the chase. "And don't go lights and siren. Let's keep things quiet."

"You're such a killjoy," said Slade, pouting.

Bourque rolled his eyes. "Very punny. Let's roll."

Wednesday evening
Wolfville

"IT'S BERNIE BROWN," SAID VAL'S CALLER. "BEV'S AUNT. I need your help."

Once Val recovered from the shock of hearing the old bookie's voice, she found her own. "How can I possibly help *you*?" she asked, wishing she had pressed record before she answered.

Val listened as Bernie took a laboured breath. "Bev isn't answering my messages. I'm worried about her."

"What does that have to do with me?" asked Val, wary. A woman like Bernie was not to be trusted.

"Let's cut to the chase. I know that you know that Bev wrote the dead prick's book," said Bernie. "I've been trying to help her out of a sticky situation, but she took off."

"I don't know where she is," said Val truthfully. "I haven't seen her since Monday afternoon, when we talked at Central Library. And let's just say, she wasn't very forthcoming."

Bernie gave a phlegmy cough. "Well, she's on the run, and the cops are calling her a person of interest in Comeau's death. I'm in the Infirmary with pneumonia. I wasn't mobile before I landed here, and I can't go look for her now."

Realization dawned on Val. "Are you asking *me* to look for her?"

"Yes," said Bernie.

Val was confused. "Don't you have someone else you can send?"

Bernie sighed. "Boris, my...personal assistant is busy tending to business here. I can't send my chef or my housekeeper. They're almost as old as I am. Also, I'm pretty sure their gun licences have expired. And my staff budget for...other purposes isn't what it used to be."

Boris, Val thought. She remembered the first note...

STOP SNOOPING OR YOU VILL DIE.

And a piece of the puzzle clicked into place.

"By any chance, would Boris happen to be Eastern European?"

"He's from Moscow," Bernie replied. "Why do you ask?"

"I don't suppose he sent me an anonymous note? With a typo in it?"

Bernie paused. "His spoken English is better than his written. But not by much. Sorry if that spooked you. I was just trying to look out for Bev."

Val stared out the windshield at Sally's apartment building. "First of all, I wouldn't know where to begin searching for Bev," she said. "And second, what would you want me to do if I found her?"

"To answer your first question, I think I know where she is. As for the second, well, you're a reporter. You talk to people for a living. So, talk to her. Tell her I want her to come home. And that I'll take care of everything."

For a few seconds, Val stayed silent. Debating her next move. Finally, she said, "Where do you think she is?"

Bernie told her. Val could hear the old woman exhale a sigh of relief before she ended the call.

As soon as she hung up, Val pointed her car toward Morden.

Wednesday evening
Morden

UP ON THE NORTH MOUNTAIN, BEV DROVE AT A SNAIL'S pace past the cottage. Her heart hurt to see it sagging with neglect. The windows were boarded up. The white paint was peeling. The roof was missing shingles. The lawn was a messy meadow of tangled wildflowers and overgrown weeds.

There was no driveway, so Bev pulled onto the soft shoulder a few metres past the place. When she was a child, the grass around the cottage had been cut regularly. In those days, there had been a parking spot for one car, on the right side of the lawn. Taking a flashlight from the trunk, she locked the car, then trampled a path through the grass to the back door. Years ago, when the family closed the cottage on Labour Day weekend, the inside of that door would be shored up with boards to help prevent off-season vandals and squatters from sneaking in.

Now, Bev would do her best to break in.

In fact, it turned out to be quite easy. The wood was weak, and Bev was strong. At dusk, it was dark inside with the windows covered by boards. The flashlight's beam led the way to a dusty lamp with an old fringed shade in the sitting room. Nothing happened when Bev flicked the switch. No surprise. The power had probably been disconnected decades ago. That was fine. Lighting up the place would indicate to neighbours and passers-by that someone was inside. She was so rattled that it didn't occur that her parking her car close to the cottage was a risky move.

Extinguishing her flashlight, Bev lowered herself onto a narrow cot covered with scratchy wool blankets. Rusty coils squeaked as they poked into her bum. Facing the boarded-up windows that overlooked the ocean, she considered her next move.

"Think," she said aloud. "Think."

Bev was hungry. And tired. And she had to pee. She pulled a protein bar from her purse, unwrapped it, and bit off the end. It was dry. Most likely the well was, too. June had been unseasonably hot. Then she remembered that the water was always turned off when the cottage was closed. Not that it would be fit to drink now, anyway.

Putting the rest of the bar in her purse for later, Bev went back outside and made her way to the outhouse. Standing in front of it, she tried to summon her courage. Even when she was young, she'd hated using it. Was always afraid she'd fall in and her screams for help would go unheard. Now, desperate times called for desperate measures. After grabbing a packet of tissues from her purse, for there was certain to be no toilet paper, she opened the door to air it out.

When Bev was finished, she stepped into the silent night. Filling her lungs with fresh air, she made her way back to the cottage as the sun disappeared over the horizon. Walking to the edge of the cliff, she closed her eyes. The waves breaking on the rocks below were a hypnotic lullaby.

Just then, Bev heard rustling in the grass behind her. Whirling around, she saw a figure emerge from the shadows at the far end of the cottage. Stepping backward in surprise, she lost her footing and screamed.

Wednesday evening
Halifax Central Library

ON THE THIRD FLOOR OF CENTRAL LIBRARY, JACKIE Oulton was surfing the internet when she saw an old photograph of herself from high school on a news report. Then another one. And another.

Jackie no longer recognized the teenager in that photo. Back then, she had carried twenty pounds of extra weight, from failed attempts to dull her fear with food, and her long hair had been bleached blond. Now, she was lean from surfing, and her natural brown hair was cut short in a flattering pixie. Only her eyes remained the same.

Turning back to the news, she saw that the police had named her a person of interest in Steve Silver's death. They were searching for her.

Jackie knew it would only be a matter of time until they found her. Pulling up her hood and heading to the nearest bathroom, she took the SIM card out of her cellphone and flushed it. Then she slipped the phone in the toilet's water tank.

After washing her hands, Jackie stood staring at herself in the mirror: Pale narrow face. Hair badly in need of a wash. Emerald-green eyes like her mother's.

"I miss you, Mom," she said to her reflection.

Jackie's next stop was the fifth floor: fiction.

When she stepped off the elevator, she turned right and headed for the letter *S*. Scanning the spines, she spotted three of Steve Silver's titles and tucked them under her arm. She walked back to the elevator, looked around to make sure there would be no witnesses, and slid the books into the garbage bin.

Jackie smiled in smug satisfaction as the intercom announced the library would be closing in fifteen minutes. Taking the stairs to the ground floor, she slipped out the side door onto Queen Street and disappeared into the night.

Wednesday evening
Morden

JUST BEFORE THE SUN SET, DETECTIVE SLADE PARKED next to the French Cross in Morden.

Grinning, she thought, *Beat him again. What a slowpoke.* Eight minutes later, Bourque pulled up behind her in an unmarked Subaru.

Not that it was a competition. When it came to homicide investigations, Slade was content to play second fiddle. For now. She knew she still had lots to learn. And she was learning from the best in the business. Even so, this small victory of beating her boss to a location was worth a mental fist pump.

Both detectives got out of their vehicles and met in between them.

"What's the plan?" asked Slade, subconsciously touching her holstered gun.

Bourque hadn't been to the site since he was a child, celebrating National Acadian Day with his family. He couldn't help but reflect on the community's history. That Morden used to be called French Cross. That the memorial stone cross was a testimony to the survival of the three hundred Acadians who took refuge there in 1755 to escape the Deportation to British-American colonies and France. All because they had refused to swear allegiance to the British crown.

There was no skirting around history. The Acadians had paid a steep price for their decision. It was a miracle they had survived.

Now, Bourque needed a miracle. He hoped his ancestors would guide him.

"Grab your Maglite, then we'll walk around the cottage," said Bourque. He was holding a heavy police-issued flashlight that could also be used as a defensive weapon. A temporarily blinded perpetrator was easier to disable than one who could see. "You take the right side. I'll go left. Meet you out back."

Once Slade had her flashlight in hand, the pair walked quietly up the road. Other cottages were lit up inside. The residents were most likely having a quiet night, watching TV or reading. Enjoying an evening snack. Letting their dogs out for a pee before bedtime.

As the detectives approached the only dark cottage on the stretch of road, they spotted a Communauto parked on the shoulder beside it. A few metres ahead was a vehicle matching the description of Bev's.

"She's here," said Slade, pulse quickening in anticipation. "And I think Val Jenkins is, too. She's a car-share member."

"Great," said Bourque, his tone dry. "That complicates things."

Suddenly, they heard a frantic cry for help coming from behind the cottage. The detectives sprinted toward it. Maglites holstered. Guns drawn.

Slowing as they rounded the corner in the dark, Bourque said, "Police! Drop your weapons."

"It's Val," said a strained voice. "There aren't any weapons. Bev needs help."

Holstering their guns, the detectives shone their flashlights toward the cliff's edge. There, they could see Val crouching next to Bev, who was lying flat on her back.

"Is she conscious?" asked Slade, pulling out her cellphone.

"No," said Val, her voice shaking.

While Slade called for an ambulance, Bourque knelt next to Bev and held her wrist. "Pulse weak but steady." Lifting Bev's eyelids, he added, "Pupils dilated. She's likely concussed." Handing Val his flashlight, he said, "Go inside and look for a blanket."

Soon, Val ran back with the blanket from the cot. Bourque tucked it tightly around Bev. The ambulance might take twenty minutes or more to reach them way out here.

"Are you okay?" asked Bourque. Val was close enough that he could sense her shaking. Probably shock. Slade was on the phone with dispatch.

"Yeah," she said. "Or at least, I'm not hurt badly. Just a few scrapes. I think I twisted an ankle. When I came around the cottage, Bev was standing near the edge of the cliff. I must have surprised her, because she turned around quickly, then slipped and fell. Thankfully, there's a lip just below the edge of the cliff. She was still conscious at that point, so I was able to help her up. Then she passed out. She must have hit her head."

"How did you know she was here?" asked Bourque. As they talked, he kept his fingers on Bev's wrist. Her pulse was getting weaker. He hoped she didn't have a brain injury. For selfish reasons: He needed to question her about Comeau's murder.

"Bernie Brown called me," said Val. "She said Bev might be here and asked me to check."

"She did?" said Bourque, surprise pitching his voice higher.

"I know," said Val, wishing it wasn't dark so she could see his expression. "I couldn't believe it either."

"Did Bev say anything before she fell?" asked Bourque.

Val shook her head, then realized he couldn't see her. "No."

"Why didn't you call me before you came to look for her?" Now he sounded annoyed.

"I didn't know she'd be here," Val replied, feeling defensive.

Bourque was right. She should have called him first. "Then I dropped my phone when I went to help Bev, and I couldn't find it in the dark. I was going to leave her to go look for help when you got here."

In the distance, an ambulance siren wailed, getting louder as it drew closer. After what felt like an eternity, two paramedics had Bev secured on a stretcher. When they were certain she was stable for transport to the hospital in Kentville, one of them examined Val. Determining her injuries were minor, she was released and advised to follow up with her doctor.

"Would you like a ride home?" Slade asked Val, handing her the phone she had found on the ground.

"Thanks, that would be great," she said gratefully. "Shit. I need to get the car back to the city."

Bourque had returned from seeing the ambulance off. He spoke to Slade. "If you can sort out the car, I'll run Ms. Jenkins home. I'd like to ask her a few more questions. I'll see you tomorrow morning at Admiral HQ."

"Ten-four, Sarge," said Slade, heading back to her car. Turning around, she added, "Take care, Val."

"Thanks," said Val, wishing she could have gone with Detective Slade. She was bone tired. A catnap on the drive back would have been nice.

"Follow me," said Bourque, heading to his vehicle.

Thursday morning
Sally's apartment

SALLY'S FAVOURITE HOME CARE WORKER, FAITH, HELPED her get dressed after a simple breakfast of half a cup of oatmeal and a quarter of a sliced banana. The medication she was taking had caused her to lose her appetite. But she also had butterflies in her stomach thinking about her confession with Father Marcellus. He would be arriving in half an hour.

"How about this?" asked Faith, holding up a yellow dress from Sally's closet.

"Heavens, no," said Sally from her perch on the side of the bed. "Something with sleeves, please. My arms look like deboned chicken wings."

Faith chuckled. "A man of God would not be paying attention to your arms, Miss MacPhee. What about this one?"

Scattered on the navy dress Faith held now were delicate white daisies. Its long sleeves fit the criteria.

"Yes, that'll do nicely," said Sally, nodding her approval. "Summery, yet subdued."

Once Sally was dressed, Faith made her a cup of tea, then left her client sitting on the loveseat. She didn't lock the door, so Sally wouldn't have to get up to let the priest in.

Ten minutes later, a familiar "Hulloo, Miss Sally!" trumpeted from the entryway. All six foot, six inches of Father Marcellus filled the living room. Back home in Nigeria, at just nineteen years old, he had been a member of the first African basketball team to qualify for the Olympics. Then God had called him to the priesthood, and he had followed that calling to Canada.

"Thank you for coming, Father," said Sally.

Holding a folder in hands the size of baseball mitts, the lanky priest squeezed himself into the armchair. Sally was grateful he didn't consider MAID a sin. His reasoning? It wasn't among the Ten

Commandments. He didn't promote it in the pulpit, but neither did he discourage nor judge parishioners who made that decision.

"It is an honour to be here with you today, Sally," he said, attempting to lower his booming baritone. "I hope my visit gives you some measure of peace and comfort. After I hear your confession, I will anoint you with holy oil, then administer absolution and the Eucharist. This will put you in a state of grace, help you transition to the afterlife, and prepare you to meet Our Lord and Saviour Jesus Christ."

Sally felt a calmness settle over her. She could listen to Father Marcellus speak all day. His accent was musical. At mass, his sermons soothed her like a lullaby.

"If you're ready, we can begin," said the priest, opening his folder.

"I'm ready, Father," said Sally.

And she was.

Sally's confession was almost the same as the story she had told Bev about her second husband, Sherman. With one exception.

Now, for the first time, she told the truth.

It was true that Frank had come over when he'd heard screaming and dishes breaking. But when he got there, Sherman was already dead at the bottom of the basement stairs.

It was Sally who had shoved him.

Father Marcellus didn't miss a beat.

"You have no need to ask for forgiveness," he said kindly. "Had your husband lived, the burden would have fallen on him to ask God for forgiveness. It was not your burden to bear."

Tears fell silently down Sally's cheeks.

"Thank you, Father," she whispered, drying her eyes with a tissue.

Confession complete, Father Marcellus carried on. When Sally had swallowed the Communion wafer, he closed his folder, clasping his hands on top of it.

"How do you feel?" he asked.

Sally paused to consider the question. Then she smiled. "I feel lighter. Like I'm floating."

The priest's face lit up. "Ah, you are filled with grace! You have been blessed. You will be prepared when it is time."

In that moment, Sally decided that Bev's confession would play no part in her own.

Standing up, Father Marcellus placed a medallion around Sally's neck.

"This is St. Joseph," said Father Marcellus. "The patron saint of a good death. It is what I wish for you."

Bending low, the priest hugged his devout parishioner for the first, and last, time.

Thursday morning
Val's apartment

VAL WOKE UP TO SHERLOCK MAKING BISCUITS ON HER belly on top of the bedspread. She glanced at her alarm clock. Eight-thirty. She'd slept in. She texted Marianne to let her know she had gotten home from Morden at almost midnight, and that she'd be at the office shortly.

Yawning, she stretched, got up, pulled on her robe, and padded into the kitchen to feed Sherlock. She was starving. After making a pot of orange pekoe tea, she placed two slices of multigrain bread in the toaster and took out peanut butter and strawberry jam.

While she ate at the dining room table, Val mentally replayed her drive home with Detective Bourque. It had been equal parts uncomfortable and comforting to sit so close to him. Uncomfortable because he was handsome and authoritative. Comforting because he made her feel safe. Not that she felt threatened anymore, now that Bernie had called off her henchman. Still. Having a smart cop with a gun in your corner (or on the edge of a cliff) was a good thing.

Bourque had discovered that Val knew about Elizabeth Silver. "Her disappearance wasn't a secret," she'd told him. "It just wasn't a news story. Lots of young people take off to travel and find themselves. Maybe especially after the death of a parent."

No, Val didn't know where to find "Jackie." Or who her friends were. Or anything more than that she was in her early thirties. With no digital footprint, she might as well have been a ghost.

When Val arrived at work, Kevin's office was her first stop. It still felt strange to see Marianne sitting in his chair.

The deputy managing editor looked up over her half glasses from the paper she was reading. "You've had a dull few days," she deadpanned.

"That's an understatement," said Val, collapsing into the visitor's chair.

"Gimme the update," said Marianne, putting her glasses on her desk. A well-worn ballcap was covering her hair. "Don't spare any details. And make sure it's in the draft you're going to file by noon. Right?"

"Right," said Val. Then she filled Marianne in on what had happened in Morden. "The cops are keeping a tight lid on the situation."

"Ah, the cops," said Marianne, leaning back and clasping her hands behind her head. "Sometimes friends, sometimes foes. My hospital source told me that Bev's under police guard in the Infirmary's ICU. Still unconscious but breathing on her own."

"That's good news," said Val. "How's Kevin? I owe him a text. Is he home yet?"

Marianne snorted. "That man would try the patience of a saint. Those poor nurses. I visited him at the rehab centre last night. Came close to sticking a syringe in his eye."

Val couldn't help but laugh. "What'd he do?"

Marianne ticked off Kevin's transgressions on her fingers. "Complained the food was inedible. Complained his room was too hot. Complained his shower was too cold. Complained physiotherapy was too hard."

Val grinned. "Sounds like he's doing well."

"Yeah, the cranky old bastard is getting sprung tomorrow," said Marianne. "Then he has outpatient physiotherapy. I told him I'd drop him off at home as long as he keeps his piehole shut. Otherwise, I'm gonna dump him in the harbour."

"When's he coming back to work?" asked Val. "I can't believe I'm saying this out loud, but I miss him."

Marianne sighed. "Yeah, I miss him, too. I'm getting paid something like five cents more an hour after tax deductions to cover his ass. Management sucks."

Val laughed, and Marianne grunted. "I'm not joking. Five fuckin' cents. Now scram. Go write me a draft of your story so I can see what you've got so far. If I don't like it, I'm giving the assignment to Joel."

"Okay, okay, I'm on it," said Val, standing up. "Hey, if your hospital source tells you that Bev has woken up, lemme know, okay?"

"Roger that," said Marianne. "Now beat it. Some of us have work to do."

The phone on the desk rang, and Marianne picked it up. That was Val's cue to leave.

Thursday morning
Halifax Central Library

JACKIE OULTON DIDN'T KNOW WHERE ELSE TO TAKE cover. Central Library was spacious and air conditioned. She could use the computers for free. Read in a chair. Catnap in a covert corner. Brush her teeth in a bathroom. Blend in with the other unhoused people who were welcome there, as long as they were sober and didn't raise a ruckus.

She didn't know if security cameras were capturing her image, so she tried to enter and exit at different times of the day. From the two street-level entrances. From the underground parkade. She started taking the stairs, in case the elevators had eyes on their occupants.

Jackie knew she had overstayed her welcome in her friend's basement. Her nights there were numbered. That was okay. The plan had never been to crash for more than a week. Just long enough to take care of some unfinished business.

On the library's first floor, she sat at a computer terminal. Typed quickly in a Word document. Hit print. As she stood in front of the printer, she glanced up. Straight into the curious eyes of a uniformed police officer. If she'd paid more attention to her surroundings, she might have noticed the posters announcing a public talk on cyber safety that day.

Grabbing the sheet of paper, Jackie took off running out the side door.

The cop was old and overweight. Used to talking to kids in schools and seniors in libraries. Pushing paper at a desk. Not chasing felons. Jackie was young and fast. Fit and strong. She still surfed whenever she could. Riding a wave was the only time she felt free. Now, adrenaline pumped extra blood and oxygen through her body. Before she knew it, she was standing in front of the *Post*'s office. Bent over. Panting. A painful stitch in her side.

The cop was nowhere in sight.

Sirens screamed in the distance.

Clutching the piece of paper, Jackie strode purposefully into the lobby. Straight to the reception desk.

"Please give this to Val Jenkins *right away*," she said. Voice tight with desperation.

A slack-jawed Robert recognized the beautiful green eyes from the news reports. He took the paper from Jackie's extended hand before she turned and fled.

Robert looked at the crumpled note. Read it. And whispered, "Holy shit."

Thursday morning
Halifax Infirmary

BIG BERNIE BROWN WAS SITTING IN A CUSTOM-BUILT bariatric wheelchair, holding her unconscious niece's hand. Boris was standing guard at the door of Bev's private room in the ICU. If Bernie was going to keep the giant Russian on the payroll, he needed something to do. Besides, she had grown fond of the loyal lug. So devoted. Like a son, or a Rottweiler.

Although Bernie had recovered from the worst of the lung infection, oxygen tubes still snaked into her nostrils. An IV pole continued to drip antibiotics into an arm. Squeezing Bev's hand, she said, "Wake up, dear. Your old auntie has something she wants to tell you."

No response. The monitors hummed a steady beat.

Bernie sighed. Guilt lay heavy on her chest like a weighted blanket. She felt responsible for what had happened to Bev. It was unfortunate that it had taken a near-death experience for her to try to turn over a new leaf. At her age, she wasn't sure if the leaf would be just as rotten on the other side. It was not in her nature to be kind.

"Tell you what," said Bernie, patting Bev's hand. "I'll go ahead and talk anyway. You just rest and listen. I wanted to tell you that... I'm sorry. For everything. For introducing you to betting when you were a kid. For not taking you to rehab when you got hooked. For not paying your debts. I guess I was trying to teach you some kind of lesson. A lesson in independence, maybe."

Bernie looked for some slight movement from Bev.

Nothing.

"If you can hear me, squeeze my hand," she said. Hopeful.

No response.

"I know you can pull through this," Bernie continued. "You're strong. Like me. When we Clarke women get knocked on our ass, we don't stay down for long. We get up and fight. We're warriors! *You're* a warrior, Bev. I promise that when you wake up, I'll make everything right. And I'll take care of you. Properly. The way a good aunt should."

Bernie was weary and weak. She nodded at Boris and he came over to grasp the handles of her wheelchair.

"I'm leaving now, Bev, but I'll be back soon," she said. "You rest and get better."

When Bev was alone again, before a nurse came in to check her vital signs, a single tear slid down her cheek.

Thursday morning
Halifax waterfront

THROUGHOUT HER LIFE, VAL JENKINS ALWAYS TRIED her best to not make the same mistake twice. Now was no different. After she read the note that a pale, breathless Robert had handed her, she picked up her phone.

"Detective Bourque," came the curt greeting. Val could hear typing in the background.

"It's Val Jenkins. Jackie Oulton just delivered a note for me at the office. Our receptionist said she took off afterward."

Seated as his desk in the Georgian Lounge, Bourque stopped typing. "Read it to me," he said. Placing the phone on his desk, he hit speakerphone so Detective Slade could listen.

Admiral Horatio Nelson was atwitter with anticipation.

Val read slowly:

STEVE SILVER ABUSED MY MOTHER. PHYSICALLY AND EMOTIONALLY. SHE DIED BY SUICIDE, BUT HE DROVE HER TO IT. VICTOR COMEAU WAS HER FRIEND. HE PROMISED TO HELP HER LEAVE STEVE, BUT HE WAS A LIAR AND A COWARD. I HATED BOTH OF THEM.

PLEASE WRITE A STORY ABOUT MY MOTHER, ELAINE JACQUELINE OULTON. SHE WAS A TALENTED SINGER AND PIANIST. A GARDENER AND A BAKER. A LOVING MOTHER. AND MY BEST FRIEND.

IF I AM FOUND, I WANT TO BE BURIED WITH MY MOM.

JACKIE OULTON

"Thanks," said Bourque. "I appreciate you bringing this to our attention. We've got an APB out, but I need you to call me ASAP if she gets in touch again."

"Roger that, detective," said Val before hanging up.

"Sarge, we just got a radio call that Jackie has been sighted sprinting down Prince Street toward the waterfront," said Slade. "Patrol cars are en route."

"Let's go," said Bourque. "We'll take your car."

After checking that their guns were holstered, they ran down to the parkade.

"Lights and siren?" asked Slade, when they were buckling their seat belts.

"Ten-four," said Bourque.

Siren and lights activated, the vehicle peeled out of the parkade.

Into a storm.

High winds were blowing the rain sideways. Small tree limbs were breaking off and falling onto the road and sidewalks. Slade turned right onto South Park Street, right onto Sackville, then left onto Lower Water. Heading straight toward the harbour. Cars pulled to the curb as they flew by.

Bourque was on his radio. "A drone spotted her heading toward Queen's Landing," he said.

Windshield wipers on high, Slade floored it.

The Queen's Landing steps were built into a new public waterfront space near the ferry terminal and led straight down into the murky harbour seawater. The massive granite steps were a popular attraction with both locals and visitors. But after videos went viral of people jumping from them into the ocean, they had also raised safety concerns.

The detectives' current concern was that Jackie Oulton might be contemplating going for a swim.

IF I AM FOUND, I WANT TO BE BURIED WITH MY MOM.

Sirens were overlapping each other. Fire trucks and an ambulance were on their way.

Unbeknownst to the first responders, Val was pedalling the short distance from the *Post*'s office to Queen's Landing as fast as she could.

Grateful that the buffeting wind was behind her. She was soaked to the skin. After showing Marianne the note from Jackie, the editor had been glued to the police scanner.

Val rolled up to Queen's Landing seconds after the first responders.

In time to see Jackie run down the steps, toward the water.

Dropping her bike on its side, Val ran to the top of the landing. "Jackie! It's Val Jenkins! I got your note!" she shouted, waving frantically.

Jackie whirled around. Feet perched precariously on a slippery lower step that was slick with rain. Waves washed over her sneakers. When she saw the police detectives run up to Val, she turned her back. And took another cautious step. The water was now up to her knees. The temperature would be bracing, likely no more than ten degrees Celsius.

"Let me handle this," said Bourque, stepping in front of Val.

"Jackie! I'm Wade Bourque with the police. We just want to talk to you. Please don't go any farther."

Jackie hesitated. Then continued to descend. Churning water sloshed onto her thighs. A growing crowd of bystanders could see her shivering.

"Let me try," begged Val.

"Make it quick," said Bourque. "Then Slade is going in after her."

Detective Slade had experience with the RCMP's underwater recovery team. She'd saved potential drowning victims before, and she'd do it again. But the goal was to get Jackie out of the water on her own, if they could.

Drenched, Val walked cautiously down the first three steps. It took all her strength to keep her footing. She was only a few metres away from Jackie. She could see the tide coming in. The wind blew Jackie's sodden hood off her head.

"I'm so sorry about your mother," Val called out.

Jackie turned around. Tears mixed with rain ran down her cheeks.

In the background, Slade inched closer to the top of the landing. Out of Jackie's sightline, she had removed her shoes and most of her clothes. Only her T-shirt, bra, and underwear remained. Muscles taut, she was poised for action.

"She didn't deserve to die like that," Jackie sobbed. Stumbling down a step. Now she was wet up to her elbows. "He should have been put in jail."

"I know," said Val. Taking one step closer to Jackie. "I'm sorry he wasn't. But if you keep walking, he wins. Don't let him win, okay?"

"I need you to tell my mom's story," pleaded Jackie. "*Please* tell her story. She was so much more than what she became because of him."

"I will, I promise," said Val, reaching out a hand. "But I need you to tell it to me."

Up on the landing, Bourque and Slade waited and watched. Alert.

Just then, the sound of a helicopter's rotor blades filled the air. Everyone looked skyward. Rain pelting their faces.

Everyone but Slade. She was laser focused on her target.

In the split second that Jackie turned her face toward the sky, a rogue wave crashed into her. Knocking her feet out from under her.

In that split second, the sea swallowed Jackie Oulton.

Flying down the steps, Slade dove headfirst into the harbour.

Thursday morning
Halifax Waterfront

BEFORE SHE DOVE INTO THE WAVES, DETECTIVE SLADE had been calibrating her breathing. So focused, she was oblivious to the storm. When she was with the RCMP, she had undergone rigorous training as a free diver. Even now, she could hold her breath underwater without a scuba tank for three minutes. Right before each dive, she purposely hyperventilated, making each exhale last longer than the inhale. Breathing that way lowered the carbon dioxide in her blood, allowing her to hold her breath longer.

Slade executed a flawless forward dive into the bone-chilling water, searching the murky depths for the body.

It took a little less than three minutes for Slade to find Jackie, grab her, and pull her to the surface. The firefighters and paramedics took over from there. Val watched from the landing as the ambulance with Jackie took off for the ER, siren wailing.

The firefighter who had wrapped Slade in warm blankets was checking her vitals.

"You okay?" asked Bourque, standing beside her.

"F-f-fine," said Slade, teeth chattering. "Go."

Bourque ran past Val. Stopped. And turned around.

"Come with me," he said.

"But my bike…" said Val, looking at it.

"I'll call someone to take it to the station," said Bourque, striding toward his car. "Let's go."

"Where are we going?" Val called out, running to keep up with him. Head lowered to brace against the wind and rain.

"To the hospital," Bourque replied. "Bev Clarke is awake."

Thursday morning
Alex's house

WHAT A DIFFERENCE A DAY MADE. IN THE ROUGHLY twenty-four hours since Alex Fitzgerald had visited Bernie Brown at the Infirmary, he had shaved, showered, and slept like a log. After a hearty breakfast and two cups of coffee, he was hunkered down in his home office working on the poetry anthology.

True to her hospital-bed promise, Bernie had gotten Boris to email a selection of her poems to Alex.

The poems were good.

Very good.

Profound, even.

Bernie's poetry plumbed the depths of her childhood trauma but without being sentimental or saccharine. If he were to review them, he'd say *They pack a powerful sucker punch to the reader's psyche.*

Alex's hypothalamus released a rush of dopamine. His feel-good hormones were firing on all cylinders. If he finished the anthology before the fall semester began, he would submit it to various poetry prizes for consideration. When it came to future grant applications, the more accolades, the better.

After devoting more than a year to crafting *Cape Breton Calls Him*, Alex was ready to take a break from long-form writing. Poetry was the perfect antidote. Hammering out an introduction to the anthology that wasn't insipid would be his most taxing task in the coming weeks. Poetry wasn't going to make him rich by any means, but the royalties from the anthology might mean he could afford a new pair of stylish eyeglasses to add to his collection. Maybe. If he bought them at Costco.

Thankfully, he could also look forward to the twenty thousand dollars he was sure to receive for being a NOVA Prize runner-up. After everything that had happened the previous weekend, he was doing his best to manage his expectations. And to let go of rehearsing his grand-prize acceptance speech. If Vic turned out to be the winner, Alex supposed he could channel his rage and resentment into a poem.

Thursday morning
Halifax Infirmary

IN HER ROOM AT THE HALIFAX INFIRMARY, BERNIE WAS also reviewing the poems Boris had emailed to Alex. Looking at the laptop on her tray table, she smiled. The writing really was very good.

Beneath her johnny shirt, a soft chuckle caused her broad bosom to rise and fall. The more Bernie read, the more she laughed. Until she had a major case of the giggles. Before long, she was full-on crying. For an entire minute, tears rained down her cheeks.

A nurse popped her head in the door. "Everything okay in here?"

Bernie was laughing so hard she couldn't speak. Instead, she offered a thumbs-up.

"Alrighty then," said the nurse, turning and disappearing down the hall.

When her laughing jag finally subsided, Bernie wiped her eyes with a tissue, blew her nose, and belched from sucking in so much air.

"Gotta love AI," she said, closing her laptop.

Thursday morning

Halifax Infirmary

AFTER SLADE HAD STOPPED AT HOME FOR A HOT SHOWER and a change of clothes, she drove to the hospital to check on Jackie. She and Bourque both felt that a female officer's presence would be less triggering. She had dressed warmly, in a T-shirt, yoga jacket, leggings, and sneakers.

At the Infirmary, Slade nodded to the officer guarding the door to Jackie's private room. When she entered, another officer was sitting in a chair, texting. After greeting her, Slade let the officer know that she could stay.

Jackie was lying in bed. Eyes open. Slade pulled a chair next to the bed and sat.

"You're the cop who pulled me out of the harbour," said Jackie. Voice flat.

"Yes," said Slade. Not rushing.

"I'm not thanking you," said Jackie. "I didn't want to be saved."

Shrugging, Slade said, "Sorry. I'm a cop. Saving lives is an occupational hazard."

A ghost of a smile played around Jackie's lips. "Touché," she said.

Slade sat in the silence, waiting for Jackie to speak.

"I suppose you want to know where I was when Victor Comeau and Steve Silver were killed," she said, after a moment.

"I am curious about that, yes," said Slade, crossing her legs.

Jackie closed her eyes. "Then I'll tell you..."

Slade interrupted. "Before you say anything else, I must advise you that anything you do say can be used as evidence at any trial against you. You have the right to consult with a lawyer before saying anything further."

Jackie opened her eyes. "I don't want a lawyer. I want to tell you. I was in Vic's and Steve's rooms. Bashing their misogynistic heads in with typewriters."

Jackie checked for Slade's reaction.

"I kind of figured," said Slade. "And I can guess why you'd want to murder Silver. But why kill Comeau? And why not drug him first, too?"

The room was cold. Jackie pulled the blanket covering her up to her neck. Both women were still chilled from their dip in the harbour.

"I wanted to make certain that Steve died, so I had a complimentary cocktail laced with ketamine sent to his room," said Jackie. "I knew he'd drink it. An alcoholic never refuses free booze. Later, I used my master key to get into his room. All of the room attendants carry one. I was just planning to check that he was dead. But when I saw the typewriter, I lost it. And you know what? Releasing that rage felt *great*."

Slade kept her composure. She'd heard, and seen, worse. "And Vic?"

Jackie sighed. "He was my mom's best friend. They'd met in university. He was probably her lover at some point, too. Didn't ask. Didn't care. All I cared about was that he promised to help her leave Steve. But the coward betrayed her. And you know what happened to her because of that."

"Why didn't you drug him, too?" pressed Slade.

"Because I didn't plan to kill him," said Jackie, voice rising. "I just went to confront him. I wanted him to apologize for not helping my mom. But he didn't. He told me to get out of his room or he'd call the police. I just…lost it. It's like I went into some sort of fugue state.

"When it was over, I wiped off my fingerprints from the typewriter and anything else I had touched with towels, filled the tub with water, and tossed them in. I didn't expect anyone to be in the bathroom. I didn't know the woman or why she was there. I told her to keep quiet or I'd kill her, too. Then I left."

Closing her eyes, Jackie said, "That's it. Now you know the story. What's going to happen to me?"

"You'll be arrested and incarcerated until your court appearance, where you'll face a first-degree murder charge and a second-degree murder charge," said Slade. "The court will determine a need for an examination based on your mental state. That decision will be made after the Crown and defence make their submission to the court."

Jackie's eyes filled with tears.

Not for herself.

For her mother.

Slade stood up. "If you can't afford a lawyer, legal aid will appoint one for you," she said. Then she left to look for Bourque.

Ten minutes after Bourque and Val left Queen's Marque, they were dripping onto the floor of an Infirmary elevator on their way to Bev's room.

"Why do you want *me* here?" asked Val, pushing wet bangs off her forehead.

Bourque looked at her. "Because you're a friendly face. Bev is more likely to open up if you're in the room. Right now, you're more of an asset to our investigation than a liability."

"Thanks," said Val, wrinkling her nose. "I think."

At the nurses' station, Bourque showed his badge to the unit clerk, who directed them to Bev's room. When they arrived, Bernie was sitting bedside in her wheelchair. Holding Bev's hand. Bev's right foot was in a cast, on top of the bedsheets. When she fell, she had broken her ankle.

Both women looked up when the detective and journalist walked in. Rain pelted at the one small window.

"Ah, Detective Bourque," said Bernie. "We've been expecting you."

Bernie felt Bev tighten her grip. She watched as fear flashed across her niece's face.

"Not to worry," said Bernie, patting Bev's hand. "I'll take care of this. We're lawyered up."

"It's okay," said Bev, looking at her aunt. "I'm ready to tell my story."

"Are you sure?" asked Bernie, her forehead wrinkling. "You don't have to."

"I'm sure," said Bev.

Bernie shrugged. "Suit yourself."

Bourque indicated that Val should sit in the lone chair. He stood next to it.

"Thanks for saving my life, Val," said Bev.

"I'm sorry I scared you," Val replied. "You wouldn't have slipped if I hadn't showed up."

Bev shook her head. "It wasn't your fault. If you hadn't arrived when you did, I might have jumped. I was thinking about it."

"Well, I'm glad you didn't," said Val quietly.

"Me, too," said Bev. "When I regained consciousness, I knew I had to make things right. I'm ready to tell Detective Bourque what really happened."

"Go ahead," said Bourque, pulling out his phone. "But I must advise you now that you're a suspect." After reading Bev her rights, he said, "I'm going to record this."

Bev nodded. Taking a deep breath, she began. "Most of my story is the same as what I said in my statement. I went to Vic's room to tell him I wanted the money he owed me for ghostwriting his book. When he refused to pay, I threatened to expose him as a fake at the ceremony. I don't know if I would have done it, but it was the only leverage I had. While we were arguing, there was a knock at the door. Vic told me to hide in the bathroom while he answered it, and that we'd finish our discussion when he got rid of whoever it was."

Bev paused to sip from a glass of water through a straw.

"Who was it?" pressed Bourque.

"Alex Fitzgerald," said Bev. "I heard Vic greet him by name. Then I heard them arguing."

"What happened next?" asked Val. Wishing she had her notepad.

"Alex left. Then, before I could come out of the bathroom, there was another knock. This time I heard a voice I didn't recognize. I couldn't tell if it was a man or a woman. It was too muffled. After a few minutes, I heard a crash. I peeked out of the bathroom door."

"What did you see?" asked Bourque.

Bev shivered. "I saw Vic. Lying on the floor. Next to a mangled typewriter."

"What happened next?" asked Val, leaning forward.

"A few minutes later, a hotel staff member came into the bathroom holding bloody towels," said Bev. "I was frozen in fear. I didn't know what to do."

"How did you know it was a staff member?" asked Val.

"I had seen her working earlier that day," she said. "And she has these unforgettable green eyes. When she saw me, she told me to go. To not call the police, or I'd be next. That she'd take care of everything. So, I ran to the ballroom."

"That's when Bev called me," said Bernie, patting her niece's hand. "What she didn't know was that Vic had borrowed money from *me* to pay what he owed *her*. Then he blew it on Botox and liposuction and whores, or whatever the vain bastard was into. I've forgiven Bev's debts. On the condition that she joins a support group for gamblers. And you'll be happy to hear that I'm retiring from my... business activities."

Bourque gave a tight smile but said nothing.

"Will I go to jail?" asked Bev. Afraid of the answer.

"That's for the courts to decide," said Bourque, standing. "When you're ready to be discharged, we'll book you at the station."

Bev's eyes filled with tears. "Okay. I'm sorry I didn't come forward before. I was too scared."

Val stood, too. "For what it's worth, Bev, you wrote a great novel."

Bev didn't reply, but her eyes overflowed.

Friday morning
The Post's *office*

VAL STOPPED TO CHECK IN WITH MARIANNE BEFORE heading to her desk. Leaning in the doorway, she watched in surprise as Kevin hammered away on his keyboard, crutches propped in a corner. Shaking her head, a grin spread across her face.

"It's a good thing the surgeon didn't amputate your index fingers or you wouldn't be able to type," Val said. "Welcome back, Lou."

Kevin turned toward her. "No one likes a wiseass, Mary. And thanks. It's good to be back. The nurses were drill sergeants, and the food was killing me."

Val plopped into the visitor's chair. "How'd you get sprung so fast?"

Kevin shrugged. "Apparently, I heal like Wolverine. Too bad I can't regenerate my toes. Win some, lose some. I'm only working mornings for a while. I'm not allowed to drive, so Marianne is chauffeuring me. I'd rather take a taxi, but the old battleaxe won't take no for an answer. I'm in outpatient physiotherapy. My foot's bandaged up like a mummy. I got the VON coming in to change the dressings. But enough yada yada. What's the scoop?"

Val crossed her legs. "Bev will likely be charged with accessory after the fact and obstruction of justice. If Jackie is deemed fit to stand trial, she'll be charged with first-degree murder for Steve's death and second-degree or manslaughter for Vic's."

"What about the NOVA Prize?" asked Kevin, drumming his fingers on the desk.

"The Westby Foundation will announce the winner sometime this weekend," said Val. "The communications director will text me when the details are posted on their website."

Kevin nodded. "So, on Monday you'll owe me a feature on the NOVA Prize winner, with sidebars on the runners-up and a tribute to the dead jerks. Then a shorter piece on the Westby's statement about the ghostwriting. Jesus. Not my circus, not my monkeys. Anyway, all of that should give you some good cud to chew on."

"The statement is coming this weekend, too," said Val, picking up her helmet and backpack. "I'll get all that to you no problem."

Kevin turned back to his computer. Paused. And swung around to face Val. "You did good, kid," he said.

"Thanks," she said, smiling. "I didn't solve the murders before the cops did, though."

"That's 'cause the perps confessed, so the cops didn't solve them either, if you want to look at it that way," said Kevin. "You dug in, did due diligence, followed clues, and talked to people. You stuck to the trail like gum on a shoe." Kevin cleared his throat. "Proud of you."

"Excuse me?" said Val, hand cupped to an ear. "Didn't quite catch that."

Grunting, Kevin turned back to his computer. "You heard me. Now get lost."

Saturday morning
Lord Nelson Hotel

ADMIRAL HORATIO NELSON HAD NEVER FELT SO fatigued.

Not even after the Battle of Copenhagen. But he had been a younger man in 1801. Now, he was relieved to find himself alone in his Georgian Lounge once again. The silence was a tonic. He needed far more than forty winks to ready himself for the forthcoming frantic wedding season. It would take him the entire day—possibly two—to recover.

Sunday morning
Sally's apartment

AT 9:00 ON SUNDAY MORNING, THE SCENE WAS SET FOR Sally's passing.

Sonya King was there.

Sally's longtime GP, Dr. Rebecca Sampson, was there.

God was there. Sally could feel Him.

Outside, the sun was shining. A gentle breeze helped cool the warm air. Chickadees and cardinals were singing. Church bells were clanging. Inside, the atmosphere was sombre, yet tranquil. Sally was ready to meet her Maker.

"Do you still want to go ahead, Sally?" asked Dr. Sampson.

Sally nodded. "Yes. I do."

Dressed in her blue dress with daisies, Sally had decided to lie on her bed, with her favourite afghan covering her. She knew that the doctor would administer three drugs. The first would relax her. The second would place her into a deep coma. The third would stop her breathing.

As Dr. Sampson helped Sally onto the bed, Sonya heard her cellphone buzzing in her purse.

"I'm so sorry," said Sonya, blushing with embarrassment. "I'll just go turn that off."

When Sonya returned from the living room, she knelt next to Sally and took her hand.

Looking into the older woman's eyes, Sonya said, "That was a call from the Westby Foundation. *Alex Cage* won the NOVA Prize."

Sally closed her eyes. Tears slid down her cheeks. Staying silent, with the remaining strength she had left, she gently squeezed Sonya's hand.

Opening her eyes, Sally looked at Sonya. Then at Dr. Sampson.

"I'm ready," she said, eyes shining.

One year later
Wolfville

ON THE LAST FRIDAY IN JUNE, SONYA KING GOT INTO her red Miata dressed in a cream-coloured pantsuit and tan strappy sandals. Traffic was light leaving Lunenburg, and she arrived in Wolfville just before 10:00 A.M. Right in time for the ribbon-cutting ceremony.

Pulling into the parking lot, Sonya turned off the engine and sat for a few seconds. Casting her eyes over the unassuming wheelchair-accessible ranch-style building off the main street in town, a lump formed in her throat.

Sally would be pleased, she thought. As for her own plan, the hospital wing with her name on it could wait.

When Sonya walked into the sunny foyer, the others were already there mingling. Holding glasses of sparkling water. Chatting. She waved at Alex, Del, Sunny, and Val. Emilie Craig, the Westby Foundation chair, was talking to the mayor. Several town councillors and residents were also present.

After greeting the guests, Sonya took her place at the podium. The room fell silent.

"Thank you all for coming," she said. "I'm Sonya King, chair of the committee responsible for this beautiful building. It is my absolute honour to officially open MacPhee House, a safe space to support local women and children in need, along with their pets."

The audience applauded.

"Sally posthumously donated her NOVA Prize funds to establish this sanctuary," Sonya continued. "I'd like to thank author Alex Fitzgerald for also donating his prize money, the Westby Foundation, and the local and provincial sponsors who have supported this important endeavour."

Sonya didn't know that Alex's prize money was meant to pay his outstanding Canada Revenue Agency bill, but that he felt donating it was the right thing to do. She didn't mention that the Westby

Foundation had donated the twenty grand that had been earmarked for Vic Comeau. She also kept quiet that she had added her own NOVA prize money, plus another eighty thousand of her own funds. Today wasn't about her.

The room filled with applause again.

After the mayor cut the ceremonial ribbon, Sonya returned to the podium.

"Sally is here with us in spirit," she said. "Please enjoy the refreshments and feel free to tour the house."

After having a number of quick conversations with guests, Sonya slipped out the back door and walked around to her car. Later, she'd meet Alex, Del, and Sunny for a late lunch at a restaurant in town. For now, she pointed her car toward Kentville and Holy Cross Cemetery.

Sonya drove up the graveyard's gravelled path and parked. Stepping out of her car, she made her way toward the columbarium. It was a cloudy, balmy day. Scanning the plaques, she found Sally's. Pressing a palm against the cool granite, she closed her eyes. Sonya didn't pray, so she said a silent hello.

Sitting on a concrete bench in front of the wall, Sonya listened to birdsong. Felt the warm breeze blow her hair back from her face. She stayed still for a few minutes, reflecting on the past twelve months.

Sonya was researching her next novel. About a woman trapped in an abusive marriage in a fictional Nova Scotian small town in the nineteenth century. In those days, domestic violence was a private matter. Wives had limited legal recourse because they were seen as the property of their husbands.

Sonya would dedicate her novel to Sally. She would donate her author royalties to MacPhee House. She would hold her launch event there. It was her way of telling Sally's story and the story of so many other women whose voices went unheard. Like Elaine Silver's. Val Jenkins would write the afterword, to tell Elaine's story and to keep her promise to Jackie.

Sonya filled Sally in on some of the other players who had been involved in last year's NOVA Prize drama. Bev Clarke had one more year left to serve in her sentence at the women's prison in Truro. She hadn't been frittering away her time. As well as leading a book club there, she was helping her fellow inmates pass their high-school equivalency tests. During her first year behind bars, she wrote the first draft of her memoir, which landed her both a literary agent and a contract with a national publishing house. The book launch and cross-Canada tour would coincide with her release date.

Soon after Bev was incarcerated, Bernie Brown had suffered a fatal heart attack. Her niece and Boris were Bernie's sole beneficiaries. When Bev got out of jail, she would be taken care of financially, forever. Bernie had seen to that.

Jackie Oulton was deemed criminally not responsible for the murders due to a complicated mix of post-traumatic stress disorder and unmedicated mental illness. She was making slow progress in the East Coast Forensic Hospital's rehabilitation program.

After the trial was over, Detective Wade Bourque brought home a spunky orange kitten from the SPCA. He named her Pippi Longstocking.

Del Davis and Sunny Patel were coauthoring a novel loosely inspired by the NOVA Prize murders. Del was tracking the word count closely.

Alex Fitzgerald published his poetry anthology to mediocre reviews. He bought a new pair of eyeglasses. At Costco.

At the *Post*, another round of early retirement packages was handed out. A disgruntled Joel Holt finally agreed to take one. And before Kevin Lewis left the building for the last time, he saw to it that Val Jenkins would be covering crime.

THE END (FOR NOW...)

Author's Note

I DON'T PLOT OUT ANY OF MY NOVELS IN ADVANCE. When I started writing this book, I only had a vague idea who the killer (or killers) were going to be, and how the murders would occur. So, I didn't intentionally set out to include story lines that touched on intimate partner violence, but my characters took me down that path. Sadly, this continues to be a timely topic—not just in Nova Scotia, where I live and where *Blood Typed* is set, but across Canada and around the world.

On Sept. 12, 2024, Nova Scotia legislators unanimously adopted a bill declaring intimate partner violence an epidemic. Over the course of just a few months following that declaration, there were more than half a dozen domestic homicides in the province.

Those who experience intimate partner violence often don't report it to the police. The most common reasons provided by victims/survivors are the belief that this type of abuse is a private or personal matter and the perception that the incident is not "important enough" to report. Other reasons may include the fear of stigma and shame, the fear of court-system intervention, or a lack of trust in the criminal justice system.

If you, or someone you know, are experiencing intimate partner violence, please know that there is help. A list of resources is available on the Nova Scotia government's website: novascotia.ca/just/victim_services/family_violence.asp

Nationally, visit: canada.ca/en/public-health/services/health-promotion/stop-family-violence/services.html.

In the United States, visit the Department of Justice's Office on Violence Against Women: justice.gov/ovw/resources-for-survivors.

Be safe. Be brave. Be well.

Acknowledgements

PROFOUND THANKS TO MY SUPERLATIVE VAGRANT Press editor, Whitney Moran (who is neither homicidal nor bitter), and the talented, hard-working Vagrant Press team for allowing me to step out of my contemporary-humour comfort zone and enthusiastically offer to publish my first murder mystery, all before I had written a single word. Whitney's confidence in my abilities always far surpasses my own. She's a crackerjack collaborator, to boot.

Artist and designer Bee Stanton nailed the cover design on the first draft. (My only request: a little more blood dripping on the skull.) You knocked it out of the park, Bee! Many thanks. I love it.

My dear friend Elizabeth Eve brainstormed ideas with me at the very beginning. I'm eternally grateful for the belly laughs that ensued and for her many years of support. I can't wait to read *her* first novel.

As always, my husband, Craig Pothier, helped me resolve sticky plot points and was an incredible sounding board and supporter of all book-related things. When I told him my idea for *Blood Typed*, he said (more than once): "A Val Jenkins Mystery"—to which I would reply, "Shut *up*!" I had only planned to write a standalone mystery, not a series. Now, well...check out the cover. I am so very lucky to have Craig in my creative corner.

Since I've never judged book awards, Marilyn Smulders generously answered a few questions about the process. I still miss you at the Writers' Federation of Nova Scotia, Marilyn, but I know you're nearby when I need you.

I owe a deep debt of gratitude to retired Detective Constable Sue Lynch of Halifax Regional Police's Criminal Investigation Division for taking the time to answer my many questions about police procedure during homicide investigations. Sue was incredibly generous with her time and the details she provided, helping make all of those scenes credible. Thanks also to retired RCMP Corporal Patrick Moran, who cast his eyes over the entire manuscript. Any procedural errors or omissions are entirely mine.

To the first readers who offered advance praise for this book (in alphabetical order by last name, so there's no fighting)—James Mullinger, B. R. Myers, C. S. Porter, Tom Ryan, Sue Slade, and Jo Treggiari, all of whom are talented writers themselves.

Confession: Not all of my lines are original. During a conversation about our hair, my pal Vic Pretty gave me a line that makes me laugh every time I think of it: "The back of my head is none of my business." And I borrowed "Human Remains" from my friend Christina Jahncke.

Massive thanks to the many booksellers, book reviewers, book bloggers, and librarians who tirelessly promote Canadian authors, day in and day out. To each of you, I shout a sincere and heartfelt "THANK YOU!"

In my previous novels, I purposely chose to not name my characters after friends, family, or colleagues. In this book, I've done the opposite, handpicking a first name here and tacking it onto someone else's last name there. If you spot a name that's the same as yours, it probably isn't a coincidence—you'll likely know who you are. This is a tribute to my most loyal readers, but to be clear: the characters only have your names—their personalities and physical features are unique.

Whitney tells me she always enjoys the banter between my characters. My real-life inspiration for that dialogue comes in part from the more than fifteen years of rapid-fire conversations I've had with my pal Pat White, my older "brother from another mother." Laughter always ensues!

Speaking of brothers from other mothers, here's a special shout-out to Joe Tinney, the owner of Open Book Coffee, the most welcoming café/bookstore in Halifax and my second home. And to Kevin O'Reilly, for his many years of friendship and phone calls (we always end up talking about cookies!), plus fellow authors Pat d'Entremont and Brett Loney, for our Open Book Coffee "tea and talk" dates about writing.

Thank you to my sister-cousin Amy Pulsifer for the (figurative) loan of her cat and her cottage. And to my dear friend and fellow author Janice Landry, for being a kindred spirit, a soul sister, and an ongoing source of support. I love you, Janice. A rising tide floats all boats.

My late mother, Mary Ann Doucet, loved murder mysteries. I'm sad that she didn't have a chance to read this one. I hope my dad, Richard Doucet, will enjoy it for both of them.

In February of 2024, Craig and I adopted a sweet thirteen-year-old Belgian Malinois shepherd mix named Duke from ElderDog Halifax. Duke snoozed by my side as I wrote almost every word of the first draft of this book. He left us heartbroken when he crossed the rainbow bridge in May of 2025, just two weeks before I wrote the final sentence. Duke was my faithful writing companion and a very good boy. This book's for him.

Jane Doucet is a Canadian journalist and author whose debut novel, *The Pregnant Pause*, was shortlisted for a 2018 Whistler Independent Book Award. In 2021, Vagrant Press published Jane's second novel, *Fishnets & Fantasies*. Jane's third novel, *Lost & Found in Lunenburg*, published in 2023, combines characters from her first two novels. Jane lives in Halifax, Nova Scotia, with her husband. When she isn't reading books, she's writing them in between walks with their senior rescue dogs, Molly and Scarlett. To learn more about Jane and her novels, visit janedoucet.com.

Photo by Snickerdoodle Photography

Also by Jane Doucet

The Pregnant Pause

Fishnets & Fantasies

Lost & Found in Lunenburg

Next in the Val Jenkins Mystery series

Death at the Petting Zoo